PRETTY FACE

AN ISABELLA ROSE THRILLER

MARK DAWSON

PART I

1

Callum Vaughn grabbed his Rolex and slipped it around his wrist, enjoying the coolness of the steel and its pleasing weight. It had cost him fifty thousand, and he had four of them, the timepieces rotating on watch winders in his dressing room and ready to be matched with whatever outfit he was wearing. He was going out this evening and wanted to look his best. He'd picked out a tailored navy-blue suit, slim fit, the jacket hugging his broad shoulders in a way that showed off his gym-built physique. The suit was paired with a crisp white shirt and a silk tie in deep burgundy, giving just the right amount of contrast to his otherwise polished look. He checked himself in the full-length mirror by the door, adjusting the collar of his shirt and running a hand through his neatly trimmed hair. He exuded power, wealth, and control: everything he'd built his brand around. The look was deliberate, calculated to impress the right people, intimidate the rest, and remind anyone else who crossed his path exactly whom they were dealing with.

He turned back to the dressing room and scanned the rack of polished shoes. He grabbed a pair of black Oxford brogues, freshly shined, and slipped them on, the leather creaking slightly as he tightened the laces. Tonight was important: he had meetings with investors, potential backers for a new expansion of his business, and he needed everything to be perfect. He was meeting a potential new girl, too, and, although he knew it would be easy to seduce her, it wasn't as if he was going to turn up in jeans and a T-shirt. That would not have been on brand at all, and Callum Vaughn was very much *all* about the brand.

He flicked off the lights and made his usual check of the building before going out. The sprawling property was on the outskirts of Dubrovnik, a converted industrial ware-house that loomed over its quieter neighbours. Its sleek, blackened windows reflected the cold sky, while the rein-forced steel doors—fitted with biometric locks—had been installed after the authorities had suggested that what Vaughn was doing here was illegal. It wasn't—at least that was what his eye-wateringly expensive lawyer had told him, and they'd backed away after that—but Vaughn couldn't be sure that the police wouldn't be back again with another trumped-up case. His sister had said he was being paranoid, but, as Vaughn had reminded her, it wasn't paranoia when they really *were* out to get you.

The building was divided into distinct zones, with each floor dedicated to different aspects of Vaughn's online empire. The ground floor housed the business's command centre: a state-of-the-art server room, its walls lined with racks of Dells and Lenovos and Hewlett Packards that managed and stored the constant flow of live-streamed webcam feeds. Security monitors displayed split-screen views of every corner of the building. Motion sensors and cameras fed directly here, where a team of three full-time technicians worked around the clock to ensure everything ran smoothly. Their screens flashed with user data, income analytics, and feed statuses from the multiple webcams in each of the six studios.

The second floor was where the production took place. It had been converted into a series of six lavishly decorated rooms, each with its own theme—exotic, luxurious, and indulgent—catering to the fantasies of Vaughn's global clientele. The webcam models, all handpicked, lived in the building's dowdier private quarters and worked shifts. It was all about soft lighting, plush furnishings, and expensive décor, creating an atmosphere designed to be visually stimulating; the girls did the rest. Microphones and high-definition cameras were positioned discreetly around each room, capturing every angle for the paying customers. There were seven girls working tonight: one each in five of the studios, and a pair in the sixth. The models made a couple of hundred dollars a day each; Vaughn made *tens* of thousands.

He watched on the bank of screens, inured to the content by so many hours of exposure. He observed it critically and reminded himself that he was going to have to talk to Katya, the blonde who'd come to him from St Petersburg, and who didn't look as if her heart was in it. She'd come to Croatia with the deluded understanding that he and she were in a relationship, he'd led her on just long enough to sink his hooks in, and now that he'd done that, she'd earn for him for as long as he wanted her to. She could bitch and moan about how she'd been tricked and how the pay wasn't fair, but it didn't matter; when she was alone, thinking about what had happened to her, Vaughn knew she wasn't half as pissed off with him as she liked people to think she was. She could go back to freezing her tits off with her alcoholic parents and her one-legged brother—his foot had been blown off in Crimea—whenever she wanted; she just had to pay back what she owed him for the flight over here and the start-up costs, plus the compound interest, and he'd let her have her passport again. Simple as that.

The upper levels were Vaughn's personal space. His private office, located at the highest point of the building, offered a panoramic view of Dubrovnik. The office was opulently furnished, with dark oak furniture, a leather-topped desk, and the latest gadgets. A wall of screens displayed real-time statistics of his business, including his favourite: a ticker that updated every minute with the day's take. He looked at it now and saw he'd made seventy thousand dollars today, the money pouring in at a rate of a dollar every second.

Sixty dollars a minute.

Three thousand six hundred dollars an hour.

He smiled.

Business was good.

Vaughn cast a critical eye over everything: the sleek, efficient technology that made him millions, the studios, the roster of models, and the impenetrable security that ensured no one could touch him. He paused outside the server room, briefly glancing at the security feed, before continuing toward the elevator that would take him down to the garage. Everything was in its place. Everything was secure.

HE'D BUILT a large garage in the grounds of the property for his collection of six supercars. His sister, Louise, had just arrived in her own Ferrari.

She gave the engine a final grumble of revs before killing it and getting out.

"All right?" Louise asked.

"All good," he said.

"Where are you going?"

"Into the city."

"That's right," Louise said. "I remember—that girl. Where's she from?"

"Tunisia. Says she's a model. Young. Fit as fuck."

"Bringing her back?"

"We'll see. Probably."

"And Smithy?"

"Seeing him before. He emailed—he wants to put another five hundred into the business."

Louise puckered her lips. "I still don't think we need it."

"I know. I'm not sure we do, either, but it'd make it easier to expand."

"We can do that ourselves without bringing in anyone else. He's not family, is he? Can't trust him the same way as you can trust blood."

"Point made," Vaughn said. "Again."

He reached into his pocket for the keys to the Aventador, then stopped.

Louise noticed. "What's up?"

"Katya," he said. "She's phoning it in. Go and have a word with her—she needs to remember that she missed her target last week."

"I'll sort it out," she said.

"She's taking the piss."

"Leave it to me—she'll be much more enthusiastic when you get back."

Vaughn raised the Lamborghini's scissor door and lowered himself into the bucket seat. He pressed the start button and felt the rumble of the engine.

"Have fun," Louise said, reaching up and lowering the door.

"You know I will," Vaughn said with a grin.

2

———

Vaughn adjusted his collar in the reflection of the restaurant's dark window and then scanned the scene inside: low lighting, polished marble tables, hushed conversations spoken in several languages. Posat was one of the more exclusive spots in Dubrovnik, catering only to those who could afford the crazy prices. He liked it for exactly that reason. The girl he had come to see was already sitting at the table, flicking through the messages on her phone.

He was late, but he didn't care. That was on brand, too; people waited for him, and not the other way around. It had been true for Alex Smith, the investor he'd just met, and it was especially true for women. You couldn't let them think they were equals; much better to make sure they knew their place in things right at the start and save the education that would otherwise have to be done later.

Recruitment was one of Vaughn's strengths. Some girls were easy, just needing a little teasing and money for the airfare, while others took more effort. Vaughn preferred the path of least resistance, but sometimes—like now—playing a longer game was worth it. Tonight would be the culmination of days of back-and-forth messaging. Amélie Dubois—a name that rolled off his tongue and just sounded sophisticated—looked as if she would justify the effort. She was beautiful, that much was obvious, but Vaughn had plenty of beautiful women chasing after him. What made Amélie different was the mysterious allure he couldn't quite figure out. She was French, lived in Tunisia, and said she was a model. She kept the details vague, and Vaughn liked that. She wasn't desperate, which only intrigued him more; more of a challenge, perhaps, more of a chase. He'd played it cool at first, making her feel like she had to work for his attention. He'd make sure it ended up the same way as the others —with her on her back in one of the studios making money for him—but he'd have fun getting her there.

He stepped through the door, the maître d' greeting him by name and leading him to the table. Vaughn appreciated the way heads turned when he entered a room. He liked that people noticed. They saw a man in a crisp, tailored suit, a man who always looked like he belonged somewhere important. Amélie would notice that, too.

"Good evening," he said.

She looked up. "Callum?"

"That's right."

He sat down, making sure his Rolex caught the dim light as he rested his hand on the table. She was more stunning in person than in the carefully curated photos she'd sent him. Vaughn noted her narrow hips, the way her dress hugged her frame. Not too tight, just right. Classy. She wore a black dress that left enough to the imagination, and her blonde hair was swept back, revealing a face that was both striking and mysterious. Her lips were painted a deep red, just enough to make a statement. She'd said she was twenty-one, but he wouldn't have been shocked if she was a year or two younger than that.

Perfect, he thought.

She smiled, her eyes studying him with a coolness that Vaughn found intriguing. "Callum," she replied. "You're late. I thought you weren't coming."

"Had another meeting," he said. "Investors. Want to give me half a million. Told them I didn't need it."

"Good for you."

She didn't look impressed. She didn't look nervous, either, which was strange; Vaughn had a reputation and knew it preceded him. She gave a light laugh and crossed her legs beneath the table, her posture relaxed but controlled. There was a subtle grace to her that suggested she wasn't intimidated by his wealth or status, unlike almost everyone else he met. The police had been nervous. The lawyers had been nervous. The girls were always nervous.

Why wasn't she?

The waiter arrived to take their orders. Vaughn ordered for both of them, of course: a bottle of his favourite wine and the tasting menu. It was a good way to assert his control, set things out the way he meant them to continue.

"So," he said once the waiter had departed, "what do you think of Dubrovnik?"

"It's all right," Amélie replied, her voice steady, eyes meeting his without flinching. "I've been here before, so it's not like it's new."

"Doing what?"

"I told you," she said. "Weren't you listening? Modelling."

Vaughn wiped the frown of confusion from his face; she wasn't remotely fazed by him.

"You've got quite the reputation," she said, taking a sip of her wine.

"What've you heard?"

"Things. I've looked online—the piece in *Slate* last year, the *Times*."

Vaughn chuckled, pleased. "You don't want to believe all that. They have an agenda. Want to make me look bad."

"We all have an agenda," she said, tilting her head, lips curling into a teasing smile. "I'm not one for gossip, though. I prefer to make up my own mind about things."

"Smart girl," he said, mirroring her and leaning forward slightly. "I prefer to show people who I really am in person."

She kept her gaze steady. "Go on, then. Who are you?"

Vaughn grinned. "Someone with lots of opportunities to share."

He let that sit for a moment. He wasn't just here to enjoy her company; he had plans for her. Amélie, with her looks and her haughtiness, her pursed lips and arched eyebrows, would be a perfect addition to the business. She'd hinted at financial struggles during their chats, and he could use that to his advantage. He just needed to bait the hook correctly.

She swallowed it. "Opportunities?"

"You're too smart to be doing whatever it is you're doing now," he said, watching her carefully. "Modelling. Come on. I don't mean to be a dick, but I've never seen you in anything. I could offer you something better. Something more lucrative."

Amélie sipped her wine again, her eyes never leaving his. "Do I look like the kind of girl who'd be on one of your webcams?"

"No," he said. "But you look like the kind of girl who'd like to make serious money."

He waited for her reaction. He knew the look: women

always hesitated at first, unsure of what he was offering, but once they saw the money, they always came around.

But Amélie didn't. She smiled slowly and put her glass down.

"No," she said. "I don't think so."

He laughed it off, though he was finding her responses difficult to reconcile with what he had expected. "It's something worth considering," he said, aware of how stupid he sounded.

She held his eye again, then gave a little shake of her head—silly boy—and picked up her glass again.

He felt a flush of anger, and before his temper took hold of him, he got up and dropped his napkin on his chair. "I'm going to the bathroom."

3

Vaughn swirled the last bit of wine in his glass, savouring the lingering flavour of the rich red as he downed the final sip. He set the glass back down, his eyes lazily wandering over Amélie, and thought about how well the night was going. It'd been good. His starter was decent, like it always was, and, once he'd worked out she was going to be more of a challenge than usual, he'd enjoyed their sparring. He'd fired out the usual battery of negative comments, all designed to make her question herself and seek validation in his approval, but rather than eliciting the response he expected, she'd responded with put-downs of her own. He'd made a comment about how muscular her arms were, and she'd responded by suggesting he must have skipped leg day. That kind of retort wasn't something he was used to hearing from women, especially not ones like her. At first, it had irritated him, but then it became clear: she was playing a game, too.

And Vaughn loved games.

The waiter was just clearing away the plates and cutlery from their starters when Vaughn started to feel unwell.

Something felt... off. A slight heaviness settled over his limbs. He blinked slowly, trying to shake the sudden fogginess clouding his mind.

"You all right?" Amélie asked.

Vaughn forced a grin, trying to shake it off, but the sensation persisted. His fingers tingled, and when he reached for his glass again, it felt heavier than before. A wave of warmth washed over him, radiating from his chest and crawling up his neck.

"What is it?"

His vision blurred around the edges, as if someone had dimmed the lights just a fraction too much.

"Callum?"

He blinked, trying to focus, but the room seemed to ripple, the walls breathing with a faint pulse. His limbs felt heavy, as though gravity had doubled. He slumped back in his chair, confused. There was a weight in his head now, thick and slow, and his thoughts—sharp just a moment ago—began to drift like smoke, slipping through his fingers before he could catch them. He reached for his glass again, but his hand missed the stem by inches, and he knocked it over. A voice, distant and muffled, drifted toward him, but he couldn't place it, couldn't make sense of the words. His heart pounded, the beat irregular and loud.

"Callum? Are you okay?"

His world tilted, his vision narrowing as the fog in his head thickened. His limbs felt like lead now, too heavy to control, and his breath came in shallow bursts. He blinked hard, trying to fight through the confusion, but it was like being trapped in slow motion.

"Sir?"

The waiter's voice floated toward him, but it was distant, distorted, like he was speaking underwater.

"He's had too much to drink," Amélie was saying. "I'd better get him home. Could you help me?"

Something was definitely wrong, but Vaughn couldn't put it into words.

The waiter had his hands underneath Vaughn's shoulders and was helping him to stand from the chair. Amélie looked as if she was taking care of the bill, leaving notes on the table, and then the next thing he knew, he was at the door, and his jacket had appeared from somewhere, and then he was outside, the valet appearing with his Lamborghini, the scissor doors raised. The cool air hit his skin as the waiter left him propped up against the wall, and Amélie took over, sliding his arm over her shoulders. Vaughn was a big guy—six four and two hundred and twenty pounds—but she managed his weight with seemingly no bother at all. He staggered, his legs refusing to cooperate, but Amélie held him steady, her arm around his waist, guiding him like he was a child.

She took him around the car to the passenger seat and lowered him into the cabin. The familiar smell of the leather interior brought a fleeting sense of comfort, but it was quickly replaced by a wave of confusion as Amélie reached across him, securing the seatbelt over his chest. Vaughn's hand twitched on his lap, but his muscles refused to respond.

She went around to the driver's seat.

"What are you doing?" he managed.

"Take it easy," she said softly, her tone smooth and reassuring. "You've had too much to drink. I'm going to help you."

He barely registered her words, his body too sluggish to respond. "How?"

"I'm going to take you home."

"You don't..." he started; then the words fell away.

His head lolled back against the leather, the familiar scent of the car mixing with a sour taste in his mouth.

He remembered what he wanted to say. "You don't know where I live."

She turned to look at him. "I do," she said. "I was there earlier."

"What?"

"I had a chat with your sister. Awful what happened to her."

He blinked, trying to focus on her, but his vision was swimming now, the edges blurring into darkness.

He felt the hum of the engine as it roared to life.

4

Vaughn's mind floated in and out of coherence. The world around him blurred, the lights of the town fading into a distant haze. He felt like he was weightless, suspended in water, but, at the same time, leaden and immobile. His vision swam, and his head lolled with the movement of the car, eyes half-lidded as he watched Amélie drive.

"I feel... I feel..." His mouth felt like cotton, and his tongue fumbled over the words.

Amélie looked over at him and smiled. "You've just had a bit too much to drink. Don't worry. I told you—I'm getting you home."

He tried to shake his head to clear the fog, but it didn't work.

His vision blurred, then swam into hazy focus again. He caught a glimpse of her face—calm, determined—and then a flash of fear shone through the fog. Something was wrong. Very wrong.

"Amélie..."

"Shh," she said.

"You said... my sister..."

"That's right," she said. "Bad what happened to her."

"What...?"

"The state she was in when I found her. Bullet in the head. You made a real mess."

"Bullet...?"

She reached forward, opened the glove compartment and took out a pistol. She held it up. "I think the police will find the bullet matches this gun. Shame what happened— the stress of the police investigation, I suppose. You've been put through it the last few months, haven't you? That kind of ordeal can make weak men snap and do things like that."

"I never..."

She put the gun back and closed the compartment. He noticed for the first time that she was wearing nitrile gloves.

"But don't worry," she said. "I've got everything under control."

Her voice was like a lullaby. His body was heavy, and he sank deeper into the seat. He was submerged in the fog and then drawn out of it, the world outside clarifying once again. He tried to focus.

The cliffs of the coastal road loomed ahead, moonlight silvering the drop to the Adriatic Sea, the black water swirling far below. Vaughn's head lolled to one side, something primal screamed at him, but it was too late.

5

His vision was still blurred, but he became vaguely aware of motion. He tried to focus, but his mind was too fogged to make sense of anything.

Was the car moving?

No.

He was.

He felt his body being shifted, hands gripping him as he was pulled from the passenger seat. There was a cold gust of air.

The smell of saltwater.

A gull crying out.

Someone was talking.

But the words were far away, like they were being spoken through a tunnel.

Was it her?

Amélie?

He felt hands beneath his shoulders and his heels dragging on the ground.

He outweighed her by a lot.

How was she moving him as easily as this?

He tried to ask what was happening, but his mouth barely formed the words, and all that escaped was a garbled murmur.

He was dropped, and, his vision sharpening, he saw he was in the driver's seat. His head slumped back against the headrest; his hands fell limp at his sides. His vision swam again as the seatbelt clicked into place, strapping him in tightly.

He felt a flicker of fear—a distant, disconnected sense of danger—but it was quickly blown away.

He heard the engine roar to life, its vibrations trembling through his body. Vaughn blinked slowly, his eyelids heavy, trying to understand what was happening.

Why was he in the driver's seat?

He'd had too much to drink.

Amélie said so.

What was she doing?

She leaned into the cabin, close enough that he could smell the scent she was wearing and see the pendant that she wore around her neck. "I want you to know something," she was saying. "I only do jobs where the person whose details I'm sent is the lowest of the low. Garbage. *Pond scum.* I'm paid well to do what I do, but for you, *Callum*"—she spat his name as if it had a bad taste—"for you, you abusive limp-dick piece of shit, I would've done you for *free.*"

He tried to move, to lift his foot, his arm—anything—but couldn't.

Panic surged, weak and distant, a flicker of lightning in the dark.

The car lurched forward, rolling slowly at first, then picking up speed. His heart raced, and he tried to shout, to scream, but couldn't. The car was moving, accelerating, the engine roaring louder and louder. The world outside the window became a blur, and suddenly, he saw the edge of the road, the cliffs, the dark expanse of the sea below.

No.

No.

This couldn't be happening.

The Lamborghini surged toward the guardrail, and now fear flooded him in an overwhelming wave. The car smashed through the barrier, and for a brief, terrifying moment, Vaughn felt weightless. He was falling—plunging through the air, the sounds of crunching metal and the wind rushing past him filling his ears—with the sea looming below, black and endless, and then everything went dark as the car hit the water with a deafening crash.

The cold swallowed him, and then there was nothing.

6

Isabella Rose went to the side of the road and, standing just behind the torn-apart barrier, looked down into the water below. The car had hit the water bonnet-first and was quickly sinking. The back end was pointing up, and she could see the red of the taillights, the glow gradually fading as the car went deeper and deeper until she couldn't see them at all.

She'd planned this all very carefully. Broker had only sent her a contract for Callum, but, as she investigated him to make sure he was morally bankrupt enough to meet her criteria, she'd found out that his sister Louise was more than disreputable enough, too. She'd decided to do them both. She didn't know who had engaged Broker, but guessed it was likely one of the girls who had been unfortunate enough to cross their path, or a parent or a boyfriend or someone else who was left with broken pieces where a loved one had once been. She doubted the client would complain that their money had gone further than they'd been told, and doing them both gave Isabella the chance to spin a more compelling story to cover her tracks, as well as making her feel a little better about the balance of good and evil in the world.

She'd got the GHB from a dealer in the medina in Marrakesh. It had been simple; no questions asked, just a wedge of cash for the small vial of clear liquid. She'd decanted it into a perfume bottle to get it through customs and then put it back into the vial in her hotel earlier that evening. She'd been practicing with water and had quickly become good enough to palm the vial and dispense the contents without drawing attention to herself. She'd waited until Vaughn had gone to the bathroom and dosed his wine. The chemical was fast-acting, and he was out of it by the time he'd finished his Crni Rižot.

Isabella had planned every detail meticulously, knowing that Vaughn was too self-absorbed, too arrogant to see it coming. Men like him always were. They thought they were in control, but their own hubris was their undoing. The plan had been days in the making, carefully crafted as she learned more about Vaughn's habits and weaknesses. She knew he liked to be in charge and had let him think he was.

But she'd turned the tables. He'd invited her into his world, sure that *he* was the one manipulating *her*, but he'd had it the wrong way around. She had set the trap, laid the groundwork, and ensured that everything unfolded exactly as she wanted it to.

There would be no way for him to escape the wreck. She'd slipped him into the driver's seat and secured the belt, and he was in no fit state to unclip it, let alone swim clear of the sunken car. She'd chosen the simplest tool for the job: a heavy brick, wrapped in an old rag, which she'd tied tightly with a length of string, creating a makeshift weight that could be wedged securely onto the accelerator pedal. It ensured that the car would speed up without his control, sending him over the edge and into the sea. She hoped it would drift free before the authorities found him; the gun in the glovebox, the same one she had used to shoot Louise, would implicate him in his sister's death. It wouldn't be hard to find a motive: Callum had been posting on TikTok about how difficult his legal ordeal had been and how even an alpha male like him had been struggling with depression.

The dots would be easy to join up after that.

Murder-suicide, open and shut.

Isabella took a deep breath, the cool night air filling her lungs as she watched the dark water ripple. It was over. Vaughn's 'business,' built on the exploitation of others, would sink with him. She felt no remorse, nor did she bother with second-guessing. Men like him didn't deserve a second chance. He'd destroyed lives without a second thought, and she had no qualms about ending his in the same way.

She wiped her hands on her dress, then turned away from the edge of the cliff. The night was still, the sound of the waves below the only reminder of what had just happened. Isabella was calm. She'd done what needed to be done. Vaughn had been a cancer, and now he was gone.

She was a mile outside of town. She took off her heels and set off, barefoot. She'd walk back to where she'd left her car and then disappear into the night. The restaurant staff would remember her, would tell the police that Vaughn had been drunk at dinner and that his companion had taken him home, but that would be that. Her communication with Vaughn had been encrypted, and she'd never shared anything that might lead back to Marrakesh. They'd never find her.

By the time the authorities realised what had happened,

found the car and hauled it out of the water, she would be a ghost.

Long gone.

PART II

7

Isabella stood on the rooftop of Riad Farnatchi in the heart of Marrakesh, watching the first rays of the morning sun break over the ochre rooftops of the medina. There was a permanent scent of dust and spice in the air, mingling with the fragrance of orange blossoms from the potted trees on the roof of the riad to the east. The souks sprawled around her, busy with the early morning clamour of traders setting up their stalls and the rhythmic clatter of donkey carts as they were drawn across the cobble-stoned streets. The muezzin's early morning call to prayer had just finished echoing across the rooftops, and the city was alive with the smell of baking bread from communal ovens and the sweet, smoky scent of tea. The hustle and bustle of Jemaa el-Fnaa, the square at the heart of the city, was just beginning; it would soon fill with snake charmers, musicians, and hawkers all vying for the attention of tourists. The Atlas Mountains loomed over everything, their peaks dusted with snow, a stark contrast to the flat, sun-baked rooftops all around her.

Isabella looked over to the roof of the riad with the

orange trees and watched a young boy in pyjamas and slippers as he went over to a small pigeon coop. He approached the wire mesh, and the pigeons beat their wings and cooed, jostling for the seeds in his cupped hands. The riad had been turned into a hotel for rich Europeans; the boy's family ran it on behalf of a Scottish man who publicised it on Facebook and TikTok. Isabella had researched all her neighbours when she returned to be sure that they had nothing to hide, and had seen the man's increasingly breathless posts about how beautiful the riad was and how life-changing a holiday in the city could be. It was all a little foolish, but harmless, nonetheless.

She stretched out the kinks in her muscles. She'd just finished her morning workout and had pushed herself harder than usual. The only equipment on the roof was a pair of fifteen-kilogram kettlebells, and she'd handled them as though they weighed a fraction of that; she had grown stronger, and now they were only good for her warm-up. She'd moved from the weights to a series of complex, balletic bodyweight exercises that Maia had taught her in the year they'd spent hiding in Mexico. The routine tested balance, breathing and basic strength; Isabella was still probing the boundaries of her unusual physical gifts, and every time she ran through the routine, she found it a little easier. She would've liked to move on to something more difficult, but Maia was dead, and Isabella couldn't very well go to an instructor without drawing attention to herself, so she'd been left with the internet. She'd scoured it until she found the training regimens of elite athletes and then mashed those together into something that felt challenging.

The boy on the rooftop opposite saw her and waved. She waved back, a little awkwardly. She didn't want to encourage him to think friendship was on the cards or for him to ask his family about the young woman who rose each morning even earlier than he did.

She descended the stone stairs to the ground floor and went to sit down next to the plunge pool. Riads like this were built around open shafts with courtyard pools at the bottom. Warm air was pulled down into the courtyard, then cooled by the water before circulating back up again. She loved to sit there, dangling her feet in the water with a book and a pot of mint tea.

She wondered what Pope would have said if he could see her now. She could guess: he would've grumbled that she should never have returned, that she was *insane* to come back here, that it was sloppy tradecraft, that she had to go somewhere she'd never been before, change her name, change the way she looked, then sink beneath the surface. Her unique genetic makeup made her incalculably valuable, and she'd already been pursued halfway around the world by people with huge budgets and no scruples who would've done *anything* to have her under their control. Maia had been their quarry, before Isabella—seemingly without any of the defects that had doomed Maia and her siblings—had taken her place.

She'd been away from the riad for months and hadn't known what she would find when she returned. She'd installed IP-enabled cameras when she had used her inheritance to buy the place, but there must've been a power cut at some point while she and Pope were in India, and the cameras had never come back online again. It was with a sense of trepidation that she had opened the heavy front door when she returned for the first time, half expecting to find the place had been ransacked. It hadn't been, and— save for the pigeons who had built a nest in one of the bedrooms and the thick layer of wind-blown sand and dust that had covered everything—the place was just as she had left it.

She looked around now. There was still a little work left to do, but most of the major renovations that it had needed were behind her. Crumbling walls had been reinforced with fresh layers of brick; rotting window frames had been replaced with new wood, intricately carved and painted by local craftsmen; the dated décor inherited from the previous owner had been stripped away; and the walls had been repainted in stylish slate grey, with colour added by vibrant artwork. Isabella had sourced everything herself: second-hand furniture from the bustling souks and rugs from the Berber markets high in the Atlas Mountains. The plunge pool had been retiled in rich emerald green, making it into the striking focal point it would once have been. She looked up now: the tranquil square of blue at the top of the shaft was her escape, a private piece of Marrakesh that felt entirely her own.

She'd paid some heed to the warnings that Maia and Pope had given her. She'd dyed her hair black, and the sun had darkened her skin, making it difficult to place her origins. She dressed conservatively, in long sleeves and loose cotton pants, and often draped a scarf loosely over her hair. Three months had passed since she'd moved back, and she hoped the locals had grown used to her presence and her quiet aloofness.

But it wasn't just discretion and modesty that she relied on to stay out of sight. It had taken time and patience, but she'd built a solid legend and a cover story to protect herself from unwanted attention. She lived in the city under the name Isabella Fischer, an internationally educated Swiss national whose parents had died in a car accident ten years earlier. She had the documentation to support the story, including a legitimate Swiss passport secured through one of Pope's old contacts in Geneva before his death. She still had a decent amount of money left from her mother, and had crafted a believable backstory to explain that, as well: she told people she worked as a model for a small agency in Paris, having supposedly been discovered on the Champs-Élysées as a seventeen-year-old, and had modelled for obscure sportswear campaigns across Europe ever since. None of it was true, but it didn't matter. She had the striking looks to make it credible, and as far as she knew, no one had ever thought to check.

Marrakesh had been kind to her.

It had given her exactly what she needed: anonymity and a life that didn't constantly require her to look over her shoulder.

She felt safe here.

It felt like home.

Safety was a new sensation for Isabella. She knew she couldn't afford to take anything for granted, and that a moment's laxity when it came to her personal security could prove fatal, but time had passed, and she'd grown comfortable with her life. She was nineteen and might once have said that mundanity was the last thing that someone her age should have sought. But mundanity and comfort were just what she'd needed after everything that she'd been through in her childhood and teenage years; she was content with the boring life that she'd built.

8

I sabella undressed and stepped into the cold shower. She watched the water running over her athletic arms and legs, noting the way her muscles rippled with every slight movement. Her forearms were defined, and the veins were pronounced, testaments to her unusual strength. Her legs were the same. She felt the familiar sense of disconnection: her body was both hers yet not hers, a blend of the girl she had been and whatever it was she'd become.

She dried off and dressed and opened her laptop, resuming what had become her daily ritual: searching the internet for any trace of Michael Pope. His body had never been found in the sea beneath Dingli Cliffs, and, although she'd accepted the fact of his death, the continued absence of certainty gnawed at her. She had a few photographs of him from the time they'd spent together, and she had run them through reverse-image searches on Google and scanned social media platforms, both the obvious Western sites as well as those with bigger footprints in China and Russia and the rest of the world. She doubted Pope would ever *choose* to appear in a photo, but there was always the chance he might be caught in the background clutter of someone else's life.

Pope had used specialised software when he had been looking for his family, but those facilities had been made available illicitly, by contacts he'd made in his career, and she didn't have his access or know-how to get it. Her more rudimentary effort was probably a pointless exercise, but it was better than not looking. She knew he was dead—she'd told herself that over and over again—but the fleeting hope that she was wrong, that he'd somehow survived the confrontation with Atari and his plunge into the sea, was something she wasn't prepared to give up.

ISABELLA LEFT THE RIAD, locked the heavy front door and set off. She lived in the Kasbah, one of the oldest districts in the city, located just south of the main medina and close to the Royal Palace. Beatrix had bequeathed her a book on the city's history, and it had become one of Isabella's favourites. The Kasbah had been a residential area for palace workers and soldiers, and that had imbued it with a more authentic, local atmosphere compared to the medina, which always had one eye on the lucrative tourist trade. It was still largely local, but, like almost everywhere else in the city, it had seen an influx of investment. Many of the large older riads had been restored and converted into boutique guesthouses, private homes, and trendy restaurants, and that had drawn in expats and investors who admired the neighbourhood's mix of history and character and saw the opportunity to make a quick buck.

It had been ideal for Isabella: the perfect blend of privacy and authenticity, hidden away from the more commercial areas but still close enough to the heart of the city. She'd grown comfortable after living here alone for the last three months. The Kasbah's rough edges allowed her to blend in, and she'd maintained a low profile while still being able to enjoy the district's charm.

She walked briskly, already planning a variation of her usual anti-surveillance measures. Today was a Wednesday, and Wednesdays were special. Isabella had left behind her phone and laptop; this wasn't the moment for leaving digital breadcrumbs that might eventually be found and followed.

Isabella took a sharp left turn into a tangle of narrow streets. Pope had taught her well: making sure she was clean was a precise art, a blend of strategy and instinct. Every turn, every pause, every face—they all counted. Going black was about noticing anyone who appeared more than once, about forcing a potential tail into the open, and about never retracing her steps.

She broke the route to Bab Doukkala into three distinct segments: the first was designed to flush out any surveillance, with sharp turns, sudden stops, and doubling back to catch anyone trying to follow; the second focused on evasion, on moving quickly and unpredictably to shake off anyone she might've missed; the final stage was confirming she was clear, choosing the most obscure route to ensure she was alone before she arrived at her destination.

She ducked into a passageway that was so narrow she could have touched both walls at the same time, then followed a wider lane between older riads that had not yet been bought up and converted. She slipped through a narrow archway and emerged into a square where locals shopped for vegetables and bread from open-air stalls. She carried on, occasionally stopping to look at a tray of oranges or lemons or to adjust her headscarf, using each pause as an opportunity to look around for anything that might have been off.

She turned into a street filled with taxis, mopeds, and pedestrians and carried on, reaching Rue El Gza, a busy thoroughfare that connected the medina with the newer parts of the city. She looked behind her, making a mental note of the faces she saw: a young woman in a red scarf, an old man with a cane, a child chasing a runaway balloon.

Isabella slipped into an open-air café and exited on the other side of the building onto a quieter street that skirted the edges of Bab Doukkala. She flagged down a beige grand taxi—a communal taxi that travelled between set points and whose price was fixed at five dirhams per passenger—and hopped into the backseat with a group of local women carrying baskets of fresh produce on their laps. The driver navigated the narrow streets with characteristic aggression, honking and jostling his way through the traffic as Isabella looked out through the window, scanning for signs of pursuit.

The taxi pulled to a halt near the Bab Doukkala market. Isabella stepped out, paid the driver the fare, and melted into the network of alleyways. She moved quickly, turning corners and darting along side streets, scaled a low wall into a hidden courtyard, and reemerged on a completely different street.

Nearly there. Bab Doukkala was a poorer district, an enclave of old housing stock that was slowly being changed as the tide of gentrification lapped at its boundaries. It was a real mixture now: shiny new buildings cheek-by-jowl with centuries-old neighbours, modernism blended with lingering decay. She passed a bakery and paused to enjoy the scent of baking dough mingling with anise and sesame seeds. She went inside. The bakery was small, with low ceilings and walls stained by years of flour dust and heat. Its shelves were lined with woven baskets overflowing with *khobz*, the traditional round Moroccan bread, their golden crusts flecked with specks of semolina. To her left, a glass display case held an array of pastries: delicate *msemen*, folded and glistening with oil; crispy *batbout* stuffed with spiced minced meat; and rows of honey-drenched *chebakia* twisted into intricate flower shapes. She joined the queue and waited while the baker worked a large wooden paddle to slide fresh loaves into the clay-lined oven that dominated the back wall. The elderly woman in front of her pointed to a stack of still-steaming *khobz*; the shop assistant wrapped one of them in a sheet of newspaper and presented it to the woman, who handed over a few coins before going back outside. Isabella bought all of the *chebakia*, the baker sliding them into a large paper bag and nodding as Isabella paid for them.

FINALLY, more than an hour after leaving her riad, she arrived at the orphanage. It was tucked away at the end of a narrow alley and looked tired and forgotten, with crumbling stone walls and faded green shutters barely hanging on by their hinges. Vines climbed up the façade, and the court-yard was shaded by a large, gnarled tree that cast twisted shadows.

Isabella pushed open the rusted iron gate and stepped into the garden at the front of the building. Above the door, a weather-beaten sign clung stubbornly to the wall, its faded letters barely readable. The sign was in Arabic: Dar Al-Amal, which, when translated, meant 'House of Hope.' It was a place where Isabella could feel useful, where her past mattered less than her willingness to help.

The sound of the children's voices, faintly audible from inside, reminded her why she had been coming here every week for several months.

"Isabella!"

She turned to see a young girl waving enthusiastically from one of the upper windows, her face breaking into a wide smile.

Isabella waved back. "Hello."

"Come and play with us!"

"I'm coming, I'm coming." She held up the bag of *chebakia*. "Shall I bring these up with me?"

9

Isabella had found the orphanage during her first week after returning to Marrakesh. She'd been on a long and aimless walk, exploring the red city without a map to get a feel for it and to reassure herself that coming back wasn't the idiotic move she knew Pope would tell her it was. She'd paused to take a sip from her water bottle when she noticed the dilapidated building set back from the narrow street. A little girl—no older than eight or nine—was playing in the small, dusty yard that passed for a garden. The swing she had been playing on had broken, and the girl was struggling to fix it. She was on her tiptoes, trying to reattach the chain to the overhead beam, but was too short to reach.

Isabella watched for a moment: the girl was frustrated but, despite that, refused to give up.

She offered to help. It hadn't been easy: Isabella's Arabic was rusty, and the girl only had a few words of English, but they'd managed to strike up a conversation that lasted for nearly an hour. Isabella would glance at her watch, thinking now was the time to leave, but the girl would grab her hand and flash a shy smile, and Isabella would stay a little longer.

The girl's name was Latifa, and Isabella would discover her story bit by bit over the following weeks: she was nine, with dark, curly hair that was often tied back in a messy ponytail, and bright, curious eyes that held a mix of sadness and resilience. Latifa's life had been upended the previous year when her parents died in a fire that tore through their small apartment while she was at school. She'd been sent to live with distant relatives who could barely afford to feed themselves, and when they could no longer care for her, she'd been sent to the orphanage. The girl's spirit had not been broken; she was resourceful, clever, and stubbornly determined, often taking on the role of older sister to the younger children, helping them with everything from homework to planning out their makeshift games.

Isabella had only been able to leave after making a promise: she would return the following week. It wasn't a promise she made lightly, and it was one she kept. She came back the next Wednesday, then the Wednesday after that, and then again and again. It wasn't long before she met Fatima, the orphanage's overworked but determined manager, who, recognising a capable and reliable volunteer, enlisted her help with everything from painting the walls to fixing broken beds.

Isabella settled into a routine without even realising it and soon became a familiar face at the orphanage. She indulged herself only after making a promise: she'd never let her own troubled world touch the children who had found refuge there. That was why she had never used her surname—not even her assumed surname—and it was why she took such careful precautions to make sure she was never followed. Pope had once told her that this kind of separation was called 'compartmentalisation'; you created barriers between parts of your life that could never mix. Being Isabella Fischer allowed her to distance herself from her past, but there needed to be another barrier between Isabella Fischer and the orphanage.

Because bringing harm to the children would be a crime for which she would never be able to forgive herself.

10

The narrow entrance hall opened into a dimly lit central courtyard covered by a skylight with cracked panels that let in natural light, revealing faded mosaic tiles on the floor. The walls were a muted, dusty yellow, chipped and peeling in places, showing patches of bare brick beneath. A once-grand wrought-iron staircase spiralled upward, connecting the building's three floors, each with narrow balconies that overlooked the central space. The balconies were lined with mismatched potted plants—herbs, bright geraniums, succulents—that added a touch of green to the otherwise worn-out surroundings.

The first floor housed a cramped classroom and a communal dining area where tables and chairs, none of which belonged together, were neatly arranged. Faded posters of the Arabic alphabet and drawings by the children had been stuck to the walls. A narrow corridor led to the dormitories on the two upper floors. Each was lined with simple metal-framed bunk beds, their mattresses thin and covered in worn sheets. Soft toys, makeshift pillows, and a few treasured mementos—tattered books and handmade trinkets and motheaten cuddly toys—lay on the beds.

The top floor also held a small library and playroom. The library's shelves sagged under the weight of old, donated books in Arabic and French, many of which were missing covers or pages. The playroom, with chipped tiles and faded murals of animals and flowers, had a scattering of well-loved toys. The large windows allowed the light to flood in, casting long shadows across the floor and offering views of Bab Doukkala.

The building had fallen into disrepair, but, despite that, there was warmth and community here, a testament to Fatima's efforts to make it feel like a home for the children.

Isabella opened the front door and went inside. It was dark and a little damp, and the scent of mildew hung in the air. She climbed the stairs to the first floor and stopped outside Fatima's office.

"Good morning," she said in French.

Fatima pushed her reading glasses up into a tangled mop of thick grey hair. "Isabella, lovely to see you."

"And you. How are things?"

"They've been better," she said.

"What's the matter?"

She waved a hand at the stack of letters and bills on the table. "I'm drowning. The minute I've paid off one thing, another thing appears. But otherwise, *alhamdulillah*, everything is fine. The children will be excited to see you." She nodded at the bag in Isabella's hand. "Especially when they see what you've brought."

Isabella pointed at the bills. "Can I help?"

"I can't ask for more money. You've already been generous—any more would make me uncomfortable."

Isabella's contract work for Broker was lucrative, and

she'd already dipped into her growing stash of money so that Fatima could ensure the children had what they needed. Fatima had asked where the money came from, and Isabella had deployed the story about her being a model. Fatima *seemed* to believe it, but, if she didn't, she kept her doubts to herself.

"I just finished a job in Tunisia," Isabella said. "Swimwear. They paid well. Please—let me help."

"No, I can manage." Fatima waved her away. "Take them the *chebakia*. I'm surprised they haven't smelled them already."

Isabella laughed. "Are you sure?"

"We'll be fine."

Isabella turned, but, before she could leave the room, Fatima yelped with sudden pain. Isabella turned back and saw that she'd opened the next envelope from the stack and then dropped it back on the desk. There was a streak of blood on her finger.

"Don't move."

Fatima swore.

Isabella angled the desk lamp to shine on the wound and saw that it had been caused by a shard of glass that now protruded from the woman's finger. It was thin but looked as if it had cut deep. Fatima reached for it, but Isabella stayed her hand.

"Better make sure it doesn't break and leave a piece behind. You don't want an infection."

Isabella leaned in to examine the wound closely, then took hold of the edge of the glass fragment between her thumb and forefinger and pulled it out.

Fatima swore again, taking a handkerchief and wrapping it around the cut.

Isabella reached for the envelope and upended it;

dozens of pieces of thin broken glass tumbled out onto the desk.

"That looks like a lightbulb. It's been smashed. That's deliberate, Fatima, not an accident. Someone's trying to hurt you."

Fatima pressed the handkerchief to her finger to staunch the blood. "Don't be so silly. It's nothing."

"No," she said. "It *is*. You don't seem surprised—has it happened before?"

"It's nothing. And I'm fine—it's just a little cut."

Isabella stared at her. "Has it happened before?"

Fatima bit her lip and looked down.

"It has," Isabella said. "Someone's threatening you. Threats get worse when whoever is doing the threatening doesn't get what they want."

"I don't mean to be dismissive," Fatima said, "but how would you know anything about something like that?"

"Do you know who sent it?"

Fatima waved a hand.

Isabella was not about to give up. "Have they sent something like this before?"

"Please, Isabella. *Please*. I'm not going to talk to you about this. I want you to forget it. I'm fine, and I don't need help."

Isabella remembered what had happened when she arrived the week before: Fatima had been standing at the back of the dining hall with a broom and was sweeping up a pile of glass from a broken window.

"The window last week," she said. "You said it was kids. It wasn't, though, was it? It was the same people who sent this."

Fatima refused to even look at her.

Isabella reached down and parted the envelope all the way so she could look inside. "There's a note."

Fatima grabbed the envelope before Isabella could take it out, and dropped it into the wastepaper bin. "Listen to me," she said sternly. "I'm saying this for your own safety. Don't put your nose into things you don't understand. You're a foreigner, and there are some things that foreigners shouldn't get involved in."

Isabella wanted to press, but it was obvious that Fatima wasn't going to say anything else. She was angry, too, and Isabella knew she'd risk their relationship if she made a fuss. It was better to give the impression that she was letting it go; that didn't mean she couldn't keep an eye out for anything else that might be amiss.

Fatima could see that her stern words had soured the mood and tried to return things to their usual footing with a broad smile. "You should go upstairs. Your treats are getting cold, and the children will be wondering what's happened to you."

11

_____

Isabella was always amazed at how Latifa and the other children could play the same game over and over and over again without growing bored. At first today it was a game of marbles; after that, they'd moved on to dramas acted out with sock puppets; and, finally, in the hour before dinner, there was football with a ball made from a sock stuffed with newspaper. They fired it again and again at Isabella as she stood in front of a goal drawn in chalk on the wall.

Latifa took another shot, and Isabella let it run under her foot so she could score. The girl whooped and ran to pick up the ball so she could try again.

Isabella put up her hands. "Enough!" she said, smiling broadly. "I've got to go."

She had business to attend to, and it wasn't something she could afford to miss. Her appointment was in an hour, and she had to find somewhere suitable for it. She needed to be on her way.

Latifa and two of the other children grabbed hold of her by the arms.

"One more," begged a young boy called Omar.

"Not now," Isabella said. "Next time."

She tickled him under the arms until he let her go.

ISABELLA WENT BACK INSIDE to say goodbye to Fatima but was stopped at the door by the sound of her voice. She was speaking with an urgent, pleading tone that Isabella hadn't heard before, and then there was silence. A phone call, Isabella thought, pressing her ear to the door. Her Arabic wasn't good enough to pick up every word, but it sounded as though Fatima was talking about the children and asking for more time.

A bank?

Could Fatima be behind on a loan?

No, she concluded. A bank wouldn't send an envelope full of broken glass.

A loan shark, then?

Had Fatima got into debt with bad people?

That seemed more plausible.

Isabella heard Ruth's voice at the foot of the stairs and then footsteps as she started up them. Ruth was an American who'd been living in the city for thirty years and who volunteered here as the chef. Isabella liked her, but didn't want her to see her listening at the door.

She hurried down, nodding to Ruth as she passed. She made a note to come earlier next week and have another try at getting to the bottom of whatever was happening. If the problem was money, it was a problem she might be able to alleviate. Fatima was proud, with reason, of what she had achieved here and had sacrificed so much in her personal life to create it. She'd made a safe place for the children, but, if she had a failing, it was that she was slow to accept help, even when it was obvious that help was desperately needed.

Like now, perhaps.

12

Isabella left the orphanage and retraced her steps. She pulled her scarf closer around her face, blending in with the locals as she cut through the streets. She paused at an intersection, allowing the busy flow of traffic and pedestrians to submerge her as she checked all around for anything that would suggest someone might have been watching her.

She needed a place where she could work discreetly, away from prying eyes and curious locals. She bypassed the trendy cafés filled with tourists and expats, remembering Pope's advice that their Wi-Fi networks were likely monitored by the government and easy to track. Instead, she went to the less conspicuous spot she had identified a month ago: a dimly lit internet café tucked between a run-down electronics repair shop and a nondescript storefront selling spare auto parts. The sign above the door flickered, one of the letters buzzing as she stepped inside.

The café had seen better times. It was sparsely furnished, with rows of ageing desktop computers set up on unstable desks, their screens casting a dull blue light in the otherwise shadowy room. The man behind the counter barely looked up as Isabella entered, his focus absorbed by the football playing on the wall-mounted TV behind her.

She paid in cash and chose a computer at the back, slipped into the worn chair and got to work. She connected to the internet using the café's public Wi-Fi, a network so open and insecure that it was practically invisible to anyone looking for serious activity. She reached into her bag for a USB drive and pressed it into the port. The drive contained a portable operating system known as Tails, a security-focused OS designed to leave no trace on the computer it was used on. Pope had taught her about it, setting her up with a secure version of the system delivered through an encrypted Dropbox by one of his trusted contacts in Berlin.

The system booted up directly from the USB, bypassing the café's old and untrustworthy Windows setup. Everything she did now would run through her own OS, ensuring that no data would be stored on the computer itself. She ran through the rest of Pope's procedure: first, she enabled the Tor network, relying on it to anonymise her internet connection by routing it through multiple encrypted relays around the world and making it nearly impossible to trace her real location; second, she set up a virtual private network to run inside Tor, adding another layer of encryption that would further obscure her activities from anyone monitoring the network traffic. She chose a VPN provider known for its strict no-logs policy, meaning that even they would have no record of her connection.

Isabella checked her work, and, happy that her multiple layers of anonymity were in place, she launched Ricochet, an encrypted messaging platform specifically designed for the dark web, where she could initiate the conversation without leaving a digital footprint. She opened a secondary Tor browser window and ran a check on the onion links she would be accessing, making sure they hadn't been compromised. Satisfied, she finally connected to the chatroom where her contact was waiting, using a pseudonym and a prearranged code phrase to verify her identity.

>> *ARCHANGEL HAS ENTERED THE CHAT*

There was a pause. Isabella stared at the screen, willing the cursor to move.

>> *BROKER261 HAS ENTERED THE CHAT*

>> *Like clockwork.*

Isabella typed.

>> *You know I like to be punctual.*

Isabella didn't know anything about the person with whom she was conversing. There had been times when Pope had been absent for a day or two, leaving Isabella in whichever safe house they were using and coming back with a fatter bank balance and a sour disposition that he wouldn't acknowledge or discuss. He'd been drunk one night, and she'd finally prised it out of him: Pope had been funding the search for his family with wet work.

The rest of the story came out the following day when Isabella wouldn't do anything Pope wanted her to do until he had explained what had been going on. Pope had been taking contract work from someone to whom he'd been introduced during his time in Group Fifteen. It was all completely anonymous: the contact didn't know about Pope, and Pope didn't know anything about the contact. They relied on cryptonyms to identify one another: the contact was Broker261, and Pope was Archangel. Pope told her that he'd taken half a dozen contracts, and each paid thirty thousand dollars. He was particular about the contracts he accepted, and the subjects had to be beyond redemption: he said he'd attended to an arms dealer, a crooked politician, and a human trafficker.

Although Isabella had money left over from her inheritance, she knew it wouldn't last forever; and that was especially true once she'd started helping Fatima at the orphanage. She was thinking of ways to top up her funds and had remembered the conversation with Pope when he had admitted what he had been doing. She had contacted Broker261, following the precise method Pope had demonstrated, and relied upon the natural assumption that whoever she was speaking to would assume that she was Pope.

The cursor flashed as Broker typed.

>> *I've transferred the bitcoin.*

>> *Using the tumbler?*

>> *Just like before. Check that you've received it.*

>> *Hold on.*

The tumbler scrambled the origin and destination of the bitcoin before it reached the new wallet she had set up, adding another layer of anonymity and making it harder to trace the transaction back to either party. Isabella opened Electrum and then Blockstream, which allowed users to monitor Bitcoin transactions without actually logging in. The money for the job had been received five minutes earlier.

>> *I have it. Thank you.*

>> *Good. And good work. The client was pleased. You were very discreet.*

>> *That's what you pay me for.*

>> *And generous. The sister, too?*

>> *Buy one, get one free.*

>> *The client is grateful.*

>> *Very good.*

>> *Want to demonstrate your discretion again?*

She paused, her fingers hovering above the keys. There was no point in being coy. It sounded like Fatima was in more trouble than Isabella had realised; she was going to need more money.

>> *What have you got?*

>> *A simple job that meets your criteria.*

>> *Price?*

>> *The usual. Want to look at it?*

There was no harm in that, she told herself.

>> *Send it.*

Broker261 was quiet for a moment, and then the chat reported that a document was ready to be downloaded. Isabella clicked to accept it, diverting to OnionShare and using the one-time link to download it. She saved it onto the USB to be opened later.

Broker261 sent a forty-character decryption key that would be necessary in order to open the file. Isabella copied it and pasted it into a fresh document, saving that to the external drive along with the file.

>> *I'll assume you're a yes unless you tell me otherwise.*

Isabella looked at the two new files and wondered who was unfortunate enough to have had their details passed to her.

>> *Fine.*

>> *You need to let me know by tomorrow if you don't want it. The client is keen that this is underway ASAP.*

>> *How long do I have before it needs to be done?*

>> *Four-week window, starting from tomorrow.*

>> *I'll be in touch.*

>> *I hope not.*

The cursor blinked again, and then the chat reported that Broker261 had left the conversation. Isabella systematically closed every program, clearing any traces of her presence from Tails before shutting it down. She pulled the USB and wiped down the keyboard and mouse with a wet wipe from her bag.

She got up, double-checked that she had left nothing behind, and then left.

I sabella took a taxi back to the Kasbah and walked the rest of the way to her riad. She unlocked the door and went inside, grateful—as she always was—for the dip in temperature. She made herself a pot of mint tea and took it, and her iPad, to the chair and table by the courtyard pool.

Isabella pasted the decryption key into the document and waited for it to load.

She read:

// Starts

Name: CHARLIE CARTER ('CC')

Age: Mid-20s

>> Current Residence:

Hammamet, Tunisia. Primary residence located in a semi-rural area on outskirts of city, within easy reach of small, local airstrips.

>> Physical Description:

Height: 6'1" (185 cm)

Build: Athletic, medium frame

Hair: Dark brown, short and slightly unkempt

Eyes: Green

Distinguishing Marks: Small scar above the left eyebrow, likely from previous injury; tattoo of compass rose on right forearm.

>> Bio:

CC is owner and operator of small air freight business—Carter Air Logistics ('CAL')—specialising in transportation of high-value, time-sensitive cargo across Africa. Primary operations involve flying to North African countries, often under guise of delivering humanitarian supplies, high-end goods, and urgent documents (although see below cf Russian clients). Business based at private hangar located at small airfield close to Enfidha-Hammamet International Airport known for light aircraft and minimal commercial oversight.

>> Known Locations and Routine:

Primary Residence: Lives alone in modest but well-maintained house on edge of Hammamet. Property equipped with basic security: CCTV at entrance, motion-sensor lights, automatic gate.

Business Premises: CAL operates from hangar at local private airstrip, known for low visibility/minimal oversight. CC spends most weekdays at hangar, conducting flight prep, handling logistics, overseeing cargo transfers.

Social Venues: Regularly seen at local bars in area. Very keen interest in scuba diving.

>> Routine:

Morning: Early riser, typically at hangar by 0700. Checks flight schedules, inspects aircraft, handles comms with clients.

Afternoon: Frequently pilots own aircraft on short-haul flights. Manages customs paperwork and oversees loading and unloading of cargo, often working directly with local agents expediting process to avoid delays.

Evening: Returns home if possible or stays in modest but

discreet accommodation near airstrips at destinations. Known to frequent local bars.

Upcoming Travel: Scheduled to fly to Algiers on Wednesday for cargo delivery. Flight logs indicate planned arrival at private airstrip on Saturday morning to oversee special consignment of goods intended for local client. Expected to remain in area until late Friday afternoon before returning. Likely to travel to coast for scuba diving.

>> KAs:

Peter Harris: Long-time friend and co-pilot, assists with secondary flights and helps manage logistics. Loyal, but has recently shown signs of tension related to more dubious nature of flights.

North African Contacts: Works closely with small network of local fixers in Marrakesh, Casablanca, and Tunis who help facilitate cargo transfers and customs clearances. Some of these contacts have been flagged for links to smuggling and low-level crime.

>> Financial Overview:

Income: Moderate but consistent cash flow from the business, largely below threshold that would draw scrutiny from tax authorities. Noticeable uptick in revenue corresponding to increased activity after Russian invasion of Ukraine and ensuing sanctions.

Assets: Owns Cessna 208 Caravan used for cargo runs. Home owned outright, no major debt. Business model suggests need for continuous cash flow to maintain operations.

Suspicious Financial Activity: Regular cash deposits, often just below reporting thresholds. Deposits coincide with flights to area, suggesting off-book dealings.

>> Security Assessment:

Personal Security: Basic awareness of personal safety but no known ties to professional security services. Relies mainly on routine and familiarity with surroundings for personal safety.

Physical Threat Assessment: Physically fit. Likely to be alert and responsive but not professionally trained in high-threat scenarios.

Vulnerabilities: Frequently works alone, often flies solo, follows predictable patterns. Known to work late at hangar, where security is minimal, providing potential opportunities for undetected access. Regular diving expeditions, often alone.

>> Russian Involvement:

Since the imposition of international sanctions following Russia's invasion of Ukraine, CAL has come under scrutiny for suspected involvement in transporting goods for Russian oligarchs and high-net-worth individuals. These activities include facilitating the movement of luxury items and other assets out of Russia to safe havens in North Africa and the Middle East. While CC claims his business primarily handles legal cargo, there is evidence to suggest that some of his operations are in direct contravention of sanctions placed on Russian nationals and companies.

Increased financial activity after the sanctions came into force aligns with CC's uptick in flights to North African destinations, including Marrakesh and Tunis. The nature of these flights has raised questions, as several have coincided with reports of high-value asset movements involving Russian nationals seeking to bypass Western financial restrictions. CAL's business model, relying on private airstrips with minimal oversight, provides the perfect cover for clandestine transport operations.

>> Potential Russian Connections:

CC's dealings include close collaboration with middlemen and fixers in Tunisia and Morocco, some of whom are known to have ties to Russian oligarchs seeking to smuggle goods out of Europe and circumvent asset freezes. These individuals are connected to shell companies used to obscure ownership of assets, a tactic increasingly common among sanctioned Russians attempting to safeguard wealth abroad. Moreover, CC's recent purchase of aircraft parts from suppliers known for dealing with embargoed countries suggests he might be retrofitting his planes for specialised cargo—potentially to carry items that require extra security or stealth, such as luxury goods or precious metals. His dealings have involved the use of cash and untraceable transactions, likely to evade digital financial monitoring.

CAL's suspected role in these operations makes it a key player in the network of illicit activities associated with Russian sanctions evasion. While CC himself maintains plausible deniability, there is growing evidence that suggests he is deeply embedded. His operations appear to be a linchpin for moving assets through North Africa, potentially offering Russian clients a way to smuggle banned items, wealth, or even people out of Europe without detection.

>> Additional:

Potential Weaknesses: Documented instances of gambling habit that may be a factor in his willingness to engage in riskier operations. His connection to these illicit activities is likely a result of desperation to maintain cash flow, as well as the lucrative payments offered by Russian clients under sanctions.

Slight estrangement from family, suggesting limited immediate support if compromised.

>> Timescale:

ASAP. Bonus for prompt (<7 days) attention.

// Ends

Isabella laid the tablet down on the table and refreshed her cup of tea. Carter sounded like bad news, and Isabella concluded that he met her criteria for intervention. Pope had explained that he'd been very open about that stipulation from day one. He had told Broker that he wasn't interested in settling personal vendettas or helping customers eliminate business rivals. He'd been clear—*crystal clear*—that he'd only take contracts where the target was a genuine, bona fide bad actor with blood on their hands.

Isabella took the tablet again and read the file for a second time. Carter was a sanctions buster, moving Russians and Russian money around North Africa. Isabella had been on the other end of Russian weapons in Syria, and, while she was not naïve enough to think that it was only Western missiles and bombs that brought misery, she'd read the reports and seen films about the situation in Ukraine and knew what side of this particular fence she was on.

The report said that Carter had been given a warning by MI6 to step back, but didn't listen; he had continued to flout sanctions, even stepping it up a notch.

That was a mistake.

The timescale was challenging, but not impossible. She opened Google Maps and plotted a route between Marrakesh and Algiers. The flight went via Paris, and there were several a day from Marrakesh.

She looked at the tablet, idly scrolling the report up and down the page, before deciding that she wasn't in a position to be fussy about the work she accepted or rejected.

She'd head east, take care of business in Algiers and fly back as soon as it was done. Broker was a prompt payer, and she'd be able to send the money—plus the bonus for prompt attention to the contract—straight to Fatima.

PART III

14

Isabella arrived at Menara Airport just as the first light of dawn began to stretch across the sky, bathing the tarmac in the muted orange glow that had become familiar to her whenever she went out on an early morning long run. She moved through the nearly deserted terminal and made her way to the check-in counter. She'd spent longer than would usually be the case on her outfit, settling for a loose, cream-coloured blouse tucked into high-waisted trousers, her hair pulled back into a simple bun. She had a pair of oversized sunglasses perched on her head, she had a small rucksack and the suitcase she wheeled behind her was Louis Vuitton. She wanted to present a specific appearance to anyone who might notice her, specifically officials at her destination who might question the reason for her trip. She had been taught well and knew that she had to live the legend she was using in order for it to be effective. Isabella Fischer had a particular kind of life with more expensive tastes than Isabella Rose, and it always took a while for her to slip back into her persona and feel comfortable with it.

She navigated security calmly and casually, putting up

with the irritation of having her case selected for further inspection without making any fuss. The early hour meant that most of her fellow travellers were still groggy, but she was already keyed up with the anticipation of attending to Broker's contract and anxious to get on her way.

The agent picked through her case—finding nothing of note—and said she was free to go. She zipped the case back up, offered a friendly smile to the agent, and continued.

She boarded the small commercial flight bound for Algiers, blending in with a mix of business travellers and a handful of tourists. She took her seat by the window, staring out as the aircraft taxied to the runway.

They lifted off, climbing above the sprawling, sunlit city, its ochre walls and bustling streets fading into the patchwork of arid landscape and scattered villages. She watched as the terrain went from rolling hills to the rugged, dry plains that stretched east. She sipped the coffee she'd been given by the stewardess slowly, flipping through the glossy pages of a fashion magazine she'd picked up at the airport; it was a prop, but also a useful distraction. She looked at the blank faces of the models in the spreads, imagining the lives they pretended to lead for the camera, and tried to imagine herself in the same kind of life. Isabella Fischer would have been completely at home in their world, so she needed to be too.

THE PLANE TOUCHED down at Houari Boumediene Airport with a soft bump, and Isabella enjoyed the familiar rush that always accompanied her arrival in a new city. She knew she was well travelled for someone her age, and that some of her destinations were not ones that many other people would have visited. Pope and Maia had both drilled into her that she would always be on the move, that settling down would be something she might never be able to do. She supposed she had thumbed her nose at both of them with her decision to go back to Marrakesh, but there were times, particularly when her anxiety at being discovered was at its highest, that she knew she would eventually have to accept that they were right.

Her life was always going to be peripatetic; she would be a vagabond, or she would be found and caught.

She disembarked quickly, following the flow of passengers down the air bridge and then toward immigration. The terminal was a sprawling maze of glass and steel, a mix of old and new that spoke to the city's own complex history. She took her place at the end of the line, passport in hand, and watched the guards to assess their attitudes. They were impassive, calling travellers forward with curt instructions, asking their questions and then stamping their passports and sending them on their way.

The queue shuffled forward, and then another kiosk opened; the officer beckoned Isabella over. He was a stout man with sharp eyes and a well-worn uniform, and he barely glanced up as he took her passport and thumbed through the pages.

"Purpose of your visit to Algeria?" he asked in French.

"I'm here for a photo shoot," she replied.

"Really?"

"That's right."

"Do you have anything to prove that?"

Isabella handed him the confected email confirmation of the shoot's details, with an invitation from a local agency, complete with contact numbers and the names of the photographers involved. The officer read the email, looked up at Isabella, then back down at the paper. He reached for his stamp and pressed it down on an empty page. "Welcome to Algeria, Mademoiselle Fischer," he said, handing back her documents.

"*Merci*."

Isabella took the passport with a grateful smile, then moved through the gates and into the busy arrivals hall.

15

I sabella stepped out of the arrivals hall and into the bright, dry air of Algiers. The sun cast sharp shadows across the pavement, and the city's energy hit her all at once: the electric hum of traffic, the scent of the Mediterranean drifting in on the breeze, a melodic tune from an *oud* from the open window of a taxi. She adjusted the strap of her bag so that it fell more comfortably across her shoulder and looked out at the taxis and private cars jockeying for position along the curb.

Algiers wasn't dissimilar to Marrakesh. It sprawled along the coast, a mixture of old and new that seemed to collide at every turn. Whitewashed buildings with French colonial façades stood beside crumbling neighbours that bore the marks of time and neglect. The streets thrummed with a chaotic rhythm: car horns honking, vendors yelling out to snag passing trade, pedestrians slouching as they made their way through the heat. Isabella remembered what Pope had told her about arriving in a new location for the first time: settle down, get a feel for the place, and only then focus on the task ahead.

She found her way to the long-term car park and followed the directions that Broker had sent her until she found the car. It was a Volkswagen Passat, and the key had been left in a magnetic key box under the right-rear wheel arch. She took the box, thumbed in the code that Broker had sent, opened the box and took out the key. She went around to the rear, checked that she wasn't observed, and opened the boot. Two items had been left there: a rucksack and a sealed cardboard box. She would check the contents when she was in a position to examine them without fear of being observed.

She'd booked a room at the Dar Tlidjene on the Rue de l'Hôpital. It looked as if it would offer the kind of anonymous accommodation of about the standard a young woman in her position would book: nice, but not too nice. The position was decent, too, offering a good place to base herself while she was in the city.

She set off, watching the city unfold as she headed north. The streets were a jumble of wide boulevards lined with palm trees, narrow alleys packed with market stalls, and steep inclines that offered glimpses of the turquoise sea. Isabella saw clusters of men gathered outside cafés, sipping espressos from small paper cups and smoking, their conversations punctuated by expansive gestures and gales of laughter. Women in flowing robes moved between stalls, haggling with vendors selling everything from fresh fruit and vegetables to counterfeit electronics.

Algiers had a vim and vigour about it, and Isabella felt at home.

16

The Dar Tlidjene was unassuming: a weathered white façade and a small, understated sign that blended easily with its similarly unremarkable neighbours. The district consisted of a cluster of low-rise buildings with white-painted walls and red-tiled roofs, all closely packed together. Utility poles and wires crisscrossed the street, and a tall palm tree swayed to the left. The sea was just to the north, and Isabella caught the occasional glimpse of the calm blue waters through the alleys that ran between the buildings. Isabella was pleased with her choice. It was exactly the type of place Pope would've picked: modest, out of the way, and with locals not likely to ask too many questions.

She parked down the street, grabbed her things, and walked back to the hotel. She stepped through the heavy wooden door into the lobby. The atmosphere was unpretentious, the lighting low and the furnishings sparse. A single reception desk, chipped and aged, was manned by an elderly man who barely looked up as she entered.

"Check in, please," she said.

"Name?"

"Fischer. I've booked a room for three nights."

He looked over at an old PC, tapped the keyboard, and, evidently satisfied, gave a curt nod and handed over the key. He told her she was on the top floor, that breakfast was served between seven and nine, and that the front door would be locked at ten but that her key would open it.

Isabella thanked him and wheeled her suitcase to the stairs. There was no lift, so she picked it up and climbed the narrow staircase. The treads creaked as she climbed to the first floor and then the second. Her room was on the third floor. She opened the door, noting that it was flimsy and wouldn't offer anything in the way of security—probably not a problem, given that she was confident she hadn't been followed—and went inside.

The room itself was small and basic: there was a single bed, a wooden dresser, and a window looking out to sea. It was perfect: discreet, unremarkable, easily left behind. Isabella went to the window and looked out; it was high enough to give a clear view over the buildings between the hotel and the beach, and she watched as a jet cut across the blue sky and a large boat—a passenger liner, she thought— traced the line of the coast. The window was open, and the smell of salt mixed with the lemon polish that the cleaners must have used.

Isabella put the rucksack on the bed and unzipped it. She pulled it open and scanned the contents. She took out the pistol first. The Glock 19 semi-automatic was light-weight, with a matte-black polymer frame and a steel slide that offered low recoil and high accuracy, making it ideal for quick, precise shots in tight situations. It had a fifteen-round magazine capacity, and that, combined with a spare maga-zine wrapped in a cloth, ensured that she would have more than enough firepower for what she needed to do. She hefted it, feeling the reassuring weight in her hand before setting it down on the bed. She went back to the rucksack and took out a compact pair of night-vision goggles, still in their case. There was a suppressor, custom-fitted for the Glock. Beneath that lay a roll of black duct tape, a bundle of zip ties, and a slim, retractable knife. There was a set of disposable gloves, a small box of disinfectant wipes, and a folded black balaclava. Last of all was a compact flashlight with a red filter.

She turned her attention to the small cardboard box. It was unmarked, plain, and unassuming. She took the knife and carefully sliced through the packing tape, lifting the flaps with elaborate care. Inside, nestled in a bed of shredded paper, was a small device. It was about the size of a coffee mug with a matte-black exterior. She lifted it from the box and felt the cool, metallic surface of the casing. She turned it over, inspecting the secure metal casing that protected the inner components. Wires were neatly tucked and secured and, according to Broker, led to a pressure sensor that would activate the detonator once the device reached the pre-programmed altitude. The small button at the base, encased in a plastic cover, just needed to be pressed to arm the device.

Isabella returned the bomb to the box, repacking the shredded paper around it.

She repacked the bag and left it, and the box with the device, in the cupboard.

She went to the bed, sat down with her back against the headboard, and took out her phone. She'd downloaded the dossier and opened it now to refresh her memory. Charlie Carter's Cessna had the tail registration of 5T-GXC. Isabella accessed a publicly available aviation database, typed it in, careful to double-check each character, and then checked the results: the aircraft was registered in Mauritania, listed under a shell company that operated out of Hammamet but had connections to several discreet business ventures across North Africa. She scanned the listed flight history, noting recent entries: frequent trips between Marrakesh, Tunis, and smaller, lesser-known airstrips that would be ideal for low-visibility operations. It was said to have landed in Algiers yesterday afternoon.

The room had a tiny bathroom with just enough space for a shower. She would refresh herself and then grab a little sleep, she wanted to go out tonight after dark, and she didn't know when she would be back.

17

Isabella woke to the buzz of her alarm at eleven. She'd left the window open, and a cool breeze blew into the room, ruffling the thin curtains. She killed the alarm and checked her messages. Broker would not have been able to contact her to call off the hit; once the contract had been accepted, the operative went dark. She looked anyway, saw nothing of interest, navigated over to TikTok for a distraction, became bored with it, and got up. No reason to wait. The sooner she did what she was here to do, the sooner she could return home to Marrakesh.

She changed into the darker clothing she'd packed—black cargo pants and a fitted long-sleeve top—and tied her hair back into a tight braid. She went to the cupboard and took out the rucksack and the box. She removed the device and, checking that it was still inert, put it in the rucksack and then slung that over her shoulder.

She took out her phone and checked her route. Dar El Beida Airfield was not a commercial facility open to the public, but rather a smaller, specialised section near the main international airport. It was located to the east, and Google suggested it would take half an hour to get there.

Isabella slipped out of the hotel and walked down the street to the Passat. The journey took her through the heart of the city, past bustling markets and the glitter of waterfront cafés. The scenery changed as she approached the airfield, becoming more industrial and less refined. The roads narrowed, flanked by warehouses and dimly lit garages, and the traffic thinned out until only the occasional truck rumbled by.

She stopped a few blocks from the entrance to the airfield and walked the rest of the way. The facility was shrouded in darkness save for a few distant floodlights that cast long shadows across the tarmac. She approached cautiously, reaching the wire mesh fence and looking through it and out onto the facility.

Dar El Beida was a far cry from the international airport next door. It had a utilitarian feel: chain-link fences topped with barbed wire, rusted gates, and a scattering of small hangars housing a mixture of private planes and cargo aircraft. The air smelled of aviation fuel, and the cries of seagulls overhead were muffled by the hum of the nearby generator that looked as if it powered the lights. Isabella moved closer, keeping low as she found a spot behind a stack of old shipping containers that provided a clear view of the runway.

She raised her binoculars and scanned the airfield methodically—left, centre, right; near, middle, far—just like Pope had taught her. There were a handful of aircraft parked on the tarmac, most of them small, single-engine planes. But it was the Cessna 208 Caravan that caught her attention: a sturdy, dark-painted aircraft that matched the description she'd been given of Charlie Carter's plane. It was parked near the edge of the airstrip, partially concealed by the shadow of a nearby hangar. The Caravan's exterior was finished in a muted grey with a matte coating. It looked rugged, and the websites she'd reviewed on the flight over suggested that its high-wing design and broad landing gear made it a good match for rough, unpaved airstrips.

She focused on the registration number painted on the tail. The black script was slightly faded but still just about legible: 5T-GXC.

The same registration that had been listed for Carter.

Broker's intelligence was right: her target was here.

Isabella watched as two men worked around the aircraft, loading crates into the hold under the dim glow of a portable light. They finished up, then clambered up into a cargo truck and drove off.

She lingered, taking mental notes of the airfield's layout and the positions of the security personnel; they were few and far between, and, given that, she decided tonight was as good a night as any to do what she had come here to do.

18

I sabella waited, pressed tight against the shipping containers, her eyes fixed on the plane. The airfield was quiet, with only the faint hum of the generator and the occasional spit and fizz of sparks from a welding gun in one of the other hangars. The two men who had been loading the Cessna had disappeared, leaving the aircraft unattended.

She took a deep breath and steeled herself as she scanned the area one last time. The fence surrounding the airfield was topped with barbed wire, designed more to discourage than to prevent determined intruders. It was about eight feet high, its metal links rusted in places, with tangles of wire that had been patched and re-patched over the years. Isabella reached out, testing the tension and finding just enough give in one section to offer her a decent foothold. She pulled herself up, gripping the fence tightly as she climbed. The metal groaned under her weight, but she moved quickly, her movements smoothly efficient. She reached the top and paused, eyeing the barbed wire coiled above her. She pulled her jacket sleeve down over her hand,

and, using it as a barrier, pushed the wire down enough to slide over.

She swung one leg and then the other over the wire and dropped down the other side, landing silently on the tarmac. She took a second to steady herself and looked for any sign that she might have attracted attention. She could see nothing and, satisfied that she was undetected, made her way toward the plane.

She reached the side of the Cessna and ran her fingers along the fuselage, the metal cool beneath her touch. She moved to the cargo door and took her lockpicks from her pocket. She found the right-sized pick, slid it into the lock, and—after a slight twist and a bit of pressure—the lock clicked open.

Easy.

She eased the door ajar, holding her breath as she slipped inside.

The interior had been repurposed for cargo, stripped of passenger comforts to leave a spacious cabin designed purely for function. The seats had been removed to make room for stacks of crates and tightly secured packages, all strapped down with heavy-duty webbing to prevent movement during flight. Metal tie-down points lined the floor, anchoring the cargo, while the walls were bare, exposing the aircraft's reinforced frame.

Isabella pulled out her flashlight, keeping the red lens on to avoid drawing attention. She inspected the cargo, finding neatly arranged bags of essential items: bandages, antibiotics, and other medical necessities. Each package bore labels indicating they were bound for the areas in eastern Algeria that had been affected by the recent earthquake.

Béjaïa.

Jijel.

Tizi Ouzou.

She remembered watching the reports from the area on CNN; these were towns with roads that had been blocked and where conventional aid routes were failing, with inhabitants cut off and relying solely on supplies from the air.

Broker had said that Carter was operating under the cover of moving humanitarian supplies, and it looked as if his intelligence was correct.

She opened the rucksack and took out the device. She found a box full of kilogram bags of rice and, taking out one of the bags, made enough space to hide the device. She turned it over, removed the hard plastic cover that prevented it from being accidentally armed, and pressed the button. A single red light shone on the fascia and then winked out. Isabella lowered the device into the space, returned the bag of rice to hide it and closed the lid of the box. She rearranged the boxes so that it was beneath another box— hiding the fact that it had been opened—and then stepped back to check her handiwork. It looked very much as she had found it, and she was confident that the device would not easily be found.

She backed out of the cabin, securing the door behind her. She crouched low, retracing her steps toward the fence. She clambered over it and landed softly on the other side.

She straightened up, rearranged her clothes and set off back to where she had parked the car. She'd only been out of the hotel for an hour and had done everything she needed to do. The next thing—but something that could wait until tomorrow—was to go and check out Carter. She needed to reassure herself that the target fit her criteria for action. She had only Broker's word that he did, and, given that she knew absolutely nothing about him, she was going to need a little more confidence that what she'd been told was true.

The only way she would be able to do that was to meet him and see for herself.

Isabella was well rested when she drove out of Algiers, merging onto the highway and heading east along the Mediterranean coast toward Béjaïa. The city's bustle faded quickly in her rear-view mirror, replaced by the long ribbon of asphalt ahead. As she drove, the landscape began to shift, the urban sprawl giving way to rugged, sun-baked hills dotted with olive groves and whitewashed villages clinging to the slopes. The air was dry, and the sun beat down relentlessly, casting shadows from the tall trees at the roadside that flickered across the road as she passed through them. The deep blue of the Mediterranean glimmered to her left.

Broker's intelligence suggested Carter had been making it his habit to indulge his passion for diving whenever he travelled to Algeria. He'd been making runs to Algiers every week for the last two months, leaving his plane at the airport for three or four days between arriving and then departing again. He spent those spare days in Béjaïa, a coastal city close to some of the best diving sites in this part of the Mediterranean. He always stayed in the same place—

Hôtel Saldae—and Isabella had booked a room there for herself for the night.

The highway cut through stretches of farmland; she saw shepherds watching over small flocks of sheep grazing on patches of parched grass, and old men in traditional robes sitting beneath the sparse shade of trees. The coastal mountains rose up, their jagged peaks cutting into the sky, and the road twisted and turned as it hugged the contours of the land.

The sun began its slow descent toward the horizon, casting a golden glow as Isabella passed through Tizi Ouzou. She stopped at a roadside stall and bought a bottle of water from a woman in a brightly coloured headscarf who greeted her with a warm smile. She thanked her, taking a moment to stretch her legs and soak in the sounds of the town: the rhythmic clink of a blacksmith hammering metal, the laughter of children playing in a nearby alley, and the faint strains of traditional music drifting from an open window.

Isabella cracked the top of the bottle and took a long drink, slaking her thirst and washing away the dust and grit that tickled her throat. She found her thoughts drifting back to Pope and the time they'd spent in Goa before they were discovered and had to run. The pace of life here seemed similar, and she remembered how they'd hoped that they would be able to stay there for two or three months, enough time for Pope to recover from the stab wound that Maia had delivered and for Pope to find more reliable leads in the search for his family. Isabella had enjoyed it, but, like everything else in her life, it had been cut short. They had allowed themselves the luxury of thinking they were hidden and safe, only for that to be shown to be illusory.

And nothing had really changed since. She thought

again about Marrakesh. She couldn't afford to feel settled. She couldn't put down roots. A normal relationship was out of the question. Kids—not that she wanted them now—would be an extravagance, and it would be unfair to bring anyone else into her world. She'd end up like her mother, with the difference that—at least for the last year of her life—Beatrix had had her. Isabella had no one and doubted she ever would. Everyone she'd cared about—her mother, Maia, Pope—was dead. She was alone, and there was nothing to suggest that would ever change.

THE FINAL STRETCH to Béjaïa took her along a winding coastal route that offered stunning views of the sea on one side and towering cliffs on the other. The road was narrow, carved into the rock, with sheer drops that fell away to the crashing waves below. As she rounded the last bend, the port city came into view. It was nestled between the mountains and the sea, its white buildings glowing in the fading light.

Isabella parked the car on an asphalt lot that shimmered with heat and stepped out, breathing in the cool sea air. The hotel was a modern, multi-storey building with an ugly design. Its façade accommodated a series of wide balconies that stretched across each level, offering what must be expansive views of the Mediterranean.

Isabella took her suitcase out of the boot and wheeled it to the entrance. Broker's intelligence had been good so far, and he'd said that Carter ought to be here tonight.

Isabella checked in and went up to her room on the fourth floor. She showered, changed into clean clothes and then took out the copy of *Dive* she'd bought before leaving Algiers. She took her phone and her AirPods and went down to the bar, a large space on the ground floor with open doors that led out onto the pool terrace with a wide view of the ocean beyond.

She took a stool at the bar, and before she could even attract the attention of the barman, she noticed Charlie Carter was three stools down from her. She recognised him at once from the photographs and videos in the file that Broker had sent over. His hair was dark brown, a little longer on top and unruly in a way that made it seem like he couldn't be bothered to smooth it down. That casual messiness suited him, as did his green eyes. His skin was the nutty brown of someone who spends a lot of time outside, and there was a small scar above his left eyebrow, though it didn't mar his appearance. She knew he was in his late twenties, but there was a youthfulness to his appearance that meant he would likely be able to pass for younger than that.

He had what looked like a gin and tonic and was fiddling with the waterproof housing around a GoPro, opening the back of the case and then switching the camera on so he could review the saved footage. He had a bulky dive controller on his wrist.

Isabella took her magazine and laid it on the bar. It was well known to scuba enthusiasts, and this one had a colourful shoal of fish surrounding a diver on the cover. She was hoping that he might notice, but he was engrossed with whatever he was looking at on the camera. She would've preferred him to make the first move, but rather than wait and run the risk that he might leave, she decided to make an approach.

"Excuse me," she said.

Carter looked away from the camera.

She pointed down at his wrist. "Sorry to interrupt you, but I saw that and thought I recognised it. It's the new Garmin?"

"Yep," he said. He turned his wrist so the dive computer was facing her. "The Descent Mk2."

"Any good?"

Carter gave an appreciative smile, clearly pleased to be asked. "Best I've ever used. Tracks everything: depth, gas mix, heart rate. The battery lasts for days, and it's solid as a rock. Perfect for technical dives." He tapped the display to wake it; Isabella saw it was showcasing a recent dive log. "Plus, it syncs with my transmitter, so I can keep an eye on my air without fumbling around. Not cheap, but worth every penny if you're serious about diving."

Isabella nodded, feigning a casual interest. "I've read the

reviews. I've been looking to upgrade. My Suunto's been giving me trouble lately."

Carter chuckled. "I had a Suunto—primitive compared to this. You won't regret switching. They nailed it."

She smiled back, pleased that the conversation was flowing easily.

He gestured down to the magazine. "You dive?"

"Not as much as I'd like."

He nodded with boyish enthusiasm. "It's my favourite thing. Been diving since I was thirteen. I try to get out on a boat at least a couple of times a month."

"You're keen."

"I love it. My job can be stressful, and you can't think about anything else when you're underwater."

"Right," she said. "Start getting distracted and you get into trouble."

He nodded his agreement. "Plus, I travel a lot with my job, so I get the chance to see different places. Take here, for example."

"Algeria?"

"I know—it's not known for diving, but there are some brilliant sites if you know where to look." He eyed her. "Is that why you're here? To dive?"

"I'm actually here for work."

"What do you do?"

"I'm a model."

He didn't know how to react. His eyes flicked over her briefly, trying to reconcile the casual way she carried herself with the glamorous stereotype he evidently had in mind. "Really?"

"Not as glamorous as it sounds. You know what I've been doing all day?"

He shrugged.

"Standing on the beach while the photographer worked out exactly what he's trying to do. I think he might have taken six pictures. Most days are like that. Long, tiring, boring."

He forced a polite smile, unsure whether to express interest or keep his distance, settling on a neutral nod that betrayed his uncertainty. He put out his hand. "I'm Charlie."

"Isabella."

She took his hand and shook it with an unforced smile. "What about you? What do you do?"

"I'm a pilot."

She raised an eyebrow. "That sounds *much* more interesting. What kind of planes?"

"Small ones. I have a logistics business."

"What does that mean?"

"I move cargo from place to place. Passengers too, but it's mostly freight."

"Fun?"

He smiled. "I can't complain. I'm lucky—most people get stuck in jobs they don't enjoy." He stopped, his cheeks reddening. "I'm not saying that's you. That came out wrong."

"No," she said. "You're right. That *is* me. I'd much rather do something I enjoyed than get paid to wear other people's clothes. And it can get old when people think that's all I'm good for."

"More to you than a pretty face," he said, fumbling the words as he realised what he had just said. "I'm sorry. That came out wrong, too. I'm making a bit of a tit of myself, aren't I?"

She smiled again, wide enough to show her teeth. "Not at all."

Isabella watched the awkwardness play out on his face, the slight hesitation in his posture telling her everything she needed to know; he was caught between curiosity and the nagging suspicion that there was more to her than met the eye.

"You were going to tell me about the best sites in Algeria."

He leaned closer to her, mock conspiratorially. "Promise not to tell anyone?"

She put her hand on her heart. "Promise."

"Out there," he said, pointing through the window to the ocean. "All this—the Taza National Park—it's amazing. Tourists don't come here—Algeria's not the safest country in the world—but it's four hours from Algiers, and it's not all that well known. I've been diving out there every weekend for the last couple of months, and I'm not kidding—it's one of the best places I've ever been, and I've been everywhere."

"Because?"

"The amount of wildlife is pretty nuts. You get big schools of grouper, sea turtles, dolphins, sharks. The water's always warm—twenty-five degrees most of the year—and the visibility's great. And there are some really challenging sites—you've got loads of wrecks, caves, rock tunnels." He finished his drink and signalled to the barman that he'd like another. "The thing about it, the thing I *love*, is that they don't have records of their underwater archaeological sites. It's the same with most of the countries in North Africa— they've never had the opportunity to log them. You can go out, find a current and drift on it and you never know what you might find."

"You ever find anything?"

"Maybe," he said, raising an eyebrow.

The barman arrived and asked Carter what he'd like.

"Same again, please," he said, holding up his glass. He looked over at Isabella. "What'll you have?"

"That's very kind. A beer would be lovely."

The barman took Carter's empty glass and went to prepare their drinks.

Isabella got up and moved around to the stool next to Carter. "You were saying you found something. Was it sunken treasure?"

"Not exactly," he said, grinning. "I was out last week, and I found an old grindstone. Big old thing, covered in seaweed and barnacles and algae. Must've weighed half a ton. I spoke to an archaeologist in Algiers, and he said it was probably being taken by a coaster to an oil mill when it either fell overboard or the ship went down. I think it sank, and I'm going to try to find it. I've chartered a boat for tomorrow. There's a skipper I know—he's taking me out just after dawn."

"You're making me jealous."

He paused, sizing her up. "How long are you in town for?"

"Until the day after tomorrow."

"Not working?"

"The job's finished—why?"

"How good are you?"

"Diving? Advanced Open Water."

"Thirty metres."

Isabella nodded. She'd been down deeper than that, although she wasn't supposed to have been; Beatrix hadn't been all that bothered with rules and regulations.

The barman returned with Carter's gin and tonic and Isabella's beer.

"It gets down to twenty-five metres there, so you'd be well within your thirty."

"Are you inviting me?"

"Why not? You should come. It's just me and the skipper —there's loads of space on the boat if you fancy it."

She winced. "Love to, but I don't have any kit."

"The skipper does," Carter said. "He'll rent it to you—won't cost much, either. Dollars go a long way here."

Isabella made a show of thinking about the proposal. She'd entertained doubts about what Broker had told her about Carter after searching his plane, and speaking to Carter had just reinforced them. He was friendly and almost Tiggerishly enthusiastic, and, while neither disqualified him from running the sort of operation that had persuaded a client to bring him to Broker's attention, there was still a jarring disconnect when she compared how he was to how she had expected him to be. A little more time with him would give her the chance to be sure that he was what she had been told he was, and that her exacting criteria before actioning a contract had been met.

And, she thought, if her standards were met... well, disposing of him out at sea would be a *lot* neater than blowing up his plane.

She took a sip of her bottle of 1664 Blanc and then, putting it down, beamed him her most winsome smile. "Where and when?"

21

Isabella woke early, the first light of dawn creeping through the curtains of her room. The faint sound of the call to prayer drifted through the open window, together with the reversing siren from a truck that was bringing something—food or fresh laundry, perhaps—to the hotel. Isabella stretched and lay still for a moment. Today was different, and she felt the familiar twinge of anticipation that came before something that had the potential to be exciting.

Beatrix had taught Isabella to dive. Isabella had been bored, and her mother had suggested it. The first few dives that the two of them had undertaken together had delivered a mixture of fear, awe, and then—in time—growing confidence. Isabella's first dive had been in the tranquil waters near Agadir, where they explored limestone formations that had been carved out over millennia. It was disorienting at first, but the quiet beauty and otherworldly serenity were addictive. She soon graduated to more challenging dives, and they ventured to more remote locations along the Mediterranean coast near Al Hoceima. The waters were warmer, teeming with sea urchins, octopuses, and the occasional ray that glided lazily beneath them. Each dive revealed new mysteries: shipwrecks lost to time, kelp forests swaying in the current, hidden marine life tucked away in crevices.

She hadn't dived since Beatrix's death, but she was confident it would come back to her.

She rolled out of bed, putting on the swimsuit that she had bought from the hotel store after leaving Carter yesterday. She pulled on a pair of lightweight trousers and a loose-fitting shirt that she could peel off once they reached the boat, then braided her hair tightly, securing it at the nape of her neck. She glanced at herself in the mirror, then grabbed her rucksack and made her way downstairs.

The restaurant was quiet, with just a handful of early risers at the tables scattered around the terrace. Carter was already seated by the pool, sipping coffee and messing with the settings on his GoPro.

He looked up as she approached, his face breaking into a warm smile. "Morning," he said, gesturing to the seat opposite. "Sleep well?"

Isabella nodded, sliding into the chair and setting her rucksack down beside her. "Took a while—I'm excited."

Carter poured her a cup of coffee from the carafe. "Me too. You're going to love it. Not many people get the chance to dive where we're going—mostly just locals."

Isabella listened as he spoke, watching the way his eyes lit up when he talked about the dive he had planned. She picked up her coffee and took a sip.

Their breakfast was simple but satisfying: omelettes, crusty bread, and fresh fruit. Carter was easy company, full of stories about the dives he had already undertaken here, the marine life they might encounter, and the chance of finding the ship that might once have carried the grindstone he'd found. Isabella listened, nodding at the right moments, her attention focused on two things: persuading him she was who she'd said she was, and working out whether he was who Broker had said he was.

22

They made their way to the car, a sturdy four-wheel drive that Carter had rented. The drive to the harbour was pleasant, the early morning sun casting long shadows across the quiet streets. Carter spoke about the equipment they'd use and the dive plan for the day. Isabella nodded along, occasionally stealing glances at him, watching the way he spoke with passion and knowledge. He was relaxed, almost carefree, entirely in his element.

The doubts that she'd started to feel during yesterday's conversation grew a little more.

They arrived at the harbour just as the morning light began to dance on the water's surface, turning it a shimmering gold. A line of boats bobbed gently along the dock, white hulls gleaming in the sun. Carter parked near a small fishing vessel that had been retrofitted for diving, the name *El Bahr* painted in faded blue letters along the side.

The captain, a weathered man in his sixties with sun-leathered skin and a permanent squint, greeted them with a firm handshake and a smile.

"This is Isabella," Carter said.

"I am Mohammed," the skipper replied. "But you can call me Mo."

"Thanks for taking us out," she said. "I'm excited."

"Charlie says you've dived before."

"Lots of times."

"But you need some kit?"

"Yes, please. I wasn't planning on going in today."

"I've got everything we need on the boat. Hop aboard—we need to get underway."

Carter jumped down from the dock to the boat and then turned, reaching back up to offer Isabella a helping hand. She took it, then found her balance on the gently pitching deck and looked around. The boat was about thirty feet long from bow to stern, with a wide, open deck designed for easy movement and gear setup. Its hull was painted a weathered white, streaked with faint rust stains. A sturdy canopy stretched over the centre of the boat, providing shade from the sun, while the back was open to the elements and allowed easy access to the water. The dive platform at the stern had a small ladder that dipped into the sea. The deck was utilitarian, with non-slip mats and cushioned benches along the sides for seating. Air cylinders were lined up against the rail, masks and fins stacked neatly nearby. Weight belts were stored in plastic tubs. A simple console near the helm housed the boat's basic navigation equipment and radio.

Mohammed went to the console and spoke on the radio with the harbour master, clipped the handset back in place and came to where they were sitting. "There's a storm coming in after lunch," he said. "We'll have three or four hours out there if we're quick now. Are you ready?"

"Let's go," Carter said.

23

Mohammed took the boat out of the harbour, passing between two rocky piers and then out into the open sea. The water was calm, a deep blue expanse that stretched endlessly away to the north, sparks of light popping off the gentle waves. Fishing boats dotted the horizon, their crews already busy with their nets, while seagulls wheeled overhead and plunged into the water in search of breakfast.

As they chugged further from the harbour, the noise of the city faded away to be replaced by the rhythmic thrum of the boat's engine and the gentle lapping of waves against the hull. If a storm was coming, it wasn't obvious yet.

"We'll be half an hour to the dive site," Mohammed called back over the sound of the engine. "Make yourselves comfortable. There are bottles of water in the fridge and some fruit if you're hungry."

Isabella went to collect a banana and then sat down next to Carter. "I was thinking about your work," she said. "I don't think I've ever met a pilot before."

"Don't get too excited. It's hardly *Top Gun*."

"What—you're saying you're *not* Tom Cruise?"

"Sorry to disappoint you," he said, his arms spread.

She grinned. "Didn't say I was disappointed."

He blushed.

"You said you moved cargo."

"That's right," he said.

"What kind?"

He leaned back against the cushion. "I started in commercial freight. I used to work for FedEx, actually, flying big jets all over the place."

"Fun."

"Not really. Let's say I was flying from Berlin to New York. We'd get into JFK, get a taxi to the hotel, stay a night—maybe get the next day off if we were lucky, but we were probably still tired and just wanted to sleep—and then we'd turn around and come back again. You don't get much of a chance to see the places you're visiting, and, after a while, you almost forget where you are."

"One hotel looks just like another?" she suggested.

He nodded. "It got to be dull, so I decided to do something for myself. Me and a friend of mine in Australia put the money together for our first Cessna. It was an old UPS Cargomaster. We'd fly it around the bush, getting stuff into places so far away from anywhere else it'd take days if it weren't for us. And it was fun, too. The terrain could be difficult, and you'd have to be on your game whenever you were landing or taking off. It reminded me why I got into flying in the first place. It was about freedom, the challenge, skill, and doing something real."

"You found your calling."

"Exactly," he said, slapping a hand against the seat in emphasis. "*Exactly*. And once you've had a taste of that kind of flying, it's hard to go back to anything else. Now, every day is different, and that's how I like it."

"But not in Australia anymore?"

"No," he said. "I missed home too much. I sold my share in the business and came back to start another one. I bought a used Cessna Caravan, went back to FedEx and agreed to a contract to handle their remote deliveries around North Africa, and went to work again." Carter leaned back, a frown creasing his brow as he recalled a memory. "But then, fast-forward to last year, I was here when they had the earthquake."

"Terrible," Isabella said.

Carter nodded solemnly. "Entire villages cut off. The aid agencies couldn't get their supplies where they needed to be, and they were looking for people like me with the kind of aircraft that could help. We were flying in clean water, medical supplies, food—anything that'd help keep those communities going. We were landing on dirt strips, old riverbeds, sometimes just open fields." He paused, his expression serious. "There was this one drop, out near Beni Ilmane. We barely had enough space to land, and the locals had marked the strip with stones so we wouldn't hit anything. You'd see the relief on their faces when we unloaded the supplies—that's when you know that it's not just another job. I know this is going to sound clichéd, but you're their lifeline. Without us, those people are in a lot of trouble. Food, medicine—life or death in some cases. And the satisfaction of making that kind of difference is something I never got flying a corporate jet or doing commercial runs."

The coastline gradually receded into the distance, giving way to rugged cliffs and secluded coves that marked the transition from the urban sprawl to the untouched wildness of the Mediterranean.

Isabella leaned against the railing, feeling the cool spray of sea mist on her face. "Is that what you're doing now?"

"This trip?" He nodded. "The last two months, ever since the earthquake, I've been doing one or two runs a week. I'll pick up supplies here and then fly them to wherever they need to go."

"Where's your plane?"

"Algiers," he said. "I'm working with Médecins Sans Frontières. They loaded it up yesterday. I'll go fly it out tomorrow afternoon. I'll pay the bills with my normal work and then do it all again next week—and it'll be that way until they don't need me anymore."

Isabella was watching him carefully, hoping not to notice anything that might give her reason to doubt him. There was nothing. She didn't pretend to be an expert in reading body language, but she'd had enough deceit in her life to know the difference between lies and truth. Carter's posture was relaxed but earnest, his eyes focused on hers without the evasiveness that she'd come to recognise when someone tried to weave a story; his gestures were natural and unforced, hands moving slightly to emphasise points, but not in the exaggerated way of someone trying to sell a line; and his gaze occasionally drifted off, as if momentarily lost in the memories he was recounting, the faint lines at the corners of his eyes deepening with genuine emotion.

Isabella bit down on her lip.

She was confused.

Broker's intelligence looked like it was wrong.

But there was relief, too.

Isabella would have killed Carter if she'd decided he was

what Broker said, and, to her surprise, she found she really didn't want to do that.

24

———

Mohammed slowed the vessel, the engine's steady hum diminishing to a low purr as they neared the dive site. Isabella could feel the change in the boat's motion, the gentle rocking increasing as the boat settled in the open water, surrounded by nothing but the deep blue of the Mediterranean.

Mohammed manoeuvred the boat into position. A small buoy bobbed nearby, marking the start of the dive route: as Carter described it, a descent along a gentle slope that led to a series of submerged rock formations and caverns and, potentially, the wreck of the coaster that he hoped to find.

Mohammed cut the engine and tossed the anchor overboard. The boat drifted to a stop, secured in the right spot. The water below was a deep sapphire, clear enough that when Isabella looked over the side, she could see faint shadows of coral and rocks just beneath the surface.

Carter checked the anchor line, making sure it was secure, and then began organising the equipment.

"We'll gear up here and do a final check before we go

in," he said. "It's a straightforward dive, but we'll still go by the book."

Mohammed brought over a wetsuit. "Try this on."

Isabella pulled it up over her legs and torso, the neoprene material snug against her skin. She adjusted the hood, making sure her hair was tucked away, and slipped a dive computer onto her wrist, tightening the strap for a secure fit. Mohammed picked up a lightweight buoyancy-control device and helped her into it, the straps clicking into place as he adjusted the fit around her shoulders and waist. The fabric hugged her frame, and the weight pockets would add just enough ballast to keep her stable underwater. He handed her a ten-litre aluminium cylinder, which she secured to the BCD. Carter double-checked the connections, making sure the straps were tight and the cylinder securely fastened.

"Here's your regulator rig," he said, passing her the breathing apparatus. "It's a DIN fit, so screw it into the cylinder valve."

Isabella took it and inspected it briefly, then connected it to her cylinder. Carter handed her a second-stage mouthpiece, which she attached to the main hose. He found a pair of fins, sturdy yet flexible, and helped her slip them over her feet, ensuring a snug fit.

"Good?"

Isabella rolled her ankles. "All good."

Carter handed her a mask with tempered-glass lenses and an adjustable silicone strap. She pulled it over her head, feeling the seal form comfortably around her face, and attached a snorkel to the side, just in case she needed it at the surface.

Carter gave her a once-over. Satisfied, he stepped back and smiled. "You're all set."

Isabella nodded, feeling the familiar weight of the equipment, the subtle pressure on her back that always preceded the plunge into the water.

Carter put on his own gear, and Isabella checked it. Mohammed checked both their pressure gauges, ensuring the cylinders were filled to the correct levels, and ran his fingers along the hoses, inspecting them for signs of wear or damage. Carter turned on his own cylinder first, listening for the familiar hiss of air as he connected the regulator, then did the same for Isabella's, watching as she took a few test breaths through the mouthpiece to confirm everything was working smoothly.

"Regulators good?" Carter asked.

"Good," she confirmed, adjusting the mouthpiece slightly. Carter clipped on his weight belt, ensuring it was balanced correctly, then put on his fins. They both spat into their masks, rubbing the saliva around to prevent fogging, then rinsed them in the sea before putting them on.

Mohammed gave a final nod, stepping back as Carter and Isabella moved to the stern. They stood on the gunwale, side by side, as the boat gently rocked beneath them. Isabella glanced at Carter, who gave her a reassuring smile before checking his gear one last time. She felt the buzz of anticipation, unspoken but palpable, a shared excitement. Carter signalled the all-clear by making a circle with his thumb and forefinger, with the other three fingers raised, held together. Isabella returned the gesture, her fingers tightening around her mask and regulator.

They jumped off the boat, hitting the water with split legs to slow their immediate descent. A surge of coolness washed over her, the sea closing over her head in a frothy burst of bubbles. She heard the usual chaotic sound of rushing water and felt the familiar tug of her BCD inflating slightly to slow her descent.

Isabella took a slow, measured breath, feeling the comforting pull of air filling her lungs. The light from above filtered down in rippling shafts, illuminating the surface like molten silver, while the deeper blues of the sea beckoned below.

She adjusted her buoyancy, gently deflating the BCD, and turned to face down. She kicked slowly as she followed Carter deeper.

They moved in unison, maintaining a steady pace, gliding easily through the water. The landscape began to take shape around them. The reef dropped away gradually, revealing a slope covered in a tapestry of soft corals and sponges, their vibrant colours muted in the dappled sunlight that filtered down. Small schools of fish darted between the rocks—flashes of silver, blue, and yellow— moving as one in a perfectly choreographed dance.

The water temperature dropped at ten metres, sending a faint chill through Isabella's suit. She glanced at her dive computer, watching the numbers tick down. The surface above was now a distant blur, the sunlight dimming and the colours around her taking on a richer, more subdued tone. She kept her breathing slow and even, feeling the gentle pressure build against her ears as they approached fifteen metres.

Carter pointed toward a cluster of rocks just ahead, signalling that they would level out there. Isabella nodded, following his lead as they moved down to twenty metres. The bottom of the reef revealed itself in stunning detail: boulders covered in a kaleidoscope of soft corals waving gently in the current like underwater gardens. Delicate sea fans spread out from the crevices, swaying with the ebb and flow, while clusters of anemones accommodated clownfish that peeked out before darting back out of sight.

The visibility was excellent, at least thirty metres, and the water was alive with movement. Carter signalled to check their depth, then gestured toward the reef wall that dropped off into the deeper blue. They hovered in place for a moment, adjusting their positions; Isabella could feel the gentle push of the current against her body. Carter signalled for Isabella to stay close, pointing out a narrow passage between the rocks that would lead them to the spot he wanted to explore.

Isabella felt calm. The rhythm of her breath mirrored the beat of her heart.

They passed through the passage, and the current became a little stronger, sending them away from the rocks toward the open seabed. Carter signalled that they should let the current take them, and, relaxing, they were both carried out.

Isabella watched Carter.

She had been right: it would have been *easy* to complete the contract here. There were sharp rocks scattered over the sandy floor, and it would have been simple enough to find one, press the edge against the rubber hose that ran from his cylinder to his regulator, and slice through it. She would be more than strong enough to stop him from swimming to the surface, and the current would take him out to sea. His body would never be found, and, when Isabella was questioned, she would be able to say that he'd just disappeared.

No body.

No witnesses.

The perfect murder was impossible, but this would be as close as she would ever be able to get to it.

And yet, despite the opportunity, despite how easy it

would be, despite the money that Broker would pay her and the good it would do for Fatima and the children, she couldn't do it. There were too many discrepancies between what Broker had told her about Carter and the impression she'd formed.

She wasn't naïve enough to think that he would have admitted to the things Broker had suggested he'd done, but he'd said a lot in the hours they'd spent together, and none of it had given her reason to doubt that he was what he said he was: a man running a small air freight business who had enough of a conscience to help others who needed him, and to help them without asking for anything in return. He seemed moral and honest, and she found it difficult to imagine that, on the one hand, he'd deliver humanitarian supplies to people who needed them while, on the other, helping sustain a war effort that had caused misery for millions.

It didn't add up.

Carter had drifted a little farther away from her, and, as she kicked to catch up, he turned, formed his hands into a flipper-like motion and pointed behind her. Isabella turned and saw a large green sea turtle gliding gracefully through the water, its shell dappled with sunlight.

Isabella gave the okay sign, and Carter did the same.

The animal drifted effortlessly past them. They watched, captivated, as it glided further into the blue, followed by a trail of small fish that swam in its gentle wake.

No, Isabella thought. This might be the perfect moment, but she couldn't do it.

The things she'd been told didn't make sense. Carter had said and done nothing to convince her that he met her criteria. She was going to ignore Broker's contract.

PART IV

25

I sabella woke before dawn, the faint light of early morning filtering through her narrow bedroom window. The air was still cool, a change from the relentless heat that was forecast to take hold later. She stretched, feeling the familiar tightness in her muscles ease. This was her favourite time: quiet, undisturbed, with the city just beginning to stir.

She dressed quickly, pulling on a pair of fitted running leggings and a lightweight tank top. She laced up her worn running shoes, checked the fit and feel before grabbing a small water bottle from the fridge and tucking it into the waistband of her gear.

She armed the alarm and left the riad, the heavy wooden door creaking softly as she closed it behind her. The alleyway outside was still cloaked in shadows, the high walls of the surrounding buildings holding onto the last coolness of the night. She set off at a steady pace, her footsteps echoing softly against the cobblestones as she made her way through the alleyways and streets and into the medina. The city was waking; shopkeepers were setting up their stalls, their conversation mingling with the occasional clatter of metal shutters being lifted. The scent of freshly baked bread drifted through the air, mixing with the earthy aroma of spices that hung like a memory from the previous day's market.

She navigated the labyrinth with easy familiarity, dodging a stray cat that darted across her path and then sidestepping a woman sweeping the entrance to a riad. She reached the edge of the medina, the narrow alleyways widening into streets, and the city began to open up around her. She picked up her pace, matching the rhythm of her breath to the beat of her stride. The road stretched out ahead, flanked by palm trees swaying gently in the early morning breeze. She passed a group of men unloading crates of fresh produce from a truck, one of them calling out to her, and ran by a small bakery, the warmth of its ovens radiating onto the street, accompanied by the inviting scent of baking *msemen* and pastries.

She turned to the south, taking Rue Azbezt and then staying with it as it drifted east and then south again. Isabella sprinted past the weathered stone walls of Cimetière de Bab Ghmat, looking out at the rows of graves: mostly simple slabs, some of which had crumbled with age, all of them surrounded by patches of dry grass and wild desert shrubs.

She drew closer to her destination. Stade Sidi-Youssef-Ben-Ali was a modest sports complex, with low concrete walls that had faded under the relentless sun. The stadium's entrance was through an arched gate flanked by bleached pillars with the surrounding area taken up by the dusty car park. It was a community space, often used by locals for casual games of football, early morning runs, and youth sports practice. The atmosphere was often lively, with the sound of children's laughter interrupted by the sharp whistle of a coach echoing in the air.

Isabella slowed her pace as she caught sight of the track: a simple, dusty ring encircling the football pitch. The stadium was still quiet save for a few other early risers: a man doing stretches by the entrance, a group of young boys kicking a worn football around, their laughter echoing off the bleachers.

She made her way to the track. The man disappeared, and the boys took their ball and left. Isabella was alone. She zeroed her stopwatch and, filling her lungs, tapped to start it and set off at a flat sprint. Her strides were long and power-ful, and she quickly reached top speed. She burst ahead with an explosive strength far beyond what would be expected of someone her age; each step launched her further than the last, her legs moving in a blur as she ate up the first fifty metres. The world around her slowed, her sensations sharpened by the rush of air against her skin, the pounding of her heart, and the thud of her feet on the track.

She reached the end of the straight and tapped to stop her watch.

Maia had spoken to her about her training. Isabella had found she could run long distances with ease and, after that, had started to explore her ability over shorter sprints. The average time over one hundred metres for a fit nineteen-year-old woman would be anywhere between fourteen and sixteen seconds. Elite female sprinters would typically complete the distance in eleven seconds.

Isabella looked down: she'd covered the distance in eleven and a half seconds. That kind of performance would place Isabella at a near-professional level; she was hitting speeds usually achieved only by top-tier athletes.

26

Isabella sat back and stretched, extending her legs and turning her face to the bright morning sunshine. She had run sprints for an hour, finishing with a final concerted effort that shaved another tenth of a second from her personal best. She was sweating and had finished the bottle of water that she'd brought with her.

She'd only been back from her trip to Algeria for a day, and after the confusion of what she'd found there, she was glad to have some time for herself. She'd finished the dive with Carter without finding the wreck he had been looking for, but, as they came back to the surface—exhilarated and buzzing with adrenaline—it hadn't mattered a bit. They had both been giddy with excitement on the voyage back, and when Carter had asked her whether she'd like to have lunch with him, she'd found the prospect impossible to resist.

They'd ended up spending the afternoon together, and it might have been longer if Isabella hadn't remembered she had something urgent to attend to. The conversation had flowed, and Isabella had had to catch herself on more than one occasion when she'd been close to saying something truthful about herself that might have undermined the story she'd given him earlier. In the end, she'd compromised and gave him a few snippets of the truth, including that she had a place in Marrakesh and visited the city reasonably often.

Carter's face had lit up at that. He'd given her his number and email and made her promise that she would keep in touch. He'd reminded her that he was scheduled to return to Algeria for the next few weekends, and that he was based in Tunisia. And he'd reminded her with a wink, he had a plane, and that meant that tacking on an additional stop so they could find another opportunity to dive together would be easy. Isabella had given him her number, biting down on the inside of her lip when she remembered what Pope would have said about such a fundamental breach of her personal security. He would have called her an amateur, and he would've been right; but it didn't matter, and she didn't care. Isabella had enjoyed the time that she and Carter had spent together and found that she wanted to do it again.

That left the small matter of the bomb that she'd left on his plane. She'd gone back to the airport that night and, thankful that the security was as lax as it had been on her first visit, had climbed over the fence again. There had been a moment of panic when she realised that the boxes had been rearranged; she'd sorted through nearly half of them before she found the one with the crumpled lid within which she had hidden the device. She removed it and, while she was inside the plane, took the opportunity to look around the cabin for a second time. Carter had told her a lot and, with more scope for him to be contradicted by the evidence around her, she'd wondered whether she might find something to lend credence to what Broker had said about him. She hadn't. There was nothing—not a *single* thing—that made her doubt that Carter was exactly what he had told her he was: a businessman with a conscience, doing his bit for people who were in desperate need of help.

She'd left the aircraft, scurried across the facility and made her way back to the hotel. She'd booked a seat on the first flight out of the country the next day, grabbed five hours of much-needed sleep and then, just before dawn, had driven across the city and flown out.

She had spent the flight wondering what she was going to tell Broker. She'd never let him down before, and she didn't know how he would react. But she knew now, for sure, that Carter wasn't what she'd been told he was, and, knowing that—that he didn't meet her criteria—there was no way she would bring harm his way. More than that, she had realised with a smile, she liked him. She had no one in her life, and certainly no one with whom she had felt any romantic connection. There was a spark, she felt it, and she thought he did, too. And that spark felt like something that might be worth kindling to see where it took her.

27

Isabella took off her shoes and went over to sit down on the third row of the bleachers. Someone had left a rolled-up newspaper there; she unrolled it and skimmed the headlines, taking the opportunity to practice her Arabic.

She noticed two people approaching the bleachers: a young man and a young woman. The man was dressed in shorts and a singlet, with running shoes laced together and draped around his neck. They stopped at the end of the track, where the man put on his running shoes, gave the woman a kiss and then set off at a steady pace.

The woman came up the steps of the bleachers and sat down in the row ahead of Isabella. She assessed her: curly black hair pulled into a loose ponytail, with a few strands escaping to frame her face. Her skin was a warm olive tone, and she wore just a little makeup; a touch of mascara accentuated her dark, almond-shaped eyes, giving her a bright, attentive expression. Her style was casual and effortless: a pair of faded jeans, white sneakers, and a T-shirt that hung loosely over her slender frame. Her canvas shoulder bag was worn and covered in small pins and patches, hints of places she'd been or causes she cared about.

Probably harmless.

The woman turned to look up at Isabella and smiled. "Hello."

"Hello," Isabella replied, forcing a polite smile.

"Nice day to be outside, isn't it?"

"Gorgeous."

"Do you mind if I sit here?"

"Please," Isabella said, cursing her luck. The girl seemed friendly enough, but she wasn't in the mood for small talk.

She watched as the young woman settled in, setting her bag down and pulling out a laptop.

"I'm Aicha," she said. "I'm supposed to be studying, but I couldn't stand the thought of being stuck inside."

Isabella gave a non-committal nod. "I don't blame you."

Aicha opened her laptop. "Been running?"

"Just finished," she said. "You're not working out?"

"No," she said, laughing. "I'm here with Bashar." She pointed to the man; he was on the other side of the track now. "My boyfriend."

"What do you do?"

"I'm a student. What about you?"

"A bit of modelling work."

"Really? That's cool."

"Not as glamorous as it sounds," Isabella said, repeating the line she'd used with Charlie. She hoped it would be enough of a full stop to end the conversation there and then.

Aicha nodded and didn't press further. Instead, she glanced at the track as her boyfriend completed another lap, his pace quickening as he came off the bend. He called something out as he went past, and she responded with a wave.

"I'm studying International Relations," Aicha said, adjusting her laptop screen. "I'm trying to decide whether to stay here for my PhD or go to the States."

"What do you prefer?"

"The States," she said. "I have the grades. It's more the money... it's not cheap."

She was easy to talk to, and Isabella found herself engaging despite her usual reservations. They chatted about Marrakesh, the city's vibrant mix of cultures, the bustling markets, and the quiet corners of the medina where time seemed to stand still. Aicha spoke of the challenges of balancing her academic ambitions with family expectations, and how her brother and sister didn't fully understand how she wanted to study abroad. Isabella listened, her usual guardedness loosening. They shifted topics to language, and she remarked on Aicha's impressive command of Arabic, French, and English. Aicha told her she'd recently started learning Spanish.

Isabella reciprocated with a few anecdotes about her own experiences with language barriers during her travels, substituting fictional reasons for visiting other countries for reality. The conversation flowed effortlessly, and for the second time in a week, Isabella's loneliness seemed a little more distant.

Bashar came around again and jogged to a stop at the finish line. He beckoned Aicha to come down to him.

She turned. "Won't be a minute."

Aicha left her laptop on the bleacher, and Isabella couldn't resist the temptation to look down at the screen. She saw an unusual cluster of VPN icons in the taskbar. She recognised one of the services from the time she'd spent with Pope; ExpressVPN was high-end and very expensive, the kind favoured by people who had something to hide. It was an odd choice for a student, especially one who appeared so casual and carefree, and even more so when she had just admitted that money was an issue in deciding where she would continue her studies.

Isabella looked down to the track to make sure Aicha was still engaged in conversation, then, on impulse, reached down and clicked to bring up a minimised window. The screen sprang to life, revealing Photoshop open with a partially edited photograph. Isabella took in the image: a stark, black-and-white photo of police clashing with protestors, raw and violent. Large red Arabic text was being superimposed across the image, incomplete but clear enough for Isabella to recognise it as incendiary: something about state violence and silenced voices.

The picture was far too pointed, too political, to be part of any casual student project. It was propaganda, and, in a place like this, that was dangerous.

Isabella minimised the window and adjusted the laptop screen back to where it had been, ensuring everything was as Aicha had left it.

She got up and started down the stairs. Aicha's boyfriend had set off again, and Aicha turned just as Isabella reached the bottom step.

"Going?"

"I have things to do. I'll let you get back to your studies."

Aicha smiled, oblivious. "See you around?"

Isabella nodded, deciding to avoid the stadium for a while. Some risks, she reminded herself, simply weren't worth taking.

28

Isabella spent the rest of the day at home. She was in the process of redecorating one of the bedrooms on the second floor of the riad, and she wanted to get most of it done before going to the orphanage tomorrow. She spread out dust sheets to protect the intricately tiled floor, which she was determined not to damage. The walls had once been painted in a soft, pale blue, but the colour had faded, and the surface had been chipped over the years. She had decided to change it to a deep terracotta that would bring warmth and contrast to the carved wooden furniture she'd sourced from the souks. After taping the edges of the windows, she dipped the roller into the paint tray and began methodically applying the new colour. Between coats, she carefully placed the large Berber rug she had purchased in one of the city's markets in the centre of the room, making sure the geometric patterns aligned perfectly with the bed.

Isabella took a break as the first coat dried, sitting on a cushion in the corner. The room was coming together, and, in a few days, she would transform it into a cosy space, layered with Moroccan textiles, two brass lanterns, and soft cushions in deep reds and ochres, reminiscent of the desert at dusk.

CHARLIE EMAILED to tell her he'd processed the GoPro footage from the dive and wondered if she'd like to look at it and have a chat. She knew she should probably say no—she was sure Pope would have told her to say no—but she'd been alone all day, and Charlie was easy to talk to. She opened her VPN to establish a secure connection and Face-Timed him. She had expected to see a hotel room in the background, but, rather than that, the wall behind him had been decorated with faded floral wallpaper, and, to the side, dark-green velvet curtains framed a window.

"Nice wallpaper," she said.

He turned to look, and when he turned back, he was grinning ruefully. "Blame my grandmother."

"Where are you? Not at home?"

He shook his head. "I'm in La Marsa."

"I don't know where that is."

"Tunisia. My grandmother has a house here."

"Visiting?"

"She's not well."

"Nothing serious?"

"Dementia," he said. "And cancer."

"Oh."

"She doesn't do things by halves. She doesn't have long left."

"I'm sorry. You should've said."

"I've been spending a lot of time with her. It's sad—she's lived a crazy life, and it's hard to watch her forgetting it all."

She felt sympathy, but also a pang of jealousy. It wasn't

the first time: talk of grandparents and brothers and family made her acutely aware of everything she didn't have. Her mother was dead, the man she'd thought of as her father was dead, and Maia—a surrogate sister, who had shared things with her that no one else had—was dead. Isabella was alone, just like the children in the orphanage.

Charlie noticed her downcast expression. "What is it?"

"Family," she said.

"You never said anything about yours."

"There's nothing to say."

"You don't get on with them?"

"I don't have one," she said. "My dad died when I was a child, and my mum died not that long ago. It's just me now."

"I'm sorry. There's me going on about mine, and... well, it wouldn't be me if I didn't open my mouth and immediately put my foot in it."

She managed a reassuring smile. "You weren't to know."

The last thing she wanted to do was open a conversation about her unusual childhood, because then she'd have to lie about being moved from foster family to foster family to keep her away from her mother, and there wasn't much distance from there to needing to explain *why* that had happened—that her mother was a state-sanctioned assassin on the run after being betrayed by her government—and that was a conversation she couldn't have with anyone.

He shook his head. "If it's any consolation, my family is completely fucked up."

"Why?"

"Money—what else? There's been a dispute over what'll happen to my grandmother's estate when she dies. It's brought out the worst in some people."

"Your relatives?"

"Mostly my brother. Her will leaves most of her estate to

me. She doesn't have any other close relatives, and she and Jack never got on. She helped me build the business, and she wants me to invest into buying another plane and *really* move into the charity sector. She used to work for Médecins Sans Frontières, back when it got started."

"Really?"

He nodded. "She was part of the first wave of volunteers in the seventies. They went into war zones without much— just basic medical supplies and determination. She saw first-hand the importance of getting aid into remote areas quickly, and she still cares about it. She's always pushing me to use the plane for humanitarian work. She wants me to do it full-time, but I'd need money to do that. She says she wants to help."

"Exciting."

"I know," he said. "And it'd be great if it weren't for Jack."

"Your brother."

He nodded again. "He wants his share. They had a big falling-out when my mother died. He's never come to any family events since then. He hasn't spoken to her, and he doesn't even send a card on her birthday or at Christmas. But now he's heard she's sick, and he's come to put his snout in the trough."

"But what can he do if your grandmother has written a will?"

"He's got lawyers. He says the dementia started a while ago, before she wrote the will. They're saying I coerced her —that I've pressured her into making me her sole benefi-ciary, whereas if she was of sound mind, she would've divided it between me and him. It's nuts."

"What does he do?"

"He's in the oil business. Incredibly rich. He's got a huge estate on the coast outside Sidi Bou Said and flies into

Algiers by helicopter. He doesn't need the money, but he's always been greedy. He always wants more, and he'll trample anyone who gets in his way."

"Sounds unpleasant."

"Very. Anyway—my problem, not yours. It's nice not to have to think about it sometimes, and it never even crosses my mind when I'm underwater. Speaking of which—do you want to watch the footage?"

"Love to."

THEY WATCHED the footage of the dive together and then stayed on the line chatting, it was two thirty when Isabella thought to check the time, and they'd continued on for another thirty minutes until she finally insisted that she needed to get to bed.

She sat up and scrubbed her fingers through her hair. She had been worrying about what she was going to say to Broker. He would want an update on the contract, and she didn't know how to tell him that she wasn't going to do it.

And she couldn't just say that, either, Broker would be disappointed, but he'd just assign the work to another contractor, and then he or she would look at Charlie without Isabella's qualms.

She needed Broker to think that she was still on the job.

And she needed time to think.

29

Isabella showered and dressed, and after making sure the riad was secure, she set off for the orphanage. She took her habitual care to avoid patterns in her route and added a few turns she hadn't made before, including a detour through a busy souk and a pause to buy a loaf of fresh *khobz* bread from a street vendor. She kept her pace steady, blending in with the flow of people starting their day, and, when she finally arrived in Bab Doukkala, she took a moment to scan her surroundings.

The orphanage and the street looked just as she would have expected, but just as she had satisfied herself that nothing was out of place, the front door opened, and two heavyset men emerged.

Isabella stepped into the mouth of an alleyway where she could watch them without drawing attention to herself.

The first man looked to be in his forties, his square jaw clenched, with a close-cropped buzz cut that accentuated the hard lines of his face. His thick neck bulged against the collar of his shirt, and his muscular frame filled the doorway as if he was used to commanding space. A small scar ran from his temple to just below his ear. The second man was slightly younger, but just as imposing. His head was shaved clean, the sheen of sweat catching the light as he stepped out. His dark eyes were cold, and a heavy brow cast a shadow over his angular features. His hands were thick and scarred. Both exuded simmering aggression, and it was obvious they weren't here for pleasantries. They wore dark, plain clothes, but their bearing and the sharpness in their eyes suggested discipline and training.

Military.

Isabella was anxious after what had gone on before. Fatima had promised nothing else had happened since, but Isabella had doubted that it was the end of the matter. She'd said they should go to the police, but Fatima had laughed. With reason, Isabella conceded; the police were corrupt, and looking into a vague threat made against the manager of an orphanage offered nothing of interest to them.

The two men walked away from the building and stopped at the café nearby, one of them taking out a phone while the other went inside to make a purchase.

Isabella made her way around them, entering the orphanage through the side door. She hurried upstairs and went to Fatima's door. It was ajar, and she carefully pushed it open with her fingertips.

Fatima lay curled up in the corner amid overturned furniture.

The bookcase had been pulled down, its books and folders scattered. Pictures had been pulled from the wall, and the desk drawers had been emptied. Fatima's laptop— the one she'd scrimped and saved to buy, the one she took to be repaired every time it stopped working instead of letting

Isabella buy her a new one—had been thrown against the wall, leaving a dent in the plaster and the computer broken into two pieces.

"Fatima."

She looked up. Her eye was bruised, the swelling forcing it half shut. Her smashed glasses were on the floor.

Isabella knelt beside her and pushed her hair back from her face. "What happened?"

"I'm fine," she said, although she winced with the effort of speaking.

Isabella picked up a chair and helped Fatima up and then onto it.

"*Now* are you going to talk to me?"

"There's no point."

"Who did this?"

"It doesn't matter."

"It *does* matter. You shouldn't be treated like this."

"It is the way of the world. We're nothing. What can I do? No one will listen to someone like me—not against *them*."

"The person who did this is important?"

"His name is Al-Masri," she said. "And some people just get what they want." She gently pushed Isabella's hand away. "I'm all right. Just bruises. If you really want to be helpful, you could help me tidy up."

Isabella stood and went to the door.

"Isabella," Fatima said, "where are you going?"

"To check the doors are locked."

She took the stairs two at a time. Her anger had been bubbling up, and now she let it overflow. She wouldn't be able to look at herself in the mirror if she let what had just happened go unpunished.

She knew how these things escalated.

This week it was Fatima.

Next week it might be one of the children.

And that was unacceptable.

She reached the side door and ducked out into the alley.

30

Isabella gambled that the men would have headed south, toward the main Avenue Hommane Al Fatouaki, and quickly saw that she was right. They'd just crossed over the road onto Rue Tétouan and were heading east. She followed behind them, staying well back yet not so far as to risk losing them as the streets became busier. They reached the busy junction where the avenue filtered into four smaller streets and made their way to Café Solo. They took a seat at one of the outdoor tables under a faded awning.

Isabella slipped into the café, taking a seat inside where she could observe them unnoticed through the window. The men ordered tea, exchanged a few words, and settled into conversation. Isabella ordered a mint tea for herself, sipping at it as she watched. The waitress hovered by their table, more solicitous than might normally have been the case, perhaps anxious to make sure these two particular customers were happy with her service. They appeared to be; one of them laughed at a joke and playfully punched the other on the arm. The waitress was dismissed with a brusque flick of the wrist and came inside. Isabella noticed how she rolled her eyes at the man behind the counter.

The two men finally stood, their tea finished, and set off again. They headed away from the busy café into the network of smaller streets and alleys to the east.

Isabella left money for her tea and left the café, following at a distance, moving with the flow of the pedestrians. The streets gradually became less crowded, the noise of the marketplace fading behind them as they turned down a series of narrower streets lined with older buildings.

She was confident they didn't know she was following them. They seemed blasé; insulated by their position, perhaps, confident that their status meant they'd never come to harm on the streets of their own city.

They reached a quieter stretch, away from the bustle of the main streets.

A narrow alley ahead offered an opportunity: no witnesses, no prying eyes.

Isabella sped up, closing the gap between them.

She moved with a speed and precision that would have defied the expectations of anyone who might have observed her. She drove her right foot into the back of the larger man's knee with such force that it buckled, sending him crashing to the ground. She stepped over him and followed up with a stomp to the back of his head, the impact driving him face-first into the cobbles.

The second man had barely reacted before Isabella was onto him. He turned into a high kick, the heel of her boot crunching into the bridge of his nose with enough force to shatter the bone. She shoved him, sending him into the wall. His hand fumbled for the gun at his belt, but Isabella followed and pummelled him with a right-hander into the mess of broken bone, snot and blood. He let go of the gun and tried to get his hands up, blocking some of the impact from her second punch, but she still landed enough of it to knock him off balance. She punched him in the gut, forcing him to lower his guard, and then grabbed his head in both hands and drove it down as she raised her knee.

He, too, was unconscious before he hit the ground.

The fight—if it could even be called that—was over in seconds.

Isabella stood over the two bleeding men, breathing evenly, barely taxed by what she had just done.

The sound of Arabic pop music drifted out of a nearby window. Isabella frisked the men, removing their handguns and tossing them away. Both had wallets. She sorted the contents, leaving the cash and receipts and taking out two ID cards that looked to have been issued by the same organisation.

Direction Générale des Études et de la Documentation.

Military intelligence.

She stared at the cards.

What were two DGED heavies doing beating up the manager of an orphanage?

Isabella pocketed the cards and retraced her steps.

31

I sabella ran back to the orphanage and climbed the stairs to the office. Fatima was on her hands and knees, the screen from the laptop in one hand and the body of the unit in the other. She'd been crying; she noticed Isabella in the doorway, reached up to her face, and scrubbed the back of her hand across her eyes.

Isabella took one of the ID cards and held it out.

Fatima squinted at it. "What's that?"

"The men who were in here. I—"

"I told you not to get involved," Fatima cut over her.

"I found a wallet outside," she lied. "This was inside it." Isabella stood with her arms folded. "I'm not taking no for an answer." She held up the card. "I know what this means. I know who those men work for. You need to tell me what's going on."

Fatima sighed. "This neighbourhood—you know it's poor. When I bought the building twenty years ago, no one wanted anything here. But it's in a good location, close to the Koutoubia Mosque and not far from Gueliz and Hivernage, places with money. Tourists, too—they want to stay in the city, and there's only so much space. It all means developers look at a building like this and see an opportunity. They see who owns it and think we must be desperate, that there's a bargain to be had and money to be made."

Isabella righted two chairs so they could sit. "Someone wants to buy the orphanage?"

Fatima nodded. "The building."

She held up the card again. "He wasn't a property developer."

"Government salaries are low. Even for someone senior in the army—they make a few hundred dollars a month. Not much. They look for other ways to make their money. Some of them deal drugs; others take bribes to let people off their military service."

"And some of them are in property development?"

She nodded.

Isabella held up the card again. "It was this man?"

"Not him," Fatima said. "That man—those men—they just work for him. The man who wants to buy the building—Al-Masri—is a general in the army. He came here two months ago and took me for an expensive lunch at his polo club. I expect he thought I'd be impressed by his flashy car and the white tablecloths and the waiters in smart suits." She laughed. "I wasn't. At the end of the meal, he tells me how he appreciates the work we're doing and how he wants to help us by finding a more 'appropriate' building. He said the children need open space and clean air. He drove me out to the desert and showed me a plot of land in a new development he's invested in. His architect was there, too. They showed me the drawings. I told them I couldn't afford to build a new site, but the general said I didn't have to buy it. He said he'd arrange for everything."

"In exchange for what?"

"This building."

"And?"

"And I laughed at him, and it was a mistake—but it seemed like such a ridiculous suggestion. We love this neighbourhood. It's not fancy, but people know us. The grocer brings us the fruit and vegetables he doesn't sell, the baker gives us day-old bread at half price. We don't want to move to the desert—why would we? We don't know anyone there."

"What did he say?"

"That was when I knew things would turn bad. He got into his car and drove off."

"Leaving you in the desert?"

She nodded. "It took me two hours to find a bus and three to get back here. The children missed their evening meal that day. The next morning his driver delivered a contract for the sale of the building, but I threw it back in his face. One week later the gas was cut off for no reason. Then it was a window that got smashed. Then the glass in the envelope. And now they're not even pretending." She gestured around her. "They hit me and trashed the office. One of them grabbed me by the hair and said that I had until the end of the day to call them to say I was ready to sell, or something really bad was going to happen. They said I needed to wake up before it was too late." She shook her head in desperation. "Can you see why I didn't tell you? Not all problems can be solved, Isabella. I know you have some money, and you've been so generous, but all the money in the world won't make this go away. The general is a proud man, and he thinks I've insulted him. I—a *woman*—said no. This will be personal for him now. He won't stop until he has what he wants, and he won't care what he has to do in order to get it."

"So? What are you going to do?"

"Am I going to sell?"

Isabella shrugged.

Fatima laughed bitterly. "Over my dead body."

32

I sabella told Fatima that she had an errand to run, but that she would be back again in time to help with the nighttime routine. Fatima said she didn't need to worry, but Isabella wasn't going to take no for an answer. Fatima had called the general's bluff before, and he had followed through with his threat and then upped the ante again. She wanted to be nearby for the next few hours in the event that he did something else.

Isabella felt as if she was bearing the whole world on her shoulders. She was worried about the orphanage, and she was worried about Charlie. Both matters were urgent, but she decided the situation with the kids was more pressing. She had some degree of agency with Charlie's predicament and just needed to win a little time with that so she could try to fix Fatima's problems.

❧

ISABELLA KNEW she couldn't return to the same place she'd used last time when she spoke to Broker; going back somewhere more than once was too risky. Instead, she slipped into a narrow alley off one of the quieter side streets in Gueliz, the modern part of the city, passed a few shops and cafés before spotting a cybercafé tucked between a pharmacy and a clothing store. It was the kind of place locals used: off the radar, unremarkable, perfect for what she needed.

She rented a terminal at the back, booted into her secure Tails OS from her USB drive, rerouted her connection through the same run of multiple VPNs before launching the encrypted messaging platform.

Broker was online and messaged her within moments of her status changing.

>> *What's happening with the contract?*

Isabella had spent an hour last night working out what she would say. It wasn't perfect—there was no getting away from the fact that she hadn't met her obligations—but she hoped it would win her a little more time.

>> *I couldn't get to the plane.*

>> *It was where I said it would be?*

>> *Yes. But the security was more significant than the file suggested. I decided to abort.*

There was a short pause.

>> *Disappointing.*

>> *Very. It was a wasted trip.*

The cursor flashed again, and Isabella found that she was holding her breath.

>> *The contract runs out next week, and the client is concerned.*

>> *Tell them not to worry.*

>> *Easy for you to say. Where is the target now?*

Isabella had known that question would come and had an answer ready for it.

>> *I'm tracking the plane. He filed a flight plan for another trip next week. He'll be in Algiers again. I'll do it then.*

>> *How?*

>> *The device. You can tell the client it'll be done.*

Isabella was in a bind. The developments with Fatima and the orphanage weighed heavily on her. Just a week ago, the work for Broker had felt like a side project, a way to stay sharp and bank some extra cash. But now, with the orphanage at risk, finding money to help Fatima carry on her work had taken on new urgency. The money in her own account, once a small fortune, now seemed as if it might be insufficient. She couldn't afford to turn down contracts, yet she couldn't see any circumstance where she would be able to fulfil her obligations under this one; she would have been stunned if Charlie was guilty of the things Broker had alleged. She needed time to think about what she was going to do, and, although this was just putting off the decision, she hoped she would be able to come up with something.

Broker was typing.

>> *It's my reputation on the line, not yours. This needs to be done. Do you need me to send backup?*

Isabella knew exactly what that meant: another operator to make sure she didn't slip up.

>> *And split the fee? No, thanks. I'll message you once it's done.*

33

Isabella left the café and stepped out into a warm evening. The streets were alive with the buzz of life: vendors calling out their final offers for the day and the hum of conversation blending with the occasional honk of a distant car. She retraced her steps through Gueliz until she was back in the older, narrower alleys that led toward Bab Doukkala. The sky was deepening into a rich, indigo hue, with the faint glow of lanterns illuminating her path. She knew there was little chance that she was being observed and let her mind wander, her thoughts going back to Charlie and what she was going to do about him.

She hadn't reached a conclusion before her daydream was disturbed by the smell of smoke.

The buildings on either side blocked any view of the horizon, and, fearful, she jogged until she was in a wider street with a broader vista.

There were trails of grey in the dark sky, and she heard the wail of a siren.

She ran.

She knew the orphanage was the source of the fire, and

her sense of dread increased with every step. She ran at full speed, ignoring the consternation of the men and women who had to get out of her way as she came barrelling through. She was eventually forced to slow down by the crowds that had gathered in the street. It was impossible not to pick up on the sense of alarm and excitement, children were running around unsupervised, and there was a steady flow of people heading toward the blaze towering above the low-rise buildings.

She turned off at the nearest alley and picked up speed again. This wasn't the time for caution, and she reached top speed once more, desperate to reach Fatima and the children before it was too late.

She neared the orphanage and was able to take in the ferocity of the fire: the flames had already consumed the top two storeys of the four-storey building, licking hungrily at what remained of the roof. Bright orange tongues of flame crackled and roared as embers rained down like sparks from a forge. Thick clouds of black smoke billowed from shattered windows, and the heat was intense, even from a distance. Isabella could feel it scorching her skin, forcing her to shield her face with her arm. The lower floors flickered with the eerie glow of the flames, which were quickly spreading downward.

She paused to grab the arm of a local, a man she recognised from the weekly food market.

"Where's Fatima?" she asked him in Arabic. "The children?"

Her sense of alarm made her oblivious to the strength in her grip. He tried to pull away but couldn't. He winced with pain; Isabella finally realised what she was doing and released him.

"Fatima?"

The man pointed to an ambulance. Paramedics were treating a group of a dozen children.

"Fatima?" she asked, increasingly desperate. "The other children?"

He shrugged and looked toward the building. "May God rest their souls."

Isabella pushed her way through the crowds to the front of the building. The sound of crackling wood and shattering glass filled the air. A line of uniformed police officers was keeping bystanders at bay. Isabella looked between them: the ground floor was largely untouched, and the fire looked as though it had started further toward the top, where the dormitories were located. A single fire engine was parked at an angle across the street. A ladder had been extended, but it only reached as high as the third-floor windows. Firemen were training hoses on the blaze, but it was out of control, and they were having little impact.

Isabella forced her way through the crowd and ran to the back of the building. The alleyways were too narrow for the firemen, so the only people there were locals who had come to watch the fire from a safe distance.

Isabella sprinted toward the neighbouring building and leapt into the air, higher than what ought to have been possible, six feet straight up. She twisted, planted one foot against the brick wall and used the momentum to propel herself forward in a perfect arc. She reached the orphanage and extended her arm toward the metal drainpipe that clung precariously to the building's side. Her fingertips latched onto the rusted metal, the muscles in her arms as taut as steel cables, and, without hesitation, she hauled herself upward. The drainpipe groaned under her weight, the metal screeching as it bowed, but she didn't pause. She grabbed hard, her arms and legs working together as she climbed. Each pull brought her closer to the burning windows above, the heat intensifying as she ascended. She reached for a fresh handhold—another pipe—but it was scorching hot. She ignored the pain, focusing instead on the children who might still be inside.

She kept climbing and, within moments, reached the third-floor windowsill. The heat from the fire hit her like a wave, but she didn't stop. She reached a window that she knew would take her onto the third-floor landing and swung a foot to kick the glass out of its frame; flames and smoke poured out. She reached with one hand to grip the windowsill, cutting her hand on the shards of glass, and pulled herself through the opening and onto the floor.

The thick smoke made it hard to breathe. She leaned back out of the window and filled her lungs with as much clean air as she could manage, then ran across the landing toward the first of the children's dormitories.

The door was shut; she kicked it off its hinges and ran in, bent low, scanning the room for any sign of life. The heat inside the room was intense; waves of scorching air hit her face. Flames licked up the walls, raced across the faded wallpaper and cast dancing shadows across the floor. The beds were on fire, too, smouldering beneath a layer of thick, acrid smoke that hung heavy in the air. Toys and personal belongings were scattered across the floor, some of them melted into grotesque shapes.

She went back out onto the landing. The flames were strongest around the stairs leading up to the fourth storey. There was liquid on the floor that was burning especially fiercely.

She returned to the window and filled her lungs for a second time.

The stairs looked weak; the flames had already licked at

the edges, leaving the wood blackened and brittle. She took a deep breath, her muscles tensing as she braced for the sprint. She bolted forward, vaulting up over the first eight treads in a single, powerful leap. Her feet barely grazed the steps before she landed on the ninth, which groaned under the sudden weight. The wood cracked beneath her, splintering as it gave way, but she pushed off just in time, launching herself into the air once more. The next set of steps was already crumbling, disintegrating beneath the relentless heat, but she cleared them and landed with a roll.

The flames crackled and hissed, consuming everything: old wood, plaster, and decades of forgotten memories. Smoke billowed thick and heavy, making it nearly impossible to see. The heat was unbearable, too, waves of searing hot air buffeting her face as the fire continued to spread. Every step felt treacherous as the boards beneath her feet groaned, threatening to collapse. Isabella pressed on. She could feel the floor shifting under her weight, but she ignored it, determined to reach the children.

Her eyes were running, and she blinked to clear them as she reached the second dormitory and forced open the door.

Fatima and five of the children were inside.

Fatima had doused a blanket with water and thrown it over the heads of the children.

She was on the floor, and she wasn't moving.

34

Isabella crouched down and lifted the edge of the blanket.

The first face she saw was Latifa's. The girl's face was sooty and tear-streaked, and she half-rose and threw her arms around Isabella's neck. Isabella prised her fingers loose, then turned to Fatima. She was breathing, but unconscious. Isabella slipped her hands beneath Fatima's shoulders and knees, lifted her as though she weighed nothing, and put her over her shoulder. She shepherded the children in front of her, telling Latifa to bring the wet blanket, and began to walk across the room toward the stairs.

She needed to get them down one storey to where the firemen had arranged their ladder.

That wasn't going to be easy.

The stairs had collapsed, and flames roared all around the gaping twelve-foot drop to the floor below.

Fatima was the priority.

She would need clean air very soon if she was going to survive.

Isabella put the children to one side.

"Latifa," she said, "you're in charge. Stay here underneath the blanket with the others. I'll be back."

She secured Fatima over her shoulder, stepped out into the hole in the floor where the stairs had once been, and dropped through the flames. She landed solidly, grateful that the floor was strong enough to bear both their weights, then ran to the window where she had seen the ladder.

A firefighter was at the top. Isabella handed Fatima through, making sure to keep her own face covered.

"There are children still up there," she said.

"We can't—"

Isabella cut him off. "Take her down and then come back up. I'll bring them here."

The fireman carefully started down the ladder. Isabella waited until his head was beneath the windowsill and then jumped high enough to reach an exposed metal joist in the ceiling above. She shuffled along it, hand over hand, until she could swing herself—legs first, her torso following—onto the landing where the children were waiting. There was pain in her hands from where the skin had been burned on the hot metal, but she ignored it. There was no time to worry about that now.

She ran back into the dormitory, collected two mattresses that hadn't yet caught fire, and hauled them out onto the landing. She dropped them into the hole where the stairs had been and carried the smallest child—a little boy called Omar—to the edge. She lowered him down as far as she could reach and then dropped him onto the mattresses. She did the same for the others, leaving Latifa until last. She cradled the girl in her arms and jumped down just as one of the firemen climbed through the window. Isabella ushered the children toward him; he picked them up, one by one, and passed them to a colleague on the ladder.

Latifa kept her arms tightly wrapped around Isabella's neck.

"You'll be all right now," Isabella said, turning to the waiting fireman.

"Where are you going?" Latifa asked her, panicked. "You'll come down with me, won't you?"

"Go with this man."

Latifa started to cry.

"He'll look after you. And Latifa—you didn't see me here. Okay?"

Isabella handed Latifa to the firefighter and waited as he carried her to the window. He turned his back, and Isabella took her chance; she disappeared into the smoke.

35

Isabella spent the next two days at the riad. She had escaped with only minor injuries, chiefly the burns on her hands. The skin had blistered, and the pain had increased as the adrenaline had receded; she had a first aid kit at home, and she used all of the tube of burn ointment, wincing as the cool gel met the scorched skin. She wrapped her hands with gauze and secured it with tape. Both nights, she took a painkiller to help her sleep. When she awoke on the second day, the ache had eased, and when she peeled away the gauze, the blisters had started to heal. She knew it was unusual, and knew she couldn't go back to the orphanage, where she might draw attention to herself and face questions she couldn't easily answer.

She scoured the internet for news of what had happened and found one article that said how a group of locals had watched a woman—described as being slim, athletic and of Arab appearance—climb into the building to rescue the trapped children. The journalist noted this hadn't been confirmed by authorities, however, and that it was likely exaggeration. Isabella saw social media posts making the same claim, but in each one the details varied just a little—it was a woman, then it was a man, then it was two men—and in the absence of any photographic evidence, the story soon turned into something of a joke. She had been lucky. There had been bystanders videoing the fire, and it was only her decision to go in through the back that had saved her from being recorded.

Isabella was able to follow news of Fatima and the children, too. Fatima was being treated for smoke inhalation but was otherwise reported as being in good health. She gave an interview and repeated the official line: her rescue was down to the mercy of God and the bravery of the local firemen who risked their own lives to clamber into the burning building. The firemen were the only ones who would've been able to confirm the presence of the mystery rescuer in the orphanage, but they had received so much praise for their heroic efforts they most likely didn't want to share the credit—or feared that they'd be laughed at if they repeated the narrative.

Better for everyone if they took the bouquets.

Isabella was happy with that arrangement.

She scoured the articles for anything to suggest how the fire had started. Some stories referred to the state of the building, with locals saying it was dilapidated and poorly maintained; others speculated the blaze had been ignited by a gas bottle with a leaking valve. There was nothing to suggest the fire had been started deliberately, although Isabella often found her mind returning to the smell she'd noticed near the stairs to the fourth storey.

She knew what it was: paraffin.

36

Isabella had been feeling more anxious after the fire, and even though she knew there was no reason to think she was compromised, she double-checked the locks on her front door, making sure each bolt was securely fastened before stepping out into the narrow alleyway.

The sun was already intense. Isabella went to an internet café she'd used before, the one with the familiar flickering neon sign proclaiming in both Arabic and French 'Café Internet & Gaming Center.' The windows were cluttered with posters advertising internet packages and cheap phone repairs. She pushed open the door and was met with the cool, artificial breeze of an overworked and dripping air conditioner. The young man behind the counter barely glanced up from his phone as Isabella approached. He was thin with dark, curly hair and wore a faded T-shirt emblazoned with the name of a video game Isabella didn't recognise.

"*Wahdek?*" he asked, meaning "Just one?"

"*Naam,*" Isabella replied.

She handed over a few dirhams, enough for an hour of

use, and the cashier nodded, sliding a small slip of paper with a login code across the counter. She took it and moved toward an empty station in the back corner of the room. She activated her VPN and navigated to Google.

She checked for messages from Broker—there were none—and then made an internet call to Fatima's number. She tapped her fingers against the table as she waited for her to pick up.

Finally, after what felt like forever, there was a click.

"Fatima?"

"Isabella." She sounded tired.

"Where are you?"

"Still in the hospital."

"Still?"

"I breathed in a lot of smoke. But I'm fine. We're all fine."

"The kids?"

"They're fine."

"Thank God." She exhaled and remembered that she couldn't claim to know what had happened without betraying that she had been there. "What happened?"

"I put the children to bed, like every night; then I went to my office to finish some paperwork. The next thing I knew, there was this noise—very loud, a crash—and then when I opened the door, I could smell smoke. It was already out of control by the time I got upstairs."

"What about the reports in the newspapers? Gas bottles?"

"I saw that," Fatima replied, her voice hardening. "Ridiculous. We don't have any. But I'm not going to argue—let them say what they want. It's easier for people to believe that than to hear the truth."

"Which is?"

"You know," she said. "We spoke about it."

She wasn't prepared to mention Al-Masri by name for fear of their call being monitored. That was possible. Fatima was afraid, and rightfully so.

There was a long pause.

"Latifa..." Fatima said.

Isabella's stomach leapt. "Is she okay?"

"Fine. But..." Fatima paused. "I know this is crazy, but she says you brought us out."

Isabella forced out a laugh. "I'm afraid not. I didn't get there until later—I had a call, and it overran."

"It was dark," Fatima conceded.

"And she would have been terrified," Isabella added.

"She was," Fatima said. "They all were. It's a miracle no one was killed."

Isabella found she was biting her lip. "What are you going to do next?"

"I don't know," Fatima said.

"Where are the kids going to go?"

"There are families in the neighbourhood who'll take them. They'll be safe while I work out how to raise the money to rebuild."

Isabella's voice softened. "Rebuild? Have you seen it? It'll take more than just repairs. It's gutted."

"I know that." Isabella could hear the resolve in Fatima's voice. "But I'm not leaving. I don't care what anyone says. If we leave, he wins." There was another pause, and then she shifted the conversation. "Will you come and see us?"

"I will," she said. "I'm working tomorrow, but I should be back for the weekend. I'll come then."

There was a beat before they said their goodbyes, the weight of the situation hanging in the air long after the call ended. Isabella moused up and closed the window with a deep sense of unease. Fatima's determination was admirable, but that same stubbornness would be her downfall if she wasn't careful.

Isabella understood her drive. She had it, too: the refusal to back down, no matter the cost. And while walking away would have been the smart move, it wasn't something either could do.

But Isabella had options open to her that Fatima did not.

Al-Masri had crossed a line.

Beatrix wouldn't have let this go.

Pope wouldn't have, either.

And neither would she.

Broker would have to wait.

Isabella had a new target.

37

She began sketching out as much detail as she could find. Al-Masri had served as the defence attaché in Washington for three years, a position that not only elevated his standing within military and political circles but also granted him access to influential figures in the U.S. defence establishment. He was well connected, close to top figures in the government, and had become an increasingly powerful figure over the years. His rise in influence had been steady, yet quiet; he appeared to be a man who preferred to operate in the background, avoiding too much public attention.

Finding an image of him was more difficult. His public appearances were rare, and he avoided media attention whenever possible. After extensive searching, Isabella finally found a few photographs: a striking man in his early fifties with greying hair, sharp, dark eyes, and a military bearing that made him look imposing even when not in uniform. In one photo, he was dressed in a formal suit, standing beside a senior American official at a diplomatic event. Another showed him on horseback, smiling, dressed in casual polo attire, and holding a mallet during a match in the Cotswolds, rubbing shoulders with European aristocrats.

The polo was interesting. It was a niche sport in Morocco, typically reserved for the ultra-wealthy. A few more searches led her to an exclusive members-only club in Marrakesh, one of the few in the country with a world-class polo field. The general was said to be a member there, frequenting the club during his breaks from official duties. Isabella sensed an opportunity. If he was this passionate about polo, perhaps it was a vulnerability she could exploit.

More searches revealed whispers about his personal life. Though he kept much of it under wraps, Isabella found information suggesting that Al-Masri had two grown children who often accompanied him to high-profile events, though their presence in the public eye was limited. His daughter, in particular, was a fixture on the polo circuit and social scene.

Isabella quickly opened a fresh email account and composed a message to the club's membership secretary, posing as the daughter of a wealthy Texas oilman looking for equestrian facilities for her father. She asked for a tour of the club, specifically during a polo match, so she could assess its suitability for her family's horses. After a few careful revisions, she hit send.

She logged out and closed the browser, then stood and stretched. There was tension in her muscles. She doubted she'd get a reply from the club today, so she would attend to the next thing on her list. She hadn't been out to the lock-up for several weeks, and she needed to make sure everything was as it ought to be.

38

The mid-afternoon sun bore down on Isabella as she sped along the quiet back roads outside of Marrakesh. Her bike—a Kawasaki Ninja—hummed with a steady rhythm, the engine's power a comforting pulse as she navigated the route to the industrial area south of the city.

It had been some time since she'd visited the little workshop near the Route de Safi. Too long, she thought. The events of the last few days had been troubling, and she needed to be sure that her cache was still secure.

She turned onto the industrial strip and slowed as the familiar row of units came into view. The workshop was nestled among vacant units with signs for cheap storage still hanging loosely on the doors of neighbouring buildings. She pulled up outside the new, reinforced door that she had fitted and killed the engine, the echo of the bike fading into the stillness of the desert.

She dismounted, taking off her helmet and resting it on the seat of the bike. The heavy padlock on the door glinted in the sunlight; it didn't look as if anyone had tried to force it.

She took out the key, slid it into the padlock, and unlocked it. She unthreaded the clasp from the hasp and heaved the roller door up. She rolled her bike into the darkened space and pulled the drawstring for the overhead light. The single bulb flickered to life, casting a dim glow over the steel lockers that she'd paid to have fitted against the back wall. They were untouched, still bolted securely to the floor, just as she'd left them. She closed the door.

She went to the alarm panel. It was a top-of-the-line setup, complete with motion detectors and high-resolution cameras; she tapped in her code and ran a quick systems check on her phone. The cameras were fine, and the motion logs revealed no suspicious activity over the past few weeks.

She approached the lockers. They were solid steel, and each was secured with a high-security seven-lever key lock. She took out the keys and unlocked the first one: inside was a neat rack of weaponry. She reached inside, brushing her fingers over the cold steel of the M-15 ArmaLite and the sleek frame of a Desert Tech MDRx bullpup rifle. Next to them sat a Mossberg 500 shotgun, its barrel polished and ready for action. Boxes of ammunition were stacked beside the guns, each calibre meticulously labelled. Below the rifles were several handguns: a Glock, a Beretta, and a compact SIG Sauer, each carefully maintained and gleaming in the low light. She pulled out the Mossberg, checking its weight, the feel of it in her hands, then returned it to its place.

Box after box of ammunition, frag grenades, and tactical gear were stacked exactly as she'd left them. There was a chance she'd need some of it soon, but for now, she was content to know it was where it ought to be.

She continued her check.

Night-vision goggles.

Flashbangs and fragmentation grenades.

Spare radios.

Her meticulous preparation had been worth it. Everything was intact.

She paused for a moment and breathed in the familiar smell of oiled steel, then locked the safes, stepped back and surveyed the room one final time. The sun was starting to dip low outside, casting long shadows through the gap at the base of the door. She set the alarm, locked the door, and climbed back onto her bike.

She pulled her helmet over her head, revved the engine, and set off.

39

L e Domaine Royal Polo Club was situated on the outskirts of Marrakesh, between the Palmeraie and the rolling foothills of the Atlas Mountains. Isabella had ordered a luxury Uber for the thirty-minute drive from the city centre, intent on making the right impression and reinforcing the flimsy legend that she'd set out in her email to the club yesterday afternoon. She'd gone out shopping for the right outfit and had settled on a tailored beige trouser suit, the clean lines complemented by a simple white blouse. She draped a cashmere sweater over her shoulders, wore a pair of Burberry sunglasses and added a finishing touch: a designer handbag that had cost an obscene amount of money. She was the daughter of a wealthy Texas oilman, and she was worried that she should have arranged for a limousine and driver. The gleaming Mercedes would have to do.

The facilities were accessible via a private road off Route de Fès, one of the city's main thoroughfares leading out into the desert. It was hidden from view by acres of olive groves, manicured gardens, and a high stone wall that ensured exclusivity and privacy. Two lines of towering palm trees flanked the long driveway leading to the main clubhouse at the end. Isabella looked left and right as the Uber drove along the road at the breathtaking views of both the arid plains and the snow-capped peaks of the distant mountains.

The driver reached the parking area and stopped. Isabella thanked him and got out.

She was struck by the understated opulence all around. The polo fields stretched out in perfect parcels of emerald green. The clubhouse was a grand building, its façade a blend of traditional Moroccan stonework and modern architectural lines. The exterior was decorated with intricate Zellige tiles, and tall arched windows allowed sunlight to stream onto the sweeping veranda that overlooked the fields. The scent of freshly cut grass mixed with the subtle fragrance of jasmine that bloomed along the garden walls. Isabella heard the thud of hooves against the turf and distant laughter. It was a peaceful oasis, almost impossible to compare with the chaos of the medina not so far away.

The membership secretary had responded promptly to Isabella's email, evidently eager to show off the club's amenities. They'd arranged the tour for three in the afternoon, and Isabella had spent the morning preparing. Her task was twofold: to convince the club she was representing someone of importance, and to gather as much information as possible about Al-Masri.

A well-dressed woman in her fifties approached and beamed out a practiced, welcoming smile. "Isabella?"

"That's right," Isabella replied.

"I'm Magda. Lovely to meet you."

"Thank you for taking the time to show me around."

"It's my pleasure. Is your father joining us today?"

"He has a meeting," Isabella said smoothly. "It'll just be me. I'll fill him in on everything tonight."

Magda hid any disappointment behind a practiced smile. "Perfect. I'd be happy to take him around another time, but I'm sure you'll both love it here. Shall we get started?"

Isabella followed Magda into the clubhouse. The interior was a blend of classic Moroccan design and European luxury. The floors were polished marble, gleaming under chandeliers that hung from the high, delicately carved ceilings. The walls bore vintage photographs of polo matches and portraits of the club's founding members, lending the space a sense of history and exclusivity.

"So," Magda said, "I'm sure you've already done your research, but Le Domaine Royal is one of Morocco's most exclusive private clubs. It was established in the nineteen eighties by a former royal, and now we cater to the country's wealthiest families, foreign diplomats, and a select group of international members—like you and your father, perhaps. The polo fields are the centrepiece of the club. We have three impeccably maintained full-size fields that we believe are the best in North Africa, with perfect grass year-round thanks to a very expensive irrigation system."

"Very keen to see them," Isabella said.

"We can do that in a moment. This way, please."

They passed through a wide corridor lined with plush, handwoven Berber rugs before arriving at the restaurant, a spacious area with floor-to-ceiling windows offering a panoramic view of the polo fields and the mountains.

"This is our restaurant," Magda said. "Our chef, Claude, is from Paris. He worked under Julien Royer at Odette. He's fabulous. Just *fabulous*."

Isabella nodded her appreciation. The restaurant had

dark wood tables set with fine china, and the room buzzed with conversation from members enjoying a late lunch. Waiters in crisp uniforms moved between tables, serving Moroccan delicacies alongside international dishes.

Magda gestured toward the windows. "The restaurant is a popular spot, especially during matches."

Isabella feigned interest while mentally noting the layout: the ways in and out and the security features she could see. They were plentiful and looked decent; that was disappointing.

They continued through to the bar area, a more intimate space with dim lighting, dark wood-panelled walls, and a grand piano in one corner. Shelves lined with top-shelf spirits were reflected in a large mirror behind the bar. The veranda was next, and Magda extended her arm, gesturing to the polo fields. The grass stretched far into the distance, the goalposts standing tall against the horizon. Horses grazed in nearby paddocks. It looked as if a match was scheduled to start, with players in crisp white uniforms preparing their mounts. Grooms stood nearby, adjusting saddles and bridles, while the players gathered in small groups, chatting and adjusting their gear. Another team— this one with riders dressed in blue—began their warm-up, trotting in tight formation, mallets swinging.

"Are they about to play?"

"They are," Magda said.

"Who's who?"

"The team in white is our first team. The team in blue is from a club in Casablanca."

Isabella looked over to a group of well-dressed onlookers gathered beneath a white marquee, sipping cock-tails and picking at hors d'oeuvres. "Who comes to watch?"

"You'll often see diplomats and high-profile businessmen among the spectators. The polo field attracts a certain crowd. You never know who you'll rub shoulders with. I'm sure your father would fit in well."

"This is stunning," she said.

"I thought you'd like it. I'll show you the pool."

"Can I come back and watch?"

"Of course. This way, please."

Magda led them to the pool area, an oasis surrounded by blossoming bougainvillea and jasmine. The clear blue water sparkled in the sunlight, and members lounged on plush recliners shaded by large white umbrellas.

They returned to the veranda just as the match began. Isabella watched and, to her surprise, spotted a man she was sure was Al-Masri. He was mounted on a powerful chestnut horse, his posture commanding as he guided the animal with a grace that suggested years of practice. Even from a distance, it was clear that he was an expert.

The teams lined up for the throw-in, and the ball was sent into play. Al-Masri was quick to react, urging his horse forward with a sharp nudge. He cut through the field, his mallet raised as he closed in on the ball. Two members of the opposing team tried to crowd him out, but Al-Masri expertly weaved between them. He struck the ball flush and sent it racing down the field.

Isabella watched as he galloped after it, his horse pounding the turf. The defenders scrambled to intercept, but Al-Masri was too fast. He leaned low over his horse's neck, pulled ahead of the defenders and positioned himself perfectly for the shot. He swung his mallet again, rocketing the ball between the goalposts. Isabella heard the crack of the mallet and then a cheer from the spectators.

Al-Masri raised his mallet in acknowledgement as he trotted back to his team.

"Who's that?" Isabella asked.

"General Al-Masri."

"He's good."

"One of our best players."

"My dad would definitely want to meet him."

Magda smiled. "I'm sure they'd get along. The general is here often, especially in the summer. He brings his family to the pool."

"He plays here a lot?"

"He does, although I think he is away soon for a tournament in Kenya. It's quite a big event. He's taking a team from the Moroccan military."

It was possible to see the parking area from the veranda. There were twenty or thirty luxury cars parked there, including a gleaming black Mercedes jeep. Two men stood beside it, obviously not part of the usual crowd of drivers. One of them lifted a pair of binoculars and scanned the polo field. There was something familiar about him, and when he turned to light a cigarette, Isabella recognised what it was: he was one of the men who had attacked Fatima before the orphanage had been set on fire.

Isabella nodded toward the match. "Do you mind if I watch for a bit?"

"Not at all. I'll send a waiter over so you can get a drink."

Isabella took a seat by the railing and watched Al-Masri and the way he directed his teammates. He barked orders and chastised mistakes with a sharp tongue. She watched as he charged after the ball once again, his horse thundering across the field. He collided with an opposing player, expertly nudging the man's horse aside with a subtle shift of his weight, clearing the path for another drive toward the goal.

40

I sabella lingered on the veranda. Magda said she was welcome to stay as long as she liked, and she ordered a mint tea from the waiter who came over to attend to her.

Isabella kept an eye on Al-Masri. The match had ended, and now the general was standing near the stables, laughing with a group of players. His team had won, and he looked pleased as he handed his polo mallet to an attendant. Isabella wondered whether there might be an opportunity to make a move against him now, and quickly discounted it. She wasn't armed, and, judging by the waiting men, the general was obviously careful about his security. She would stay where she was and see whether there was a chance to learn anything about him and his routine.

Magda appeared from the clubhouse and approached with a bright smile. "What do you think?"

"It's beautiful."

"Do you think your father will like it?"

"Definitely."

"As I said—let me know if he'd like to come and have a look himself. I'd be happy to arrange another visit."

Isabella glanced again at Al-Masri. He looked at his watch, gave a curt nod to his companions, and began to walk toward the parking area. It looked like he was leaving.

"I'll speak to him tonight," she said. "I'll email you tomorrow, if that's all right?"

"Of course."

"Thanks again."

Isabella smiled politely, then got to her feet and walked away from the veranda just as the waiter returned with her tea. She kept her movements casual until she was sure no one was watching, then made her way to the staff compound that she had noticed behind the club. The area was a collection of low buildings where the stable hands, gardeners, and maintenance workers stored their tools and equipment. They had bypassed it on the way to the polo field, and Isabella had taken note of a small motorbike parked near the compound wall. It was exactly what she needed.

She approached the bike and glanced left and right to confirm that no one was nearby. She pulled out the lock-picking tools that she'd put in her bag, and within moments, she had the ignition lock popped and the bike's engine rumbling to life.

She straddled the seat, kicked the bike into gear, and steered toward the side exit of the compound. As she approached the front gate of the club, she caught sight of Al-Masri's black jeep pulling onto the road.

IT WAS RUSH HOUR, and the city streets were a tangle of cars, mopeds, and pedestrians. Isabella kept her distance from the jeep, weaving between vehicles to remain unnoticed.

The traffic slowed as they approached a crowded intersection, and she used the opportunity to drop a few cars back. The jeep soon picked up speed, heading toward the main road that would lead to the heart of Marrakesh. It took Isabella through the bustling streets until, eventually, the road narrowed as they approached a more affluent area on the outskirts with quieter, tree-lined streets.

The jeep turned into a well-hidden driveway and disappeared behind tall, wrought-iron gates. Isabella didn't stop; she continued past the property, taking note of the high walls and the security cameras. She parked just along the street and watched as the gates slid closed, leaving only the faintest hum of the vehicle's engine as it continued up to the house.

Today had gone about as well as Isabella could have expected. She had only intended to scout the club but had had the benefit of an hour watching the general, and now— the cherry on top of the cake—she knew where he lived.

Now she just had to work out how to get closer.

41

Isabella rode to a mall she knew in the upscale district of Hivernage. She parked the bike and went inside, finding a clothes store, where she bought a traditional abaya. She went into the mall's bathroom, changing out of the outfit she'd worn to the polo club. She folded the clothes, took out the abaya and slipped her arms into the wide sleeves. The garment fell down her body, covering her from her shoulders to her ankles. She took the matching black hijab, carefully placing the centre of the scarf at the top of her forehead. She draped the fabric over her head, making sure it concealed all of her hair, crossed the ends under her chin and tucked one end over her shoulder, securing it with a pin. The remaining fabric covered her neck and shoulders, ensuring her appearance was inconspicuous. She put the clothes she had worn earlier into the bag she'd been given in the store before going back to the bike.

She returned to Palmeraie. She approached the general's property and continued down the street, checking again so she could identify the security measures in place: concrete bollards blocked off both ends of the road; a red-and-white striped military sentry box stood at the entrance to the short driveway leading to the three-storey house beyond; cameras everywhere. Isabella parked in a secluded spot between two large palm trees, hidden from view by thick foliage around their trunks. The area was quiet, with only the occasional pedestrian walking along the pavement.

She went back toward the villa, this time on foot. There was a small café across the street: a perfect place to sit and observe without drawing attention. The abaya provided her with the anonymity she needed, allowing her to blend in with the locals who were already in the café or at the tables arranged on the grass outside.

She chose a seat near the window, offering her a clear view of the villa's entrance, ordered a coffee—thick, strong Moroccan espresso—and settled in to watch.

She noted everything: two vehicles that entered and then left and the comings and goings of staff. She saw that the villa was well defended, but even the most secure homes had weak points. The smallest details could reveal secrets to those who knew where to look. The way the security personnel moved, the condition of their uniforms—whether they were crisp or unkempt—told her how alert and disciplined they were. Cigarette butts littering the ground spoke to a casual attitude that could be exploited. On the other hand, state-of-the-art earpieces suggested the security team was well-funded, their equipment regularly updated. Vehicles left in plain sight hinted at carelessness, while cars parked in garages reflected a higher level of caution.

The general's setup looked to be at the better, more effective end of the spectrum.

Annoying.

Isabella paid for her coffee and went back onto the street. She could hear the faint sounds of a radio playing in the guard booth at the entrance to the property. A young soldier, barely out of his teens, stood up to stretch his legs. His uniform hung loosely on his thin frame, and he absently hummed a tune. His eyes flicked over her, dismissing her as just another passerby, an anonymous woman of no consequence.

She observed the villa carefully. The palm trees and greenery surrounding the estate had grown thick, their branches offering a natural cover that made it difficult to see through to the second-floor windows. The glass was tinted with a protective film, letting in light but obscuring any clear view from the outside; it would be useless for a sniper looking to take a precise shot. She counted seven small security cameras positioned at strategic points around the exterior of the house. The Mercedes she had seen at the polo match wasn't visible, but a high-end BMW sat in the driveway, its engine idling and a driver at the ready. Other personnel patrolled the grounds; all were well built and obviously armed.

Very annoying.

Isabella scanned the neighbouring properties, considering whether any might offer a suitable vantage point for a sniper. But someone had already thought of that; bollards lined the pavement, preventing cars from being parked too close; and identical security cameras were mounted on the surrounding villas, no doubt connected to the general's own surveillance system. The flat roof of the villa directly opposite was likely just as secured, with access restricted by heavy locks and chains under the watchful eye of his men.

She continued on.

The general's security was too tight here; any attempt to infiltrate or attack him at the villa would be suicidal.

She needed a different plan.

The polo club.

Magda had mentioned that the general was a frequent visitor, using the swimming pool and shooting range as well as playing polo. That presented an opportunity, but Isabella would need to find a way to access the club without attracting suspicion. She'd already played the role of a potential member, and now that angle was closed. She needed a way to blend in, to move freely around the club without supervision.

She needed help.

Someone who could get a job there.

Someone local.

She wondered.

Aicha?

She had the right profile: she was Moroccan and evidently had the inclination to strike against the regime. The files Isabella had glimpsed on her laptop suggested she was already involved in dissident activities. Could she be convinced to help with something more direct?

Isabella pushed the thought aside for now. She hadn't decided what her next move would be. Threatening the general wasn't an option, it would just provoke retaliation, and she couldn't risk Fatima and the children coming to harm.

Threats wouldn't be enough.

If she acted, it would have to be decisive and final.

She thought back to the fire at the orphanage: the smell of smoke, the children's cries for help, and Latifa's tear-streaked face.

She was in no doubt that Al-Masri had ordered the fire-bombing, and he didn't care who lived or died.

Whatever she decided to do would be justified.

42

Isabella returned to the riad, still dressed in the disguise she'd worn to scout the general's house. She reached the front door and, conscious that her neighbours would not be used to seeing someone dressed in an abaya going inside, made sure no one was watching before taking out her key and unlocking the door.

She disengaged the alarm, checked her hidden security measures had not been touched, and, satisfied that everything was exactly as she'd left it, went to the kitchen and took yesterday's leftover tagine from the fridge and heated it up in the microwave. She ran a glass of cold water and downed it in one thirsty gulp. It had been a long day, and although she had intended to go up onto the roof and lift some weights, she found that she didn't have the motivation. The microwave beeped; she took the tagine and a beer from the fridge and climbed the stairs to her room.

Solving Fatima's problem was going to be challenging. She had been thinking—again—of whether there was any way she could do it without bloodshed but had decided that there was not. She might have been open to an attempt at persuasion, but Al-Masri had ceded any right to a civilised outcome when he had nearly killed the children. And, anyway, would she really have trusted him even if she had made him realise the good sense of backing away? He would see her point of view if she had a pistol against his head, but what would happen when she had gone? He would be outraged at being threatened by a woman, and he would react. Isabella couldn't watch the orphanage all the time, and, even if that had been possible, giving the general a reprieve would also give him the opportunity to gather his resources and make a more forceful attack that she would not be able to resist.

No, she was sure. He didn't know she was coming, he couldn't possibly prepare for it, and she wouldn't pass up the benefit of surprise because she was queasy about what she knew she would have to do with him. She'd killed people like him before—for herself and for Broker—and a man like that didn't get to tweak her conscience.

He was going to get exactly what was coming to him.

SHE FINISHED her dinner and was taking the empty plate down to the kitchen when her phone buzzed with an incoming FaceTime call.

She looked down at the screen: it was Charlie.

She paused, wondering whether she should answer; she couldn't think of a reason why not and, besides, she hadn't spoken to him since the day before yesterday and missed their chats. She glanced behind her to make sure that there would be nothing in shot that would cast doubt on the story she'd told him or give him anything that might enable him to locate her, and, happy that everything was bland and anonymous, she tapped to connect.

The screen flashed black, and then, as the call connected, she saw his smiling face.

"Hey," he said.

She frowned. His left eye was swollen, surrounded by dark bruising that extended down to his cheekbone, which was itself marred by a thin, red gash. A deep cut ran along his temple, partially hidden by the bandage that was wrapped around his head.

"What happened?"

He tried to strike a cheerful tone. "Car accident."

"Sorry?"

"I was rear-ended." He tapped a finger against the bandage. "My face bounced off the wheel when I went off the road and crashed."

"What happened?"

"I'd been to see my grandmother—I told you I was going back, didn't I?"

"You did."

"I'd just left her. It was late, and there was some fog. It was a straight road; everything was fine until this car came racing up behind me. I was doing fifty; he must've been doing seventy, maybe eighty. He tried to overtake, got it wrong and clipped me. Sent me off the road and—*bang*—into a ditch." He paused. "Could've been worse. I managed to control the impact but, if I hadn't, I would've driven into the trees at the side of the road. I was lucky."

There was no question in Isabella's mind that what had happened had been deliberate.

"Jesus," she said. "That's awful."

"You should see my car. The whole left side has crumpled where I went into the ditch. Insurers say it'll be a write-off."

Isabella bit her lip. "Can I ask you a question?"

"Sure."

"And do you promise you'll be honest with me?"

"Of course."

She pointed. "Has anything else like that happened to you recently?"

"Like what?"

"Like something you thought was an accident but maybe looked a bit suspicious?"

He was quiet.

Her stomach fell. "That's a yes?"

"It's a maybe."

"Tell me."

"When I picked up my plane, right after you left, I flew to Malaga. I was above the Alboran Sea when I realised something was wrong. I thought the fuel gauge was faulty, but you have to take these things at face value, so I turned around and made an emergency landing at Oran."

"And?"

"There was a hole in the tank. It looked like someone had punctured it deliberately. Looked like it might've been a screwdriver."

"Shit."

"I know," he said. He chuckled, evidently determined to make light of it. "Probably one of my competitors—I don't know if I told you, but there's *so* much money to be made flying humanitarian supplies into disaster zones."

"Don't joke," she said. "It's not funny. It's sabotage. And you could've been killed."

"I don't know—it might've been something else entirely."

"Like what?"

"An accident?"

Charlie didn't sound convinced, and Isabella certainly wasn't. She knew this was Broker. Even though she'd taken the contract, he'd given it to another contractor at the same time. Pope had said that happened sometimes—it was called a redundancy—but she'd never noticed it before. But now? There couldn't be any doubt about it. There was someone else on the case. They'd tampered with Charlie's plane, and then, when that didn't work, they'd tried to run him off the road.

Isabella closed her eyes. Things had been neat and tidy six months ago, everything in good order and free of complications. She'd been making good money and was happy with a life without friends or romantic entanglements.

But now there was chaos everywhere she looked.

There was a man she needed to kill—quickly—before he finished what he'd started with Fatima.

And there was Charlie—a man she'd *refused* to kill— being stalked by one of Broker's other contractors.

She wasn't blind to the irony.

What a *mess.*

"Isabella? What's up?"

She remembered it was a video call and that Charlie could see her. She opened her eyes and smiled at him. "What are you doing tomorrow?"

"Not much—the doctors say I can't fly until they're sure I'm not concussed. I'm supposed to go back and see them at the end of the week. Why?"

"Can I come and see you?"

He brightened. "Sure... but—"

"My agency's been pestering me to do a shoot in Tunisia, but the money's not great, so I've always said no. But they'll cover my plane ticket, and I could come and see you before I go and do it. What do you think?"

PART V

43

The boat was called the *Osprey*, and it looked as if it was held together with string and glue. Charlie explained that he had bought it for a song from an Australian who had used it for his dive school before being forced out of business by rising costs. He kept it in the harbour at Hammamet, the town on the northeastern coast of Tunisia where Charlie lived.

Isabella had flown into nearby Tunis and booked a room at a hotel that overlooked the Mediterranean. She had met Charlie for dinner the previous night, he had suggested a seafood restaurant overlooking the beach, and they had enjoyed a spectacular meal. They would have carried on into the night, but they had arranged to take the boat out for an early morning dive, and cast-off had been scheduled for six.

It was a beautiful start to the day. Seagulls coasted on the strong wind above them, and white clouds scudded across an otherwise blue sky. The *Osprey* rocked gently beneath their feet as they moved around the deck. Charlie was busy checking the air cylinders, securing them in place with practiced hands, while Isabella laid out the masks, fins, and wetsuits.

Charlie glanced up from the dive console, a digital display flashing the current depth and the surrounding water temperature. "How's your gear?" he asked, nodding toward the regulator Isabella was testing.

"Good," she replied, glancing over at him. She watched as he adjusted the straps on his buoyancy-control device, the weight of the dive cylinders sitting comfortably on his back. Isabella reached for her own BCD and began securing it around her shoulders.

The salty wind whipped through their hair, the smell of marine fuel blending with the freshness of the ocean.

"How far is it?" Isabella asked, securing her gear and checking the straps on her cylinder.

"Not far," Charlie replied. "We'll be in the water in about twenty minutes."

"Are you going to tell me what we're going to see?"

He'd been coy about it all last night, save for telling her that she would be impressed. He smiled at her now, laughed and relented. "I suppose it won't hurt if you have an idea before we go down." He tapped on his dive slate, sketching a quick outline of the dive site. "There's an old Italian frigate down there. It went down during the war." He pointed to the slate and his drawing of the ship. "The hull's mostly intact, and you can swim right through the passageways. It's only about eight metres down, and it's still in decent condition. Tons of sea life. I've seen dolphins there, big rays, and there was a pilot whale a month ago."

Isabella glanced over at him. He still looked beaten up after the accident. The left side of his face had been badly bruised from bouncing off the steering wheel, and she'd noticed the stiffness in his posture as they had boarded the boat earlier.

"Can I ask you a question?" she said.

"About the dive?"

"No." She pointed to his face. "About that."

He waved the question away. "I told you—it was an accident."

"Come on, Charlie. It wasn't. You know it wasn't."

"He was driving too fast, probably drunk, and he—"

"But it wasn't just that," she cut over him, "was it? Come on—do I really have to spell it out? First there was the hole in the fuel tank. You could try to say that was an accident, too, but we both know that it wasn't. Right? Holes don't just appear like that, do they?"

He didn't answer.

"And now there's the crash. They both could've killed you, and they both happened in the space of a week. We both know this isn't just a run of bad luck."

He glanced away. "I know. It's weird."

"It's deliberate, Charlie. Both things are deliberate. Someone wants to hurt you."

He sighed. "I know. I mean, it got me thinking... I've been back over all my clients and trips from the last twelve months to look for anything that might have landed me in trouble like this, but there's nothing. I can't think of anything." He started counting on his fingers. "No one's got a grudge against me, at least not as far as I know. I haven't overcharged a client. I haven't broken an agreement. And I'm not a big enough fish for a competitor to try to force me out of business. In short," he said, scratching his head, "I'm stumped."

Isabella nodded. She was in a difficult situation, and she still wasn't quite sure how to manoeuvre herself around it.

She was convinced the client behind the two attempts on Charlie's life was his brother, and that his motive was as old as time: greed. But it was one thing for her to suspect that and another thing entirely to find a way where she could tell Charlie without compromising herself. She would have to tell him that she knew because she'd also been given the contract to kill him.

"Let's think laterally," she said. "Is there anyone who might stand to benefit if you weren't around?"

"Seriously? I'm nothing special. I couldn't be more ordinary if I tried. There's nothing that would make me a target."

Isabella knew she would have to lead him to the same conclusion she'd reached. "What about your grandmother and the inheritance? What about that?"

"What about it?"

"It's a lot of money—right?"

He nodded. "It's a lot."

"How much?"

He spread his hands. "A million. I don't really know—it might be more."

"See—that is a lot. What if someone wanted it?"

"You mean my brother?"

She nodded. "Why not?"

"Jack's a shit, but would he run me off the road? No. And how would he know to puncture the fuel tank? He doesn't even know where I am half the time. He thinks my business is pointless—he makes sure to tell me that every time I see him. It's not him, Isabella." He shook his head firmly. "No way."

"I'm not saying he'd do it himself. Look—I've been around a bit. I've worked in some unpleasant places, and I've met some unpleasant people. There are places where, if you've got enough money, you can find people who'll do that sort of thing for you."

"Come on—be serious."

"I am being serious. There was this one time, last year, I was booked to do a shoot in Cairo. The client had a night-club, and he had a run-in with someone who was trying to open a rival club down the street. The second guy hired someone to kill my client. It didn't happen—the police stopped it—but you can find loads of stories online of that kind of thing happening. The dark web makes it possible to be anonymous, and people do things they wouldn't normally do when they think there's no way they'll be found out. You said it yourself—Jack has the means to do it, and he definitely has the motive. I'm just saying—I don't think you should write him off."

Charlie shook his head. "That's nuts. I'm the one who bumped his head, not you."

"Money makes people do stupid things."

Isabella had tried, but she could already tell it was useless. She knew her life was beyond unusual, and that she'd seen and lived through things that Charlie would never have believed. She understood better than most how dangerous the world was, and how people were often driven by darker motives. The fact that Jack had probably paid for the murder of his brother wasn't shocking to her; given the line of work she followed, it was almost mundane.

But for someone like Charlie—an innocent—it would be harder to accept. It sounded like something from a trashy novel. But that was the problem; his refusal to face reality wasn't just naïve, it was dangerous. He wouldn't take measures to protect himself, and that would leave him wide open for the next attempt by Broker's current contractor, or the one after that.

He'd been lucky so far, but that luck wouldn't last forever.

Isabella hadn't wanted to get involved, but had always known it was probably going to be necessary. The options for doing that were limited: she could go dark, tell Charlie that she was leaving and then follow him in the hope that she'd spot the contractor before they tried again. She could identify them and then remove them as a threat. It might work, but there were uncertainties, and it could take a while. It might be days or weeks before they tried again, and that was time she didn't have; Fatima and the children were vulnerable, and she needed to attend to them, too.

And wouldn't Broker just put the job up again and send someone else?

She thought about Broker and what she knew of him. It wasn't much. He—or she—was in business with a simple model: his clients paid him to kill people, and he made it happen. But what if the client—in this case, Jack—cancelled the contract? What if Jack contacted Broker and told him he'd changed his mind, and he didn't want Charlie killed? Jack wouldn't get his money back, but that would be his punishment for doing something so stupid. And Broker? The hit itself meant nothing to him, and he'd still have the money. He'd call off the contractor, reassign him or her to another job, and that would be the end of it.

Charlie would be safe.

Charlie cut the engine, and the boat started to drift. Isabella adjusted the strap on her dive mask, checking for any leaks, while Charlie lowered the anchor, the chain rattling as it disappeared into the turquoise water below. Isabella pulled her fins from the mesh bag and slid them on, then double-checked her dive computer. Charlie, meanwhile, hoisted the air tanks and positioned them next to the stern, ready for when they'd make their backward roll into the water.

She often thought about what Pope would do, and here, right now, it was easy.

He'd go after Jack, scare the shit out of him, sort things out that way.

Charlie switched on the oxygen tank valve, checking the pressure gauge.

"Ready?"

She was distracted.

"Hello?"

"Sorry," she said. "Million miles away."

"Penny for your thoughts?"

"Forget it," she said. "Doesn't matter."

"Don't worry about me," he said. "I mean it. It's nothing. I'll be fine."

He held her gaze for a moment, then pulled off his T-shirt and zipped up his wetsuit, but not before Isabella saw more bruises on his chest.

She'd made up her mind: she'd enjoy the rest of the day with Charlie and then make her excuses and leave.

And pay Jack a visit before she made her way to the airport.

PART VI

44

J ack Carter lived in a large villa on the outskirts of Sidi Bou Said, a coastal town just outside Tunis. The villa was nestled atop a hill that overlooked the Gulf of Tunis, providing panoramic views of the Mediterranean. Isabella researched the estate from a quiet café. She started with satellite imagery from Google Earth. The house sat behind a high stone wall, partially obscured by thick bougainvillea and cypress trees. A long driveway wound up the hill, leading to a gated entrance that, in turn, opened onto a courtyard. The house itself was sprawling, with multiple wings, terraces, and balconies. It was the kind of property bought when a person had more money than they knew how to spend.

Isabella zoomed in on the estate's surroundings, noting possible entry points and weak spots. The rear garden backed onto a public footpath that wound back down the hill toward the coast. There were olive trees and a small citrus grove that would provide useful cover, and, as she switched to Street View, she saw the walls were not as impenetrable as they had first seemed. They were tall, but without any impediments—wire or spikes—at the top. Isabella fancied she would be able to scale them.

She turned to OpenStreetMap and the various estate agent listings for similar properties. She found the listing for the villa that must have been prepared for when the property was last on the market, before Jack bought it, complete with floor plans and photos. The main house was as expansive as it had looked from overhead, with a reception hall, marble floors, and a sweeping staircase that led to the upper floors. There were multiple guest suites, a private cinema, and a pool house next to an infinity pool overlooking the sea.

She switched to social media and scrolled through the profiles of Jack's wife and children. Though Jack himself maintained a low online presence, his daughters and wife were frequent posters. Isabella reviewed their posts and continued to fill in the blanks with regard to the villa's layout and daily routine. A tennis court, private stables, and expansive gardens appeared frequently in their photos.

The estate had recently undergone renovations, and a filing with the local planning office revealed that the security systems had been upgraded as part of the work. The installation included high-definition surveillance cameras positioned strategically around the perimeter, covering all entrances and blind spots. In addition to the cameras, there were motion sensors embedded along the walls and in the gardens, designed to trigger alarms if anyone attempted to enter the property at night. These sensors were linked to a central monitoring system that alerted both the on-site security team and a third-party response unit. The filing also indicated that the panic room had been upgraded with reinforced doors, biometric access, and an independent power supply, ensuring it could remain operational even in the event of a power failure or deliberate sabotage.

Isabella noticed a potential flaw: the system relied on external power, meaning any disruption to the local grid would compromise its effectiveness. Additionally, the angles of the cameras, while comprehensive, looked as if they might leave small gaps near the tree line at the back of the estate. Isabella ought to be able to move unseen if she timed her approach correctly.

She leaned back in her chair and checked the time.

It was half six, and the café was about to close for the day. Isabella would go back to her hotel room and prepare, she was booked on the first flight out of Tunis tomorrow, and she wanted to take care of Jack tonight. She'd wait until the household was asleep before she did what she had come here to do.

45

It was a little after two in the morning. Isabella had been busy; aside from the planning and research, she'd found a store and picked up the gear she would need. She was dressed all in black: a fitted, long-sleeved top, black cargo pants with deep pockets, and, over that, a light-weight matte-black jacket with a high collar that could be flipped up to obscure the lower part of her face. She wore a pair of black tactical boots with rubber soles, flexible enough for running and climbing, and black gloves to ensure she left no fingerprints. She'd tied back her hair into a tight braid and tucked it inside the balaclava that covered her face.

Jack Carter's property was even more imposing in person than it had appeared during her research. The main house loomed ahead, its pale stone façade illuminated by the soft glow of discreet uplights. The tall hedges and olive groves created a natural barrier from the road, but it was the walls that gave the place its fortress-like feel.

Isabella saw the wrought-iron gate at the entrance and

counted the security cameras discreetly mounted along the perimeter.

She scouted the property as thoroughly as she could, concluding that her plan to use the garden at the back of the estate as her way in was the right one. It was hidden behind dense hedges and groves, difficult to observe from the main house and road.

She went back down to the foot of the hill. The electrical substation that served the property was there, and, after satisfying herself that there was no one else in the area, Isabella took out a pair of insulated wire cutters and a small toolkit and forced the panel. She identified the circuit that fed power directly to the security system and cut into the cables. She looked up the hill and saw the house plunge into darkness before the backup generator kicked in, the alarm was still powered, but the cameras—not connected to the backup—were not.

She made her way to the tall stone wall that marked the boundary at the back of the property. It was ten feet tall, but that was not even remotely challenging for her. She jumped up, catching her hands against the lip of the wall, and then swung a leg over, crouching once she landed on the other side.

She paused, scanning the area for any sign of movement or additional security measures that she might have missed. The garden was empty except for an abandoned croquet set, and the grounds were quiet.

She'd memorised the floor plan and knew that the ground floor was expansive, laid out with interconnected rooms. The front door opened into a wide hallway that led directly to the heart of the house. To the left was a spacious drawing room, and beyond that a formal dining room connected to the kitchen, which stretched the full width of the house and led out to the garden. A glass-walled garden room overlooked the lawn and was another potential point of entry. On the right side of the house was a grand sitting room and a private study. The upper floors were just as expansive, with bedrooms spread across multiple wings. The master suite was positioned on the far side of the house. A secondary staircase led up to the attic, converted into additional guest rooms and a small office.

Isabella saw the security cameras and, trusting that they were still disabled, she sprinted across the lawn until she reached the cover of a nearby tree. She took a moment to steady her breath and continued until she reached the glass doors of the garden room.

46

Isabella crept toward the garden room door, crouching low and keeping close to the walls of the house. She shucked the backpack from her shoulders, opened it and took out the latch slip tool she'd brought with her. It was a narrow strip of steel, about twelve inches long and just a fraction of an inch thick. She inserted it between the door and the frame and, after a few seconds of gentle pressure, felt the latch give way. She opened the door just wide enough to slip inside, then closed it softly behind her.

It was dark save the soft glow from the moon, and the only sound was the faint hum of the air conditioning. Isabella moved quickly and silently through the space, passing into the kitchen. It, too, was quiet save for the low hum of the refrigerator in the corner. The dining room and hallway stretched out in front of her. She knew the master bedroom was on the right-hand side of the first floor, away from the other bedrooms. It was unlikely anyone would be awake at this hour, but she wasn't prepared to take chances. She moved through the dining room, careful to avoid any possible creaks in the floorboards, and reached the base of the staircase. She listened for a moment, attuned to any sound that might indicate movement upstairs, but the house remained still.

She climbed the stairs, her body low and balanced to distribute her weight evenly on each step.

She reached the top and paused again to listen.

Still nothing.

The door to the master bedroom was slightly ajar. She pushed it open and looked inside: the layout was exactly as she had anticipated from the floor plan. The large bed was positioned against the far wall, its headboard facing the door, with large windows on either side allowing a faint glow from the night sky to filter in. The room was sparsely decorated, in keeping with the minimalist style of the rest of the house, but still spacious and luxurious. She could see the en-suite bathroom door to the right.

She slipped inside, her footsteps soft against the thick carpet.

There was a single figure in the bed, snoring loudly.

Isabella reached into her pack and took out the knife she'd brought with her, then reached into her pocket and took out her phone. She tapped her finger against the screen to wake it, opened the voice memo application, started a recording and then put the device down on the bedside table, angling it so the microphone was pointing directly at Jack's head.

She checked her balaclava was covering her face, sat down on the edge of the bed, took Jack by the shoulder and gently shook him awake.

He mumbled something she couldn't understand.

She shook him again.

He awoke.

"Nice and quiet," she said.

He sat bolt upright in bed, blinking furiously, struggling to see her in the darkness.

He panicked. "Who are you?"

He reached for the bedside lamp, but Isabella slapped his hand away.

He tried again, and she punched him in the face. He yelped, his hands going to his face, and was unable to stop her as she pushed him back down onto the mattress.

"I'll call the—"

Isabella took a handful of his hair and yanked, exposing his throat. She laid the blade against the skin, just below his bobbing larynx.

"You won't," she said evenly.

She had whetted the blade before coming out, and now she let him feel how sharp she'd made it.

"Please," he said. "I'm sorry."

"What are you sorry for?"

"I... I..."

"I mean," she said, "you must be sorry about something. You wouldn't have said that if you weren't."

"Please—don't hurt me."

"Is it Charlie?"

"What?"

"Are you sorry about Charlie?"

"What are you—"

She pressed down with the knife. "Let's not be silly about this, Jack. It won't go well for you."

"Charlie?" he stammered.

"That's right. *Charlie.* Your brother."

The pause before his reply and the flicker of recognition

in his eyes told her he knew exactly what she was talking about.

"I don't have much time for him," he said.

"You paid to have him killed."

"No. That's ridiculous."

She pushed down on the blade and slid it up his neck so that the edge caught against the stubble running up to his chin.

"I won't have to push too much harder to break the skin. Do you want to keep lying to me?"

"Okay," he said. "*Okay*. Please."

"Going to tell me the truth?"

"Yes."

"All of it?"

"Yes," he said. "I swear."

"I'm listening."

"He thinks he's entitled to money."

"Your grandmother's?"

He stared up at her in surprise. "You know about it?"

"Go on, Jack."

"He thinks he's going to inherit it," he said, "but he's not. Is that really what this is about? That little shit doesn't need the inheritance. He'll piss it away on his stupid little business."

Isabella angled the blade a little more and drew it a quarter inch to the left. The edge cut into the skin, creating a little furrow into which blood quickly welled.

"And so you paid someone to murder him."

It wasn't a question, Jack realised that, and that it wouldn't do him any good to pretend she was wrong. "What else could I do? He wouldn't listen to reason, and I need the money more than he does." He began to snivel.

She looked around. "A lovely house like this? I doubt it."

"It's not mine," he said. "It's the bank's. I'm in debt. My business is in trouble, and I had to take out a loan to keep it afloat. Had to secure the loan on the house, and it didn't work—now they want to repossess it."

"That doesn't sound like that's Charlie's problem," she said. He started to protest, but she silenced him by holding up her free hand. "I just wanted you to know that hurting him would be bad for you. Not just bad—very bad. *Life-shorteningly* bad. That's why I'm here. I want you to understand there will be consequences if that happens. I want you to understand that there will be consequences—for you—if anyone so much as *looks* at your brother in the wrong way. Do you understand that, Jack?"

"Yes."

"Are you *sure*?"

"Yes—I'm sure."

"Good. Now—I want you to call the man you paid to kill Charlie and tell him the deal is off. He'll tell you that he doesn't do refunds, and you're going to say that's fine, he can keep the money, you just don't want him to carry out the contract. Do you understand?"

"Yes."

She stepped back, surveying her handiwork. It wasn't pretty. She'd taken no pleasure in making a grown man cry, but people like him needed to learn that they couldn't do whatever they wanted.

"I'm giving you a chance, Jack. You've seen how easy it was for me to get to see you tonight. It won't matter what you do tomorrow—it'll still be easy. You won't get another chance. I'm going to trust you to make things right. Don't make me come back again. That'll inconvenience me, and I won't be nearly as friendly."

"You won't need to come back," he said, his voice high and tight. "I'll sort it out."

She pointed the blade at him. "See that you do."

She picked up her phone, backed away, quickly checking that she hadn't left anything behind and, happy that she hadn't, left the room and made her way back down the stairs to the door and the garden beyond.

PART VII

47

Isabella flew back to Morocco. She was confident that her session with Jack would help focus his mind and that he would quickly contact Broker to call off the hit, but, beyond that, it was hard to know what would happen next. She didn't know how Jack communicated with Broker but knew that if Jack disclosed the reason for his radical change of mind—that someone broke into his house and threatened him with a knife to the throat unless the job was cancelled—there was a risk that Broker might dig for more information. If he did that, was it possible he might make a connection with her tardiness to action the contract? Would Broker realise it was her? Surely not.

She didn't know what would happen, but perhaps it was irrelevant. Her performance might already have given Broker reason to doubt her, and perhaps he would be less likely to send new work her way. But, she reflected, would she even be prepared to take on new contracts? Because either Jack had lied to Broker about Charlie—and why would Jack do that?—or Broker had lied to her, knowing that the contract wouldn't be accepted unless there was some sort of moral turpitude to condemn the subject.

Broker wouldn't trust her.

She didn't trust him.

Much better for all parties if they left things as they were and went their separate ways.

She took out her phone and opened her messages. Charlie had promised he would let her know when he was next in Morocco and had said he was looking forward to seeing her again. That would be fun. She would take him to the souk and then Majorelle Garden, and then they could finish with sunset drinks at one of the rooftop cafés in the medina. She sketched out the day and found, to her pleasant surprise, that she was looking forward to it. She'd been on her own since Pope's death and had ignored the fact that she was lonely. Having company to enjoy the city with her would be a refreshing change, and the fact that her potential company was so easy on the eye was no bad thing.

Her thoughts ran away from that to the pressing concern that she had been putting off. Fatima and the children were in danger, and that danger would continue until either the general had been persuaded that he wasn't going to get the orphanage or the threat he posed had been neutralised in another way. She'd considered ways that she might be able to persuade him but doubted that the approach she had taken with Jack would work a second time. A man like Al-Masri would feel slighted if he were threatened by a woman. Morocco was a spectacular country, but there was no getting away from the fact that it was a patriarchy and that antediluvian attitudes toward women had been ingrained over centuries. The general was a soldier too, and would feel the weight of his office behind him; a man like him, grown fat on corruption like a pig at the trough, would not react well to the prospect of having his latest money-making scheme ripped away.

That was bad for him: it was more than likely that Isabella would have to end his life. Neither he nor Fatima showed any signs of backing down. The children were at risk. They'd been lucky she had been there to get them out during the fire, but they might not be so fortunate if—*when*, she corrected herself—the general tried again.

And Isabella couldn't take that chance.

48

Isabella woke before dawn; the call to prayer from the mosque nearest to the riad was just audible. She lay still, running through what she'd decided to do. Today was important, and if she was going to get what she needed, she'd have to approach it carefully. She wanted to be sure about Aicha before she involved her in the plan she was still sketching out, and that was going to require some subterfuge on her part.

She slipped out of bed, feeling the chill of the tiled floor against her bare feet. The soft glow of early morning light filtered through the shutters, casting patterns across the walls. She picked out a practical outfit of nondescript clothing: a loose linen shirt, dark jeans, and a lightweight jacket. She braided her hair and tucked it beneath a hijab, intent on looking like just any other local going about her day.

She found her backpack and filled it with the things she thought she might need: her phone, a notebook, a camera with a telephoto lens, and a pair of sunglasses. The camera would remain in the bag unless absolutely necessary, she doubted she'd need it, but it was better to have it and not need it, than need it and not have it.

She spared five minutes for a quick breakfast of strong coffee and a piece of fresh flatbread and checked the time: it was six. Aicha would be on her way soon to get to the campus for the start of lessons at nine.

Isabella needed to get going.

Isabella reached the university campus with time to spare. The district had a very different feel to the chaotic energy of the medina; it was quieter, more orderly, with modern buildings and neatly arranged streets lined with palm trees.

A café opposite spilled out onto the sidewalk, with tables and chairs set under awnings to provide shade. Isabella found an empty table where she could sit unnoticed among the locals. She had a clear view of the entrance to the campus and up and down the street.

Isabella scanned the area and assessed whether anyone else—apart from her—was taking an interest in the building. Nothing seemed out of place. A few children were playing in the park next to it, and a vendor was setting up a stall selling fresh fruit. It looked normal and exactly as she would have expected.

She sat back, her sunglasses concealing her eyes as she pretended to read from her phone. Her attention stayed on the entrance.

Aicha arrived thirty minutes later. She was dressed casually in jeans and a light jacket, and the backpack

Isabella remembered from before was slung over one shoulder. She seemed distracted but at ease, and her gaze was downcast as she checked her phone. She crossed the main street and entered the campus through the main gates, joining a group of students heading toward the central academic buildings.

Isabella was happy.

Nothing was out of the ordinary, and she was confident that Aicha was not under surveillance by anyone else.

She looked up and signalled for the waitress's attention so she could get another coffee. She needed to wait until Aicha emerged.

49

Isabella had been at the café for more than four hours, doing her best to melt into the background while still watching the students as they made their way along the pavements in front of her. The waiting staff must have noticed her, but no one asked her to move on. She had tipped the waitress who had served her first, and that same girl had seemingly reserved her for herself; Isabella had added a little extra payment to each new check, and the girl seemed happy enough not to disturb the arrangement.

Aicha finally emerged at just after two, walking alone and at the same casual pace as before. Her expression was anxious. Her head was low, and her phone stayed in her pocket.

Isabella stood up slowly, tossing a final tip onto the table as she adjusted the hijab around her neck.

She set off, keeping a comfortable distance behind as they moved away from the university.

Aicha crossed Avenue Allal El Fassi and headed toward the busier commercial streets. Isabella followed, weaving through the thickening crowd. Aicha went down Rue el Kadi Ayad and turned in at the entrance to a small car park. Isabella slowed her pace, hiding behind a row of fruit stalls. Aicha approached a dark-coloured scooter parked on the side, unlocked it with a key she took from her pocket, and put on the helmet she took from the top box.

Isabella frowned.

She was going to have to find another way to follow.

She scanned the street; a line of taxis idled nearby, the drivers smoking and chatting as they waited for fares. Isabella hurried over and slipped into the backseat of the first one.

"I need you to follow that scooter," she said, pointing toward Aicha.

The driver, an older man with greying hair and a sceptical expression, glanced at her in the rear-view mirror.

"Money first."

Isabella handed over five hundred dirhams. "Stay back," she said. "But don't lose her."

The driver put the taxi into gear and pulled out into traffic just as Aicha set off herself. She darted between cars, but the driver was skilled and deftly manoeuvred them through the traffic without drawing attention.

They moved further from the centre of Marrakesh, and the scenery began to change. The clean, orderly streets faded behind them as they travelled down Boulevard Mohammed VI, the palm-lined boulevard delivering them into the outskirts of the city. The industrial zone loomed ahead, the roads becoming more deserted, lined with warehouses and factories.

Isabella's eyes stayed on the scooter, fingers tapping on the armrest.

"Back a bit," Isabella said.

The driver nodded, slowing down as they turned onto Route de Safi with its worn-down warehouses and empty lots.

Aicha turned sharply onto a narrow, unmarked road just off the main route. She pulled over.

"Stop here."

The taxi stopped, too, and Isabella handed the driver another hundred dirhams.

The man glanced at her, his curiosity clearly piqued, but nodded and pocketed the money. "You want me to wait?"

"It's fine," she said. "Thank you."

Isabella got out, waited until he drove away and then made her way cautiously toward the warehouse outside which Aicha had parked the moped. Aicha locked the helmet in the top box and then disappeared through the large metal door at the front of the building.

Isabella approached. The doors were worn and rusted, and the concrete walls were weathered. There were just a handful of windows, all of them small and reinforced with metal bars. The surrounding area was just as run-down, with cracked asphalt and overgrown weeds pushing through the pavement. The air was thick with the scent of dust and oil, and it was loud with the rattle of machinery from a machine in the neighbouring building.

Isabella turned into the alley at the side of the building and went around to the back. She found a narrow, grime-covered window and jumped up, grabbing the bars with both hands and hauling herself up so she could peer inside.

The interior was dimly lit, with just a few flickering strip lights. Large metal shelves lined the walls; most were empty save for a handful of unmarked boxes, some wrapped in plastic sheeting. A table in the middle of the space bore scattered papers and electronic equipment. She saw crates stacked against the far wall, some of them open, revealing what looked like cannisters of chemicals. The air was heavy with the smell of oil and rust.

Aicha was speaking with two men, her voice too low to hear; their backs were all turned to the window.

50

Isabella came back out to the road and looked left and right for somewhere she could observe the warehouse. The street was quiet, with just the occasional rumble of machinery and distant clatter from other buildings. An old brick building opposite caught her eye: it looked as if it was abandoned; the windows were cracked, and there was paint peeling from the walls. It sat directly across from the warehouse, and it looked high enough to offer a clear view.

Isabella crossed the street and tested the rusted side door. It was locked; she picked a spot just below the keyhole and stepped back, making enough room for her to drive her boot at it.

The lock gave way with a snap, and the door cracked back.

She went inside.

The interior was dark and damp, and she could smell the mildew. She climbed a narrow set of metal stairs, avoiding debris scattered across the treads, and, at the top, she found an empty office with a broken window that looked down on the warehouse.

Perfect.

The sun was beginning to dip lower, casting long shadows across the cracked pavement. She could see the front of the building where Aicha was, including the parked scooter, and saw the occasional flicker of movement through the grimy windows.

She settled into position, crouching near the broken window and waiting.

An hour passed and then another, and then, slowly, the warehouse's front door creaked open again. The two men who had been inside with Aicha emerged, one of them carrying a box to the back of a van parked along the street. Isabella watched them closely as they loaded the van with more boxes, their movements purposeful but unhurried.

She got a decent look at both of them: one of the men was old and walked with a limp; the other man was younger and, judging by the number of boxes he managed, much stronger.

She recognised him: it was Bashar, the runner who had been with Aicha at the track. Her boyfriend.

Isabella stayed where she was. She was well hidden and not concerned that she could be seen, but itching for them to leave so she could break into the warehouse and look around.

ANOTHER THIRTY MINUTES passed before all three people—Aicha, Bashar and the other man—came outside for the last time. The old man looped a chain through the handles of the door and secured it with a padlock while Bashar said something to Aicha, emphasising whatever points he was making with stabs of his finger.

They said their goodbyes and parted company; the two men went to the van while Aicha got on her moped. The men drove away and, after struggling to get the moped started, Aicha turned around and headed back into the city.

ISABELLA WAITED for another ten minutes, and then, satisfied that the building was empty, she climbed back down the metal stairs and went outside.

51

Isabella stood across from the warehouse for a few moments, it was quiet, and so was the rest of the street.

If she was going to go inside, now was the time.

Isabella inspected the padlock: it was rusted and bore the scrapes and scratches of repeated use. Rather than trying to snap it with brute force, she reached into her bag and pulled out her lockpicks. She knelt closer to the door, inserted the pick into the keyhole and felt for the tumblers. She heard a soft click as the lock disengaged, and the padlock slid open; she unhooked it from the chain.

She set the lock aside and slipped through the door, closing it behind her.

Isabella paused, listening for any sign that the sound had been noticed.

There was nothing.

The air inside was warmer, stuffy from the heat that had built up through the day. The faint scent of chemicals lingered, sharp but familiar. Isabella let her eyes adjust to the dim light filtering through the windows and saw the stacked crates and scattered materials that she'd noticed when she had looked in previously. She moved cautiously, her steps soundless on the concrete floor.

The warehouse wasn't large, but it was cluttered: rows of crates and makeshift shelves lined the walls. She made her way to the nearest stack of boxes and scanned the labels. Some were marked with chemical warnings, others left blank. Isabella pulled at the top of one of the crates, flipping the lid open to reveal bags of fertiliser, the type commonly found in agricultural supply stores. These were the precursors for crude explosives. Nothing sophisticated, but still dangerous.

She continued through the room, picking out more materials. There was a small stash of glass bottles stacked neatly near a table with a jerrycan of petrol and torn rags that would serve as wicks, most likely for Molotov cocktails. A few metal canisters stood against the far wall, their labels barely visible through the layers of dust. Isabella ran her fingers over the nearest one, cleaning the label enough to see that it was filled with low-grade fuel. There were thin rolls of copper wire bundled beside a row of old kitchen timers. Isabella picked up one of the timers, turning it over in her hand; it was rudimentary, the kind of thing anyone could buy at a market, but effective enough for what the group evidently had in mind: small, targeted explosions, bombs that could be set and then left to detonate when the timers hit zero.

There was a workbench against the far wall. She went to it and saw it was covered with papers. There was a map of Marrakesh, marked with several key locations: government offices, police stations, busy intersections.

Isabella had known that Aicha was involved with the dissident movement, but this was beyond what she had expected. The Moroccan security apparatus was all-present and ruthless, with sources and agents everywhere. A series of low-level attacks on army checkpoints in rural and desert areas had caught the popular imagination recently before the state censor ordered that newspapers should stop running stories on the subject. And then an explosive device had detonated outside an empty military recruitment centre, forcing it to close. On every occasion they had struck, the group responsible had spray-painted the stencilled image of a bright green fist held aloft, a broken manacle hanging from the wrist.

Isabella opened a cupboard and took out an aerosol can with dried green paint spattered on the outside.

She made a final sweep and then made her way back to the entrance. She slipped through the doors, pulling them shut behind her and securing the chain with the padlock.

She stepped back into the late afternoon sun; she'd seen enough. She had wondered whether Aicha might be persuaded to help with the general, but now she could see that she might be able to ask for more than she had intended.

52

Isabella went back to the riad, prepared a pot of coffee and took her laptop up to the terrace on the roof. She opened a VPN and began her research on the group of which she suspected Aicha and the others were members.

The movement had been dubbed the Dawn of Liberty and had begun as a small and secretive network of dissidents, intellectuals, and activists in the early 2010s. Isabella knew about the uprisings that had swept across the Arab world around then; local impetus in Morocco was provided by grievances over government corruption, police brutality, and economic inequality. The movement was said to have been founded by a mix of university students, human rights lawyers, and disillusioned former members of the ruling party. What started as peaceful protests and clandestine meetings quickly evolved into something more dangerous as the government cracked down, driving the movement underground.

Isabella searched again, and, after starting with the Wikipedia entry, followed links to more in-depth articles. The Dawn, as it was known, was focused on mobilising public sentiment through protests, speeches, and online campaigns. They advocated for democratic reform, transparency, and an end to the exploitation of the working class. But the government's heavy-handed response—including arrests, forced disappearances, and the torture of activists—forced the group to reimagine its tactics. It fractured into cells, each operating independently to avoid infiltration by government spies.

A brutal government crackdown following a mass protest in Marrakesh led to the arrest of many of the group's original leaders and marked a turning point in the movement's history. With much of its leadership in prison or in exile, the younger, more radical wing of the group took control. They moved away from peaceful protest and began planning more direct, disruptive actions designed to undermine the state and expose its vulnerabilities.

Cells were scattered across the country. The movement no longer staged public protests, instead focusing on covert operations designed to embarrass the government, sow chaos, and bring attention to their cause. Membership was now reputed to be a mix of students, labour organisers, and disillusioned members of the military, all united by their opposition to the corrupt elite who controlled Morocco.

Isabella clicked again, following a link to a piece just published in the *New York Times*. The group's activities were varied but all designed to disrupt the government's grip on power. They relied on old-school methods of resistance: distributing underground newsletters, organising strikes in the city's factories, graffitiing anti-government slogans in the medina. While the movement said that it would remain non-lethal, there was an increasing willingness to employ sabotage. Dawn of Liberty cells were responsible for small-scale attacks on government infrastructure; nothing deadly, but enough to create confusion and force the authorities to allocate more resources to internal security. These included targeted power outages in wealthy neighbourhoods, hacking traffic systems to cause gridlock, and disrupting government ceremonies with carefully timed explosions. They aimed not to kill but to inconvenience; their goal was to show Moroccans that the government could be embarrassed, its control shaken, and that their dissent could not be silenced.

Isabella navigated to a report on CNN where a journalist was invited to speculate on the structure of the group. She said it was organised into decentralised cells to minimise the risk of infiltration. Each cell operated independently, with only a few leaders in contact with the wider network. The structure ensured that even if one group was compromised, the entire movement would remain intact. The leadership communicated through encrypted channels, using dead drops and coded messages to avoid detection by the government's intelligence agencies. Its activity was said to focus on Marrakesh, with meetings taking place in secret locations: in the alleyways of the medina or in buildings rented under false identities. Isabella noted, with a nod, that the group also made use of safe houses in the industrial district, blending in with the area's factories and warehouses. The commercial units doubled as storage for the materials—chemicals, electronics, and printing equipment—that supported their sabotage campaigns.

The movement's ultimate goal remained the same as when it was founded: to see Morocco liberated from corruption and authoritarian rule. The Dawn planned a more just, democratic society, where resources were shared equally and the voices of the people were heard. Their tactics had evolved to match the repression they faced, and now they sought to disrupt the image of stability that the government projected, both to its citizens and the lucrative tourist trade.

Isabella put her laptop down and ran her fingers through her hair. She hadn't expected anything like this; it had been obvious at their first meeting that Aicha was a firebrand, and Isabella had been confident that she would be interested in the offer she was intending to make. But what she had learned in the last day—both in the warehouse and now, from her research—suggested Aicha was much more radical than she had given her credit for.

She wondered whether she would need to adjust her plan to take that into account.

53

Isabella was up early the next morning. She worked out on the roof and then went to the bakery for a loaf of freshly baked *khobz*, the traditional round Moroccan bread, and toasted a slice over a small flame until it was warm and slightly crisp. She cut up a handful of juicy, ripe tomatoes, drizzling them with olive oil and a sprinkle of sea salt. She prepared a small bowl of *amlou*—a rich spread made from almonds, honey, and argan oil—and spread it over the bread. She took a glass of freshly squeezed orange juice, the sweetness of the local fruit complementing the food. She was going to be busy today, and she didn't know how easy it would be to stop and find something to eat. Better to fill up now.

The day was due to be particularly warm, so she dressed appropriately, and, locking the riad behind her, she set off to the university for the second time in two days.

~

Isabella made her way to the same café she'd been to the day before and took a table where she could see down the road so she could see Aicha approach. She ordered a small glass of *nous-nous*—'half and half' in Arabic, reflecting the balance of strong dark espresso to creamy milk—and settled in to wait.

It didn't take long. She noticed Aicha making her way along the pavement, and, finishing the coffee and leaving a note on the table to cover the bill, she let her walk by before catching her up.

Isabella feigned breathlessness. "I thought it was you."

Aicha turned and smiled. "Good morning. How are you?"

"Hot."

"I know," she said. "It's going to be warm today."

"Nothing changes."

"What are you doing here?"

"Just passing," Isabella said.

"How have you been?"

"I'm good."

"Still going to the stadium to run?"

"Not for a few days," Isabella said. "I've been away for work."

"The modelling?"

"That's right. I've been in Tunisia."

"Jealous."

"Don't be. I was standing in a freezing cold warehouse all day, and the clothes were awful."

Aicha seemed pleased to see her, and the two of them fell into an easy conversation.

Isabella asked her where she was going.

"The Apple Store," Aicha said. "My laptop is on its last

legs. I've tried to patch it up, but I think I'm going to have to accept it's time to get another one. What about you?"

Isabella thought quickly. "Clothes shopping. I'm going your way—want to walk together?"

"That would be nice."

Isabella knew she was approaching the moment beyond which there would be no going back. She had considered the strategies she could employ with Aicha. She could have played the long game, presenting herself as someone of similar ideological bent who could be recruited to the group. But that would have taken weeks—months—and Isabella had no way of knowing how Aicha's friends would react to the idea of bringing someone new—a *foreigner*, no less—into the group. That kind of development was too uncertain and would take too long. It was better to approach the matter head-on.

They reached a café that had recently become popular.

"Want to get a coffee?"

"Why not," Aicha said. "I'll get them. What would you like?"

"My treat," Isabella insisted.

Aicha said she'd have an iced tea, and Isabella went up to the counter to order, adding an iced coffee for herself. She thought about how Pope would have gone about something like this. He'd explained once how he tried to make people feel like they were the ones in control, gently nudging them toward his own goals without them realising. It was never about forcing or demanding; it was about planting the right seeds. Pope would ask the right questions, make the other person feel heard and understood, even when he was carefully steering the conversation to where he needed it to go.

Isabella collected the drinks and took them to the table.

She put them down and then sat. "Have you been to the States?"

"Never."

"But you said you wanted to go, right?"

"One day."

"I remember—was it Stanford or UCLA?"

She smiled. "You've got a good memory. Either would be amazing. But it's not realistic for someone like me. I'd need a visa, and the chances of that... Well, there's basically no chance."

Isabella frowned. "Why do you say that?"

"Come on. Don't be naïve. Why would they give someone like me a visa? And even if they did, there's no way I could afford to study there. My parents aren't around anymore, so there's no help coming from them, and I can barely afford to pay my rent. I don't have any money—certainly not enough for something like that."

"Your boyfriend?"

"Bashar? A student. Same as me."

She pursed her lips. "Maybe it's something I could help you with."

Aicha stopped and stared at her. "How?"

Here we go, Isabella thought. No going back now.

"Look, Aicha—I haven't been entirely honest with you."

Her posture stiffened. "What does that mean?"

"Promise me something—you won't say anything until you've heard me out."

She looked at Isabella with concern. "You're worrying me."

"Don't be—there's nothing to worry about. But please listen carefully. I know what you and your friends are doing in the warehouse."

The blood drained from Aicha's face. "I don't know what—"

"Yes, you do," Isabella cut over her. "The one near Route de Safi. I know about it, and I support you. What you're doing is brave."

Aicha's mouth fell open. "You must be mistaken. Route de Safi? I don't think I've ever been to Route de Safi."

"You were there yesterday," Isabella said gently. "I was waiting for you outside the university. I followed you there. I waited until you and your friends left, and then I went inside and looked around. I know everything, Aicha. Everything. I know what you've been doing. I know about the Dawn of Liberty."

Aicha looked as if she was going to be sick and, for a moment, Isabella was fearful that she was going to leave.

She didn't. Instead, she reached across the table and gripped Isabella's wrist. "You can't say anything. If they found out... I would go to prison for a long time."

"I haven't told a soul, and I won't."

"So... so why are you saying this?"

"I told you I haven't been honest, and I haven't. Let me tell you the truth. I'm not a model. That's what people who do the work I do would call a legend—a cover story. Something we make up so we have a reason to be in places like this. I work for an organisation whose values and objectives align with yours. I know you don't know this, and you might not believe me, but you have friends. Influential friends with power and money who are cheering you on. Friends who want to help."

Aicha held up her hands. "I don't believe you."

"Why would I say any of that if it wasn't true?"

"How do I know you're not working for the government?"

"Because you would already have been arrested, wouldn't you? They would have picked you up yesterday. They didn't."

Isabella could see the emotions playing out across Aicha's face: fear at the thought that someone knew her secret, anxiety at what that might mean for her, but also a flicker of excitement. She remembered what Pope had told her: she'd need to understand Aicha's motivation, build credibility with her, establish trust and minimise risk. She would highlight shared goals and make an appeal to Aicha's —and the group's—self-interest; in this case, she could hint at the promise of resources: money, intelligence, protection.

But Isabella's story was completely false, and she knew there was a risk it'd be seen for what it was.

She needed to be confident and persuasive.

"This is crazy," Aicha muttered.

"But you're still here."

Aicha said nothing.

"Here's what I'd do if I were you," Isabella said. "I'd have a conversation with Bashar and the older man you were with yesterday and then come back to me once you have an answer."

Aicha stared at her for a long moment. "Who are you? Not who you said you were."

"No," Isabella said with a smile. "That should be obvious."

"Who, then? I need to know."

"I'm a friend. That's all you need to know."

"What do I call you?"

"Isabella," she said.

Aicha stood up and swung her bag over her shoulder.

"Speak to your friends. I'll come here again tomorrow.

We can have another coffee, and you can tell me what you think."

Aicha set off without looking back.

54

The sky was overcast, with the promise of rain in the air. Isabella returned to the coffee shop at the same time the next day. Aicha was already there, sitting at the same table they had sat at the day before with a nervous expression on her face.

"Morning," Isabella said. She sat down and picked up the menu. "Want something to drink?"

"No," she said curtly. "It's better that we go somewhere else."

"Okay," Isabella said. "Where would you like to go?"

"You want to talk to my friends?"

"Did you speak to them?"

"Yes. And they'll speak to you, but it has to be somewhere else. This is too obvious."

"Where?"

"You'll have to trust me," she said.

"I'll need a bit more than that."

"Not if you want to meet them. I'll take you."

"When?"

"Now. They're waiting for us."

Aicha led the way to the road, held out a hand and waved at a taxi that was parked next to the pavement. The driver flashed his lights, drove over to them and pulled over. Aicha spoke through the window to the driver in Arabic and then got in, leaving the door open for Isabella to follow.

Isabella sat down on the seat and glanced over at Aicha. Something was off in her manner. There was a tightness in her posture—visible tension—although, she supposed, that might very well be down to fear. Isabella had taken her by surprise and then made a vague offer that would have given her cause for anxiety. A little tension was to be expected; it would have been more concerning if there was none.

Isabella could tell that Aicha didn't want to talk, so she looked out of the window. The taxi proceeded south, turning east after a while to cross a bridge over one of the irrigation canals that formed part of the *khettaras*, the system of irrigation—mostly underground—used for water management around the city. The manicured gardens and orderly streets of central Marrakesh slowly gave way to more rugged terrain. The palm trees grew sparser, replaced by parched shrubs and patches of dusty earth. The streets were less congested, and, as the taxi wound through a series of roundabouts, the outline of factories and warehouses emerged on the horizon, their bulky, rectangular shapes silhouetted against the backdrop of the mountains beyond. The buildings had a haphazard look to them: graffiti streaked their walls, and weeds grew untamed along the edges of cracked pavements.

"How far are we going?" asked Isabella.

"Not far," said Aicha.

Isabella felt it again: that same sense that something wasn't quite right. The car seemed normal. It had the same plastic-covered seats as every other local taxi and played the same tinny pop music. There was a copy of the Qur'an on the dashboard. A string of worn prayer beads dangled from the rear-view mirror, swaying gently as the car navigated the uneven streets. But the driver's eyes, reflected in the mirror, seemed to linger just a little too long on her.

They passed by empty lots filled with piles of discarded construction materials—broken bricks, sheets of corrugated metal, wooden pallets—evidence of unfinished projects or forgotten ambitions. A lone street vendor with a rickety cart waited by a junction, selling fruits and bottled water to motorists while they waited for the lights to change.

Isabella paid a little more attention to the driver. He was young, around the same age as Aicha, with thick stubble covering his jaw. But what caught Isabella's attention were his hands. His knuckles were white from gripping the steering wheel so tightly. Marrakesh taxi drivers were dare-devils, among the most fatalistic Isabella had met, and they wouldn't last long in the job if crazy driving made them nervous; yet this one was as skittish as a kitten.

The scenery grew even bleaker. The road was pocked with potholes and ruts and was badly in need of repair. Soon, a row of dilapidated warehouses came into view, their rusted metal doors closed. The driver slowed down and then turned into a narrow side street.

Isabella's suspicions were quickly justified.

The driver swung the wheel hard and turned the cab off the street and into a garage. Bashar had been waiting outside, and as soon as they were inside, there was a rattle and a clang as he pulled a metal shutter to the ground.

Isabella turned to look at Aicha. She had taken a small pistol from her bag, and now it was pointing at her.

"Easy," Isabella said.

"Get out of the car."

Isabella did as she was told. She looked around: tools were scattered across a wooden workbench, and chains hung in long loops from the ceiling. The floor was stained with oil and grease. Dust coated the walls, and the air smelled faintly of gasoline and metal, with a hint of something mustier, like damp rags left too long in a corner. In the dim light cast from a flickering bulb, she noticed a pile of tyres stacked haphazardly against the far wall. A rusted jack sat unused near an old engine block, its once bright paint long since faded. Isabella turned to the garage door and saw that it had been bolted shut from the inside.

The driver got out, came around the car, and grabbed Isabella roughly by the arm. He pulled her toward the back of the workshop as Aicha followed with the pistol—a miniature Mossberg MC2sc 9mm—still trained on her.

Now Isabella noticed an older man dressed in a *gallabiyah*—a long traditional robe—and resting his weight on a walking stick. Isabella recognised him from the warehouse.

She wasn't nervous; she could stop this at any moment she chose. The man with the stick was unarmed, as was the taxi driver, who held her arm in a tight grip. That left just Aicha and the pistol, and it was obvious that she was uncomfortable with the weapon.

Taking control would have been easy: disarm Aicha, use the gun to hold off the men.

None of them had any idea of what Isabella was capable of, and that moment of surprise—which would then become shock—would be all she needed to assert her will over them.

But she wasn't here to overpower them.

She needed their help.

She was here to persuade them.

"Sit down," said the older man, pointing with his stick to a single wooden chair.

Isabella did as she was told.

55

Aicha kept the pistol on Isabella. The taxi driver spoke to the older man and, without saying a word to Isabella, left the warehouse through a pedestrian door.

Two men and Aicha. The odds were even more in Isabella's favour now, yet she still wasn't interested in taking advantage of them.

The man with the stick stepped from the gloom into the light. His skin had a grey pallor, and scarring was visible under the collar of his *gallabiyah*, the marks trailing up his neck. He moved slowly, each step deliberate, the worn wooden stick tapping at the ground ahead of him. His face was lined with deep creases that suggested a hard life spent outside, and his sunken eyes, nearly lost beneath heavy lids, gleamed with a cold intensity. A thick, grizzled beard, streaked with grey, framed his face, and his lips were thin and cracked and looked as if he had forgotten how to smile. The fingers of his free hand twitched; they were gnarled with age. He was old—she guessed in his mid-sixties—but there was something dangerous in the way he carried himself.

"Questions," the man said. "I ask; you answer."

"Fine."

He came closer, the light from the bulb falling onto his face, and she realised she'd seen his photograph before. He'd been in her research: his name was Abraham Azabal, a former engineer turned revolutionary, and he'd spent two years in Tazourit, one of Morocco's brutal desert prisons, during the Years of Lead. There had been a profile of him that suggested he'd emerged from detention hardened, his ideals sharpened by the suffering he'd witnessed both inside and outside its walls. Now he was one of the leading figures in the Dawn of Liberty.

"Let's start with something simple. Who are you?"

"I told Aicha."

"Tell me."

"Isabella Fischer."

"And who do you work for?"

"Not easy for me to tell you that."

He smiled. "You're not in a position to refuse. Look around." He gestured with his walking stick toward Aicha, who held the pistol pointed at the centre of Isabella's chest. "We're speaking to you politely for now, but that can change quickly if I doubt your cooperation."

Isabella held his eye. "Violence wouldn't be a good idea. And there's no need for it. I have an offer for you. I wanted to come and see you in person to make sure you understand it, but it'll be for you to decide whether you accept it or not."

Azabal smiled. "And if we refuse? You'll just walk away?"

"That's right. That's exactly what'll happen." She nodded at the garage. "This place is obviously temporary— you haven't lost anything by bringing me here."

"But you've seen *us*, now."

"I hate to rain on your parade, Abraham, but we knew about you before today."

He raised an eyebrow, no doubt surprised at Isabella's calmness and the casual manner in which she had dropped his name.

"What are you? British?"

"That's right."

He shook his head. "This is all very unlikely. How old are you?"

"How does that matter?"

"Nineteen?"

"Older than I look."

"Twenty, then."

"It doesn't matter how old I am."

"But it *does*. It goes to your credibility. It is extraordinary that you'd be employed by the sort of organisation who would do such a thing as this. MI6? *Please*. And it is even more extraordinary that they would select *you* as their envoy."

"And yet here we are. Someone of my age comes with lots of advantages. I'm the last person anyone would suspect. You'd walk past me on the street and say I was harmless." She pointed to Aicha. "The same is true for someone like her. Easily dismissed. Easily overlooked."

"You don't know anything about me," Aicha muttered.

Isabella could see why she'd adopted a more hostile tone. She must've been worried that the others would think she'd been too loose with her tongue in her previous interactions. "I know enough," she said.

Azabal rapped his cane against the concrete floor. "Tell us what you told her."

"The regime here is corrupt and brutal. It's bad for the

Moroccan people, it's bad for North Africa, and it's bad for the wider Arab world. My employers would like to see things change, but it's not something that can be done in the open. We effect change by supporting local efforts."

"And how do you do that?"

"Cash, equipment and advice."

"Advice?" said Azabal. "Really?"

"You can take it or leave it."

"I think I'll leave it."

"That's up to you, but I think that would be naïve."

Azabal turned to smile at Aicha and then Bashar. Azabal shook his head and spoke in Arabic, perhaps under the impression—wrongly—that Isabella wouldn't understand.

Teach her some respect.

"That'd be a bad idea," she said, fixing Azabal with a level gaze.

Bashar took a step toward her and clenched his fist.

Azabal held out his stick to stop him. "How can we trust you? You say you work for an organisation that supports our aims—yes?"

"Yes."

"The Israelis, then. They say they support us."

"Not Israel."

He ignored her. "And if you are a Mossad agent, you must know that you are not among friends."

"I'm not Mossad."

"He was right, then." Aicha jabbed the pistol. "MI6."

Isabella was content to have them think that, and didn't demur. The sound of a siren came from the street outside, and all three of them stiffened. Bashar hurried to the shutter, pressing his ear to the metal. They were quiet as the siren faded from earshot.

He turned, his face set in an ugly frown. "This is stupid. How do we know this isn't a trap?"

Isabella spread her hands. "A trap? Come on. If I worked for the government, they'd have kicked down the doors and dragged you off to prison months ago. You weren't difficult to find."

"You want information," Aicha said. "About us and what we do."

"No," Isabella said. "I really don't. And think—you know I'm not with the government. They don't run undercover operations like this. They're not subtle. They hang people upside down from chains and beat them for hours until they confess." She turned to Azabal. "Abraham knows that. They'd dump you in one of their prisons and batter you senseless until you tell them what they wanted to know— isn't that right?"

Isabella knew that the smallest detail about someone, divulged just at the perfect moment, could throw that person completely off balance.

"Be careful," he said.

Bashar spat on the floor. He went to a workbench and picked up a large monkey wrench.

"No, Bashar," Abraham said, holding up his stick to bar the way.

Bashar pushed the stick aside.

He stepped up close to Isabella.

Isabella nodded toward the old man. "You should listen to him."

Bashar slapped Isabella hard across the face.

"Tell us the truth. Enough bullshit."

Isabella felt the sudden sting but ignored it.

Aicha grabbed Bashar by the shoulder.

He pushed her back and slapped Isabella again.

Isabella let her head hang down, then looked up at him and fixed him with a baleful expression. "Last warning."

Bashar's eyes bulged with anger. "I'm going to start with your legs and then work upwards. One broken bone for every lie you tell."

He lifted the wrench and swung it hard toward Isabella's left knee.

She stayed seated, lifting her left leg and using the sole of her foot to block the wrench. She followed that with a sharp kick with her right foot to Bashar's ankle that swept the leg from underneath him. He lost his balance and toppled over.

He looked up at her, his face deformed by fury. He scrambled up and swung the wrench again, but, this time, he aimed it at her head. Isabella blocked his swing with her left hand and then repeated the kick a second time, striking his ankle hard enough that his foot slipped from underneath him again.

She still hadn't moved from the chair.

He was on his hands and knees.

"Don't make me stand up," she said.

Bashar clambered up again and swung the wrench for a third time.

Fine. I warned you.

She hopped up, stepped into the wild swing and caught his arm.

He froze, his eyes wide, as Isabella applied force to his elbow, isolating it at an unnatural angle. She held his eye as she applied more torque, the pressure building at his elbow and shoulder until he grunted with pain. The wrench slipped from his fingers and clattered to the floor.

Bashar strained, but she was much too strong for him. She shifted her weight, locking his arm against her chest, her hand pressing just above his elbow. She leaned in slightly, her voice low and calm. "If I wanted to break it, it'd already be broken."

He grunted as he tried to wriggle free.

She applied more pressure; an ounce or two more and the ligaments would pop. "This really is your last chance."

Bashar stopped struggling.

Isabella released her grip and pushed him away. She kicked him in the side of the knee, and he fell to the floor.

She looked at Abraham. "Tell him if he tries that again, I won't be so nice."

56

Aicha hurried forward to help Bashar to his feet and, for a moment, forgot to train the gun on Isabella.

She didn't take advantage of her lapse. "I'm on your side," she said. "I understand the stakes you're facing, and I'm not here to waste your time. We're not interested in direct involvement, but that doesn't mean we can't help you *in*directly. I'm offering access to our intelligence network: real-time data on government movements, potential vulnerabilities, satellite imagery when necessary. We can also assist with training: counterintelligence, urban tactics, anything that keeps you alive and effective. And if logistics are an issue, we can secure equipment, transport, and safe houses. Discreetly, of course. Everything will stay under the radar. You'll get what you need, and we keep our hands clean. Think of it as a silent partnership."

Azabal eyed her. She allowed herself to hope that she might be getting through to him.

"And advice," she said. "There are lots of things we can tell you that'll be useful. For example, you're not storing your chemicals properly. I'm sure Aicha told you that I was in your warehouse yesterday, after your meeting. I took pictures and sent them back for analysis. We've seen the kind of setups you're using—fertilisers mixed with solvents. If you're not careful, you'll blow yourselves up before you can get the bombs into your cars. The heat alone will cause a reaction if those chemicals aren't kept cool. Your containers aren't sealed, either, so you're risking contamination. I could go on."

Azabal looked irritated. "Please do."

"The wiring—you're using kitchen timers, basic ones. That's fine for small-scale disruption, but if you're aiming to really cause a distraction, you'll need more precision. We can help with that. We can get you the right components—undetectable, untraceable—and show you how to use them."

Bashar glared at her. "You think we need your help?"

"I haven't made it clear enough? I *know* you do. You have passion, but passion without the right tools will get you caught—or killed. You've been lucky so far, but that luck won't last forever. Do you know how easy it was to find you? It was *very* easy—it took a couple of days. We—me and the others in the city with me—we've been in places like this before. We've worked with groups like yours, and we've kept them alive." She paused, letting her words sink in. "There was a group in Damascus, in your exact position a year ago —idealists, smart, but sloppy. They thought they had a secure setup, but their communications were being tracked without them even knowing. We taught them how to use encrypted systems, how to set up dead drops, and gave them new equipment that made them invisible. They're still operational now, even though half the groups around them have been shut down."

Azabal shifted slightly.

"And a cell in Alexandria. Similar problem to yours—improper storage of chemicals. One wrong mix, one bad spark, and they were sitting on a bomb. Boom—the whole safe house blown to bits. We helped them find a secure location for their materials, taught them to disguise what they were doing so it looked like a legitimate business. Still there, still causing problems, still hitting their targets. Same goes for the opposition in Tripoli and Algiers."

Bashar glanced at Azabal and then at Aicha.

Aicha turned to Isabella, finally remembering to bring the gun back up again. "You still haven't told us why we should trust you."

Isabella met her gaze and held it. "Because I don't need to be here, do I? We're offering you something no one else is —experience. The kind that can keep you alive and keep the government off your back. But if you want to do this alone, like happy amateurs... it won't be long before you all end up in somewhere like Tazourit. Abraham can tell you how that'll be for you." She paused, letting her words sink in. "I'm here to make sure that doesn't happen."

The room was silent for a moment. Azabal's eyes flickered with a mix of scepticism and consideration. "This wouldn't be for free, though, would it?"

"No."

"So what's your price?"

"We need your help. We need you to work with us on something that'll align with your goals, too. There's a general in Moroccan military intelligence. We have our own reasons for wanting him out of the picture, but when you look into him and what he's done, you'll see he's a brutal and effective tool of the regime. Removing him will win you friends among those he's terrorised. It'll be much more effective than leaving a pipe bomb outside a recruitment centre."

Abraham, Aicha and Bashar exchanged glances. "What does that mean? 'Removing'?"

"We'd like to take him out of the country."

"To kill him?"

Isabella didn't know how they would react if she told them the truth—that she was going to kill Al-Masri—so she played it more carefully with the line she had already rehearsed. "No. We just want to speak to him."

Abraham looked unconvinced. "This is... this is difficult. A senior officer will be well protected. Armed guards. Armour-plated cars. To reach a man like him is not an easy task. And we have never done anything like that before."

"We have. And we have a plan. We've done the surveillance and the reconnaissance. We just need two people to play key roles." She nodded at Aicha and then at Bashar. "And the two of you are perfect."

57

The next week was busy.

Isabella and Abraham agreed that they would use the warehouse as the venue for their planning, taking comfort in the fact that the area was deserted after dark. Abraham always brought food, usually a slow-cooked tagine with rich, savoury lamb or chicken stewed with vegetables, couscous, and warm, fresh *khobz* bread. The aroma filled the space as they sat around the makeshift table, a small radio crackling in the background with local music or news to obscure their conversation.

After eating, they'd sip mint tea as they got down to work. Isabella had laid out the urgency of the situation. Time was short, she said, and they needed Al-Masri to be in their custody by the end of the week.

There was no room for error.

They began to make progress.

Aicha got a job at the polo club. They were looking for young, presentable waitresses with a good command of English, and she fit the bill perfectly. She came back from her first day with a new black skirt, white shirt, and a list of instructions on how her appearance should be maintained. The rules were strict: her hair had to be neatly tied back at all times, with no loose strands; makeup was to be minimal —just enough to look fresh but not so much as to draw attention; nails were to be kept short and clean, with no bright colours or patterns allowed; and jewellery was limited to a single pair of stud earrings and no visible neck-laces or bracelets. Her uniform had to be impeccably pressed, and she was to wear low, polished black shoes with no embellishments. She was told to carry a small notepad at all times to take orders quickly and correctly, and was reminded to greet all members formally, addressing them as 'sir' or 'madam' in both English and French. Smiling was mandatory, but only in a polite, reserved manner. Most importantly, she was to remain invisible when not required; staff were to blend into the background and never draw attention to themselves.

Isabella was impressed; Aicha had proven herself invaluable. She had sharp instincts and a gift for detail. Her eagerness to learn from Isabella was apparent, and every evening she came back from the club brimming with fresh intelligence. She noted everything, down to the tiniest detail: the way Al-Masri greeted certain members with more warmth than others, the specific routes he took around the club, and even his peculiarities, like how he always requested a specific table facing the stables when dining.

Bashar was different and made it clear how he resented the idea of applying for a service job. His father owned a series of riads in the coastal town of Essaouira, and Bashar was accustomed to being served, not serving others. He refused point-blank to wear a waiter's uniform. It was fortu-nate, then, that Aicha noticed a position was advertised for a trainer at the club's gym. Bashar had obtained the necessary qualifications during his teenage years, mostly as an excuse to frequent the gyms in his father's properties and mingle with foreign women. Though he carried an air of entitlement, he was capable enough for the role and managed to adapt to the position with relative ease.

The two of them settled into their new jobs and began gathering intelligence. A large map of the club, taped to the wall, became the centre of their operation. Aicha and Bashar filled in new details, slowly giving Isabella what she needed. The map was cluttered with scribbled notes: security rotations, blind spots in the surveillance system, back routes used by staff members during off-peak hours. Isabella pressed for specifics, drilling Aicha and Bashar on the layouts and asking them to walk her through their interactions with key personnel.

Aicha explained that the supervisors maintained a watchful eye over the staff, particularly during peak hours when the club was busy. They hovered during the rush—lunchtime until late afternoon—but once things subsided, they retreated to the back offices, leaving the staff with more freedom.

Still, Aicha said, the supervisors knew the regulars well, and while they trusted the experienced waiters and waitresses to handle things, there was always an air of caution when it came to the more prestigious members, like Al-Masri. He rarely interacted directly with the staff unless something went wrong, but his presence at the club was enough to make everyone alert. He typically entered through the main doors, but his private parties were hosted on the back terrace, shielded from everyone else by lush greenery and high walls.

His security was another layer entirely. Bashar noticed how the guards operated. They were discreet but not invisible, moving with a professionalism that indicated they weren't the usual hired muscle. While they didn't interfere much with the day-to-day workings of the staff, they kept a steady patrol of the grounds with a focus on the main entrances and exits. Bashar said they worked in rotations, making sweeps of the property every hour, but their attention was mainly on the perimeters so they could stay out of the heart of the club, where the members dined and mingled.

Isabella mapped the weaknesses and gaps in their routines. The security might be competent, but their predictable patterns left openings, especially in the quieter parts of the club like the staff-only areas and the rear-of-house corridors. Aicha and Bashar's information gave her a clearer picture of how she could navigate, but there was more to consider.

If Al-Masri's men flooded the club after she had done what needed to be done, the real challenge wouldn't be getting in but getting out.

She needed to know the exit points and how quickly she could disappear without drawing attention. They built a picture of the club's layout and routines; Isabella constantly pressed for more, focusing on how they could control the chaos that would follow once the plan was set in motion.

They drew a large map of the club and the grounds. Each evening, Aicha and Bashar added new details based on their observations. They used their phones to take discreet photos, which were printed and pinned to a corkboard beside the map. The visual aids helped them form a clearer picture of the layout.

Staff gossip also proved to be a rich source of information. Al-Masri was well known, his reputation as a polo player and rumours of his volatile personality preceding him. Some staff spoke of his generosity when it came to tipping, while others warned of his explosive temper.

One waiter recounted how Al-Masri had publicly berated a colleague for a minor mistake, demanding that the staff member be fired on the spot.

More disturbing still were the stories about those who had crossed him. One man, a polo player who challenged him for the team captaincy, had got into a heated argument with two of the general's men over a parking space. The argument escalated into a brawl, and the rival was beaten so badly that he had to be hospitalised. Al-Masri made a show of reprimanding his men publicly, but not long afterward the rival's prized horse fell ill. Poison had been slipped into its feed, and the infection that followed ended its polo career.

Al-Masri's protectiveness over his children was even more notorious. His daughter—a fixture on the club's social scene—was known to flirt with the younger staff. One evening, after noticing her speaking with a handsome barman, Al-Masri sent her out to the car and then leapt over the bar and beat the young man to the floor. The staff knew better than to question him, and the barman, after being dismissed, was never heard from again.

Isabella listened to the stories and felt the pieces of the puzzle falling into place. The general was dangerous, his power significant, but he wasn't invincible.

With each new detail, her plan began to take shape.

The only question left was how—and when—to do what needed to be done.

58

They'd been working for three days by the time Isabella was happy that they had everything they'd need. They were enjoying dinner together when Isabella told them she had decided they needed to go beyond preparation.

"We have to use what we know to work out a plan. Where do we think Al-Masri is most vulnerable?"

Aicha put down her fork. "When he's not with his men."

"Which isn't often," Isabella said.

"It isn't," she agreed. "He travels with at least one other vehicle and at least four soldiers."

"Who are all armed," Bashar added. "They're good, too. Scary. They use the gym to work out, and they know what they're doing. One of the trainers used to box professionally. He was lightweight, and the guard was middleweight, but he knocked him down easily."

"We can agree on that, then," Isabella said. "Stay away from Al-Masri's men."

"The restaurant is too public," Aicha said. "Same for the polo field."

"What about when he works out?"

"He's always with a trainer and at least one guard."

"The shooting range?" Bashar said.

Isabella raised an eyebrow. "Go on."

Bashar nodded. "He does a session once a week without fail. The club closes the range to other members, so it's just him."

"For how long?"

"Usually for an hour."

"And he's alone? Totally alone?"

"Yes—but armed, obviously. That's probably why they leave him alone. He's safe because he's literally carrying a loaded gun."

Isabella studied the map of the grounds. "Two entrances to the range," she said. "One here, from the direction of the health club."

"That door is always locked," said Bashar. "Everyone uses this door here."

He pointed at a door that opened into a courtyard.

"What's inside the range?"

"Exactly what you'd expect." His truculence had not disappeared entirely.

"Anywhere someone could hide?"

"There's a storeroom—here." Bashar pointed at the map again. "Not big, but enough space for one. They use it for cleaning materials, extra targets, things like that."

Aicha looked down at the map. "What are you thinking?"

"I'm thinking this has potential."

"How will you get in?"

"Do you think you could steal someone's pass for me?"

"That's simple. Staff get changed after their shift and

often leave their passes hanging on a hook in the changing room. It's the easiest thing in the world to take one."

Isabella nodded, running through the sequence of events in her mind before speaking them aloud. "So—how's this?" She laid a finger on the map. "I come in through the staff entrance here using a stolen pass. Security is lax. There are new staff all the time, and as long as you have your pass and you're wearing the uniform, nobody asks any questions."

"Correct," she said. "And you're the right profile: young and female."

Bashar shook his head. "But there are metal detectors everywhere. There's no way you'll be able to get through the arch without them spotting a gun."

"I don't need a gun."

"What do you mean?" he said. "How will you get him to come with you?"

Abraham spoke for the first time. "She won't need to bring a weapon into the club because she's going to take Al-Masri's—is that right?"

Isabella shrugged. "Rude not to."

I sabella woke up with a familiar feeling of apprehension and excitement. They had been working on the plan for days, and today would be the first—and only—rehearsal. Every detail had been scrutinised, analysed, and repeated. But now it was time to test it out for herself.

Bashar had argued against it, his pride bruised by Isabella's single-minded insistence. He'd tried to persuade her that he and Aicha had already checked everything and that going over it again would be a waste of time. Isabella had shut him down quickly. Her mother, Pope and Maia had all drilled into her the same thing: preparation was everything. Isabella had learned the same lesson from each of them. Someone else might say they knew the plan, that it was solid and that it would work, but only a fool would put his or her life into the hands of another's opinion. Abraham had backed her up, recognising Bashar's impetuosity, urging patience and siding with Isabella's more cautious approach.

Isabella arrived at the club at nine in the morning. She was wearing the uniform that Aicha had stolen for her: a simple black skirt, a crisp white shirt, and a modest head-scarf. She flashed the stolen security pass at the guards; they barely glanced up from the screen in the corner, nodding her through with no more than a casual wave. Aicha had worked out the timing and had got it just right; the guards were used to the humdrum routine of staff arriving and didn't question a thing.

The general wasn't due to attend the club today, and Isabella would spend an hour or two running through the plan herself. She crossed the restaurant and bar and went outside. She knew the layout—both from her previous visit and from the descriptions and notes Aicha and Bashar had provided—and knew exactly where to go: the shooting range was at the far edge of the club, concealed behind a nondescript door.

She approached the corridor leading to the range and saw a familiar figure: Magda, the woman from the member-ship office who had shown her around on her first visit. Isabella looked for an exit, but there was none. The narrow corridor offered no escape, and Magda was coming straight toward her. Her eyes narrowed, her gaze locking onto Isabel-la's face, and then—to Isabella's relief—Magda reached out to tuck a loose strand of hair back under Isabella's head-scarf. She told her to do better, patted her on the shoulder, and sent her on her way.

Bashar had said the door to the shooting range would be open, and it was. The range was quiet, the early hour ensuring that the first session of the day hadn't yet begun. Isabella slipped inside and took in the space. It was just as Bashar had described: dimly lit and utilitarian, with concrete walls lined with targets and gym mats on the floor.

She found the storage cupboard in the corner and opened the door. It was crammed with life-size targets, old plastic chairs, and an assortment of cleaning supplies. It wasn't well organised and ought to be easy enough for her to hide inside. She'd told the others that she would force Al-Masri outside at gunpoint and take him through a quieter part of the grounds to a service road where one of Isabella's colleagues would be waiting with a car. That was a fig leaf for their benefit; she'd take Al-Masri's gun, shoot him with it and then disappear.

They wouldn't see her again.

The only thing still to check was how she would leave the range without attracting the attention of Al-Masri's guards posted outside. She scanned the room, searching for an idea, and quickly found one: a narrow window on the far wall, high up and slightly ajar. Isabella tested the water pipe leading up to the window; it was sturdy enough to bear her weight, and she was confident it would take only a few seconds to pull herself up, slip through the window, and disappear onto the roof beyond. It would be easy from that point on, and, by the time the general's team realised something was wrong, she'd be in the wind, and he'd be dead.

60

Bashar—who had access to the bookings for the range—confirmed that the general was due to attend the club the following morning, and Isabella was up in plenty of time to make sure she was ready for him.

She left the riad dressed in her usual clothes, the stolen uniform in a shoulder bag that hung loosely from her shoulder. In the event that Al-Masri's men tracked backwards from the shooting, she didn't want to leave anything that would lead them to her door; she took two different taxis across town to a busy shopping centre, where she used one of the public toilets to change. From there, she used another two taxis to zigzag her way toward the club, walking for thirty minutes between each car so that it would be impossible for investigators to connect the journeys.

The final taxi dropped her a mile from the club, on the side of a busy thoroughfare, and she walked the rest of the way.

Her phone buzzed as she approached the staff entrance.

She took it out and looked at the screen: it was a message from Aicha.

>> *My doubles partner is ill. Nothing serious. Shall we postpone the game?*

They'd discussed the code they would use the previous evening. The 'doubles partner' was Bashar, and the game was what they were planning to do today. 'Nothing serious' told Isabella that Bashar was genuinely ill. If he'd been detained by the police, Aicha would have said that he was 'seriously' ill.

She tapped to reply.

>> *Let's go ahead.*

Bashar wasn't crucial to the operation; his role had been to provide background intelligence, nothing more. They'd agreed that Aicha and Bashar would make sure they were working so they could provide updates or in case there was something that would force her to change the plan. But Aicha could do that herself, and more capably than the still quarrelsome Bashar.

Isabella adjusted her scarf and pushed open the door to the security booth, holding up her pass and lanyard in one hand while walking toward the opposite door.

"Good morning," she called out in Arabic.

A grunted reciprocation followed.

She was through the other door and into the club. She walked to the shooting range, looking to the left and right to check for anything out of the ordinary: a staff member who looked unusually nervous, a new camera installed overnight.

There was nothing.

Everything seemed exactly as it had been yesterday.

The door to the shooting range creaked as she pushed it open. The morning sunlight through the high windows reflected off the lime-green walls. The lights were switched off in the main room, but she could see that the range stretched away into the distance to where the targets were hung. Isabella checked for anyone else who might have been there as early as her, but there was no one. She had the place to herself.

She walked to the cupboard, opened the door and worked her way into the far corner, sliding behind a stack of multi-coloured gym mats.

Now it was a waiting game, she thought, checking her watch.

Al-Masri would arrive in half an hour with his security and the instructor, but once the room had been checked and the general was set up with his weapon, ammunition and targets, they'd leave him to it.

Isabella's phone vibrated. It was Aicha again.

>> *My friend has arrived early.*

The general was here.

61

Isabella waited in the dark. The first thing she heard was the sound of conversation from outside, then the creak of the door, and then the sound of footsteps as —she counted—four men entered the range. Their voices were calm and relaxed, as she would have expected. The words were too muffled for her to make out, but she thought she could hear Al-Masri talking about his horse, and another man—the firearms instructor, perhaps?—asking the occasional question.

The other two men were silent. Isabella imagined they would be the general's security.

She heard the sound of retreating footsteps, the door to the shooting range opening and then closing, and then silence.

Isabella waited, closed her eyes and listened hard.

She heard the clicking of a pistol being loaded, then the crisp reports of eighteen gunshots as Al-Masri fired an entire magazine at the target. Isabella felt the usual buzz of violence as it tingled up and down her arm, starting at her fingertips and reaching her shoulder. The general was close

—feet away—and it wouldn't take much now to bring Fatima's dilemma to an end and win the future of the orphanage.

Isabella slowly extricated herself from her hiding place behind the gym mats, making sure to be as silent as she could, and worked her way toward the door.

She heard the noise of rounds being thumbed into a magazine as Al-Masri reloaded.

Isabella reached for the handle.

She heard the click of the magazine as it was shoved back into the well.

Isabella's fingers slid around the handle.

Al-Masri started to fire again.

She counted six shots and then eased the door open.

The general was at the foot of the range, his back turned to her. His arms were outstretched, the gun in a two-handed grip, his arm and shoulder absorbing the recoil from each new shot.

Isabella stalked him.

She would act quickly, deny him the opportunity to make a sound that might alert his bodyguards.

Ten steps.

An arm around the throat, squeezing it hard enough to close the trachea.

Seven steps.

Wrap her legs around him, take him to the ground, choke him out.

He fired again and again.

Take his gun, put a bullet in his head, leave.

Three steps.

Two.

One.

She looped her right arm around his head and drew it

down beneath his chin, cinched in the hold, squeezed so hard that her muscles bulged. She clasped her left hand over his mouth and pulled him back. He toppled over, landing on top of her. She held on. The gun fell from his hand. He pawed at the arm around his throat, trying to weaken her grip; she squeezed harder, locked her legs around his waist and squeezed harder still.

He started to choke.

He struggled harder, desperately.

The door opened behind her.

"Get away from him!"

She glanced over.

Two men, both armed.

She let go of the general, grabbed the pistol, aimed it and pulled the trigger.

The gun barked and jerked in her hand, but the guards kept coming.

She fired again, too close to miss.

Nothing.

Fuck.

She looked at the useless pistol in her hand and knew.

Fuck.

She knew what had happened.

She'd been duped.

The gun was loaded with blanks.

He knew she was coming.

He'd known everything from the start, laying the trap with himself as the bait.

And she'd fallen for it.

"Let him go now."

The guards were on top of her, their guns pointed down.

She released the hold, slithered back and raised her hands.

A third man came in through the door.

She closed her eyes and groaned at her own stupidity.

Bashar was dressed in military fatigues instead of his usual jeans and T-shirt. He had a pistol, and he pointed it at her head.

"Up."

She did as she was told.

"Not so clever now, are you?"

He held the muzzle of the pistol to her forehead.

"I've wanted to do this for a long time," he said.

She half-closed her eyes, but he didn't pull the trigger. Instead, he drew the pistol back and cracked the butt into the side of her head. The room spun, and there was blinding pain as she staggered backward. Her vision blurred, and for a moment, everything became a swirl of colours. She tried to steady herself, one hand reaching out to grasp the edge of the table with boxes of ammunition and a stack of used targets, but her knees buckled, and she fell, the table coming with her and the brass rounds raining over her.

62

Isabella awoke with no idea where she was.

The air was thick and stale with the faint smell of motor oil and sweat. She could hear the low rumble of an engine and felt the occasional thud and bounce.

She blinked.

It was dark, with just the hint of light to her right.

Her hands were behind her back. She tried to move them but couldn't; they'd been well secured. She leaned back and lifted a foot, using it to probe the space. It was tight, with metal enclosing her on all sides, not enough room for her to be able to extend her leg all the way.

She was in the back of a van, locked into some sort of cage.

Her head felt sore, and it came back to her: Bashar had been there, and he'd pistol-whipped her. She twisted her neck, rolled her shoulders, breathed deeply. She was fine. No lasting damage, and certainly nothing that wouldn't heal.

She tried to get a better idea of the van and the cage. It was probably a police meat wagon, the cargo area fitted out so that prisoners could be moved without the risk that they might get away.

She thought she heard a sniffle.

"Hello?"

There it was again.

She repeated the message in Arabic. "Hello? Can you hear me?"

"Hello?"

It was Aicha.

"It's me," Isabella said. "Isabella."

There was no response.

"Are you all right?" Isabella asked.

"No," she said. She sounded close to tears.

"Did they hurt you?"

Nothing.

"Aicha? Talk to me."

"They hit me."

Isabella ground her teeth.

"It was Bashar," Aicha said.

"I know. He's working for the government."

"I feel so stupid," she said. "I trusted him. I told him everything."

"You'll be able to take that up with him later."

"How?"

"Because I'll get us out."

Aicha managed a weak laugh. "Are you mad? Do you know where we're going? It'll be somewhere they take political prisoners. Oukacha, maybe, or somewhere like that. They'll beat us until we tell them everything, and then they'll beat us just because they can. They'll throw us into a box that is so small we can't move, and they'll leave us there in the heat for days and days. People don't come out of there the same as they went in. Many die. And those who don't are broken."

The van bounced over a deep pothole, throwing Isabella against the metal divider.

"What happened?" she said.

"The manager called me to his office," Aicha said. "They were waiting for me there. They'd already caught you—they dragged you out by your feet. I thought you were dead."

Aicha groaned.

Isabella laid a hand against the divider. "Are you okay?"

"I think they broke my nose. And maybe my ribs."

She lowered her voice. "What about Abraham?"

"They'll have him."

Isabella searched for silver linings. She was confident that she'd been careful enough to be sure Al-Masri and his men couldn't find a way to connect what she had tried to do with the orphanage, so it seemed unlikely that Fatima would suffer the general's retribution. They would question Isabella, but she would hold out.

But they might take her fingerprints, take her photograph, and that would be a problem. The people looking for her would see that, and then there was no telling what would happen next. She remembered how quickly they'd found her in Mexico when she'd been the bait to lead them to Maia. Who would find her first? The Americans? The British? The Chinese?

There was a dark humour in that; Al-Masri would have no idea what would be unleashed when the scientists realised she was still alive.

Aicha started to cry.

"I mean it," Isabella said. "I'm going to get out, and, when I do, I promise I won't leave you."

"You have no idea," she said. "There's nothing you'll be able to do. We're both as good as dead."

63

The van rumbled to a stop. The metal cage rattled with the vehicle's deceleration, and Isabella braced for what would come next. The doors were unlocked and opened, letting in a flood of daylight. Two uniformed officers stepped forward; both were large men, their faces impassive as they unlocked the cage, grabbed Isabella and dragged her out of the van.

They had come to a stop in what she guessed was a parking area outside a police station. The building was an imposing concrete structure, its walls pockmarked with age and splashed with graffiti. The air outside was thick with heat and the smell of exhaust fumes. Isabella glanced up at the building. They were still in Marrakesh, but it was hard to be sure where. She had no idea how long they had been travelling. She guessed they were on the fringes of the city, somewhere far from the medina.

Isabella was left with one of the guards while the other went back to the van and collected Aicha. Her face was bruised, and she walked with a stoop to one side, her arm close to her torso to protect her ribs. She was crying.

They were marched through the doors; the smell of stale cigarette smoke hit her. The station was dimly lit, and she could hear the hum of cheap fluorescent lights overhead. A large desk sat at the centre of what must have been the reception area; a bored-looking officer sat behind it, scribbling something on a form. He glanced up briefly as they were brought in, then gestured with a nod toward the back of the station.

Isabella felt the grip on her arm tighten as they were led down a narrow corridor, the walls lined with cracked tiles. The deeper they went, the more oppressive the atmosphere became. She heard muffled voices and the distant echoes of metal doors as they clanged open and shut.

They were taken to a small, windowless room. Inside, a female officer with a stern expression waited for them. She was flanked by two more guards, one on either side of the door. Isabella's cuffs were removed, and she was shoved forward toward the desk.

The officer took her time as she finished writing something.

Finally, she looked up at Isabella. "You first," she said. "Name?"

There was no point in resisting, not yet. "Isabella Fischer."

The officer scribbled something down, not looking at her. "Nationality?"

"British."

The officer's eyes flicked up briefly, studying her face, before she looked back down at the paperwork. "Reason for being in Marrakesh?"

Isabella knew she had to tread carefully. "I'm here on business."

"What business?"

"I'm a model."

The officer raised an eyebrow. "Really?"

"That's right."

She chuckled. "Who are you working for?"

"Freelance. Different clients. I was between jobs when this happened."

She shook her head. "Any local contacts? Anyone we should tell about what happened?"

"No."

The officer leaned back in her chair, eyeing Isabella with a faint suspicion. "You must think I was born yesterday."

"I don't think that."

"Never mind. No point wasting time now—it'll all come out." The officer tapped her pen against the desk and turned her attention to Aicha. "And you?"

Aicha hesitated, her voice trembling as she gave her name.

"You are Moroccan?"

"Yes."

"Then you are even more of a fool." The officer gave a final glance at the two of them. "Take them to holding."

They were led deeper into the station. The cold, damp smell of the cells became more obvious. They stopped at what looked like a holding pen. Metal bars creaked as one of the officers slid open the door. The small, dark space inside was as grim as Isabella had imagined: stained walls, a single narrow bench along one side, and a dim bulb that flickered overhead.

They were both pushed inside, the cell door slamming shut behind them.

Aicha slumped down on the bench, her face pale, tears still fresh in her eyes.

Isabella stood and assessed the situation. She knew they

were being watched—probably through hidden cameras— so she had to be careful what she said. She put her hands on the bars and pulled, but they were solid, and there was no give. But it wouldn't have made any difference; getting out now would win her nothing save another beating.

She knew what was coming would be unpleasant, but she was going to have to steel herself and get through it.

She was going to have to be patient.

There would be a moment, a window when she might be able to exploit their ignorance of who she was and what she could do, but it wasn't now.

64

She heard a set of footsteps; they stopped outside their door. A key was inserted into the lock and turned, and the door opened. The two guards from earlier were standing outside: one held a baton, and the other had a pair of handcuffs.

The man with the baton pointed it at Isabella. "You," he said. "Come with me."

ISABELLA WAS LED through the facility to a room that looked like it was used for interrogations. She had been cuffed outside the cell and knew that even if she was able to free herself, it would do her no good. She was curious, too, to find out what they would ask her. She would bide her time.

Isabella was shoved inside. The walls were bare save for a single clock ticking steadily above the door. There was a table with one chair on one side and two chairs on the other; Isabella sat down on the single chair and held out her hands so that the cuffs could be removed. The guard unclipped one of the bracelets, fastening it to a metal bracket that had been cemented into the wall. She tugged it; there was no give. The fluorescent light buzzed, casting harsh shadows across the table.

The door opened, and another officer walked in. He was tall, broad-shouldered, and wore a crisp uniform. There was a faint sheen of sweat on his brow from the heat. His eyes were hard, unblinking, as they focused on Isabella. He carried a folder in one hand, which he placed on the table with deliberate precision before sitting across from her.

He didn't speak for a moment and just studied her, letting the silence stretch.

Finally, he broke it. "Miss Fischer," he said, his voice calm but edged with suspicion, "you know why you're here."

She remained silent, meeting his gaze but offering no response.

He opened the folder, pulling out a photo of Al-Masri. He slid it across the table toward her. "You were planning to kill him, weren't you?"

Isabella glanced at the photo but didn't touch it.

The officer leaned back, crossing his arms. "You'll do yourself no favours by playing games with me."

She took a breath, carefully choosing her words. "I'm a British citizen," she began, "and I'd like to speak to my embassy."

The officer raised an eyebrow. "Really?"

"My embassy and then a lawyer."

The officer narrowed his eyes, his fingers tapping lightly on the table. "Remarkable."

"What is?"

"Do you have any idea how much trouble you're in?"

"Embassy."

The officer snorted, a smirk playing on his lips. "You're

an outsider, a foreigner meddling in things you don't understand. You came here to kill a general, and now you think you can wait for your *embassy* to get you out? You're not getting out. Not *now*. Not *ever*."

She didn't flinch.

The officer leaned forward now, his voice lowering to match hers. "Who else is involved?"

She stared him out.

He tapped the folder again, eyes narrowing. "We know about your meetings. We know about Abraham and Aicha. You've been conspiring with known dissidents."

"Embassy."

The officer stood up, pacing slowly around the room, his hands clasped behind his back. "You're walking a dangerous line. I'm asking nicely now." He stopped behind her chair, leaning down slightly. "There are other ways I can ask."

Isabella knew she ought to play scared, but she found she didn't want to give him the pleasure of thinking that she was frightened of him.

He rested his hands on the back of her chair, his knuckles grazing against the spot between her shoulder blades. "Last chance," he said.

"Embassy and lawyer."

He let go and stood up. "I gave you a choice," he said.

The door opened again, and two more officers stepped inside. The senior officer made his way around the table and flicked his fingers at Isabella in a dismissive gesture. "Take her to the cell. She'll have plenty of time to think about how much she wants to help us."

65

Isabella was taken to a different cell, and Aicha wasn't there. The door banged shut behind her. The cell was almost identical to the one she had been in before: bare walls, a narrow cot bolted to the floor and a flickering fluorescent light overhead. She sat down on the cot and tried to work out what to do.

Pope had schooled Isabella on the sort of tactics she might expect if the two of them were ever captured and held in circumstances like this. Isabella knew that they were likely separating her from Aicha to break their solidarity, to see if one or both of them would crack under pressure. Isabella leaned back against the wall, forcing herself to remain calm. She wouldn't crack, at least not for a while. Aicha probably would, but she didn't know anything about Isabella that could be damaging.

Isabella knew she would be able to withstand more punishment than they would expect, but also knew it was in her interests to hide her resilience for as long as she could. It would serve her no purpose to provide them with even the slightest inkling that she was unusual; that meant she was going to have to play the role of a young woman who was out of her depth and frightened, terrified of what had happened to her and what might happen next. She would have to play it well enough that they were fooled while she waited for the right opportunity to get out. She was surprised—and relieved—that they hadn't yet taken her photograph or fingerprints, and hoped they might wait a little longer before doing that. She hadn't expected much of a window before all hell descended on wherever it was she was being held, but perhaps their negligence—or willingness to ignore proper procedure—would mean she had a chance to get away without any of the people who were looking for her seeing the flare that would be sent up the moment her details went online.

HOURS PASSED. The hum of the light was the only sound save the occasional footsteps from the corridor outside the door. Isabella knew better than to let the silence unsettle her. This was a waiting game, but she also knew that it wouldn't last forever. They would want answers soon, and, when that time came, they wouldn't be shy in the choice of tactics they'd employ to break her.

She knew they wouldn't have separated her from Aicha unless they planned to interrogate them one-on-one. Isolation was a classic technique, intended to make a subject feel vulnerable. It was possible that Aicha had already been taken in first, forced to endure questioning while Isabella waited.

She had to focus on herself. She planned on saying nothing—Pope would have described it as 'playing a straight bat'—and asking for her rights to be observed. She would once again request contact with the embassy and a lawyer, not expecting that her request would be considered, but making it because that would be what they would expect.

She couldn't let fatigue or frustration get the better of her. She needed to be stoic until they let their guard down, and then she would need to be ready to move. There would be a moment when they grew overconfident, and then she would take her chance.

THE HOURS STRETCHED ON. The fluorescent light burned into her eyes, making it impossible to rest.

She stood up and began to pace, counting her steps, trying to keep her mind sharp.

Eventually, there was a key in the lock, and then the door opened.

A guard stood there, looking in at her.

"Come with me," he said.

66

I sabella was cuffed again and then shoved down the corridor. The guard led her to the same interrogation room as before, jabbing her from behind with his baton when she slowed, and keeping up a steady stream of muttered insults.

Bashar was there, leaning against the back wall, his features twisted into an ugly smirk. Two holsters had been fitted to his belt: one held a pistol and the other a Taser.

There was a second man, too, seated at the table. Isabella recognised him at once.

Al-Masri.

The general was wearing a crisp blue blazer with a white shirt, and his leather shoes gleamed with fresh polish.

The guard pushed her roughly into the metal chair, unlocked one bracelet and clipped it to the bracket as before.

He said something in Arabic over his shoulder to Bashar and then turned to Isabella with a grin.

"I am asking Bashar if this is really the right person." His English was heavily accented, but otherwise perfect.

Isabella remembered from her research that he had been posted to Washington as a military attaché. "I'm wondering if I am remembering things correctly. *This* is the woman who wants to kill me?"

Isabella's instinct was to show obstinance, but she knew that would be counterproductive. Instead, she bit her lip and looked down at the table.

"You are Isabella Fischer?"

Isabella glanced up and gave a timorous nod.

"I will call you Isabella," he said. "Is that okay?"

She nodded again.

"Let me tell you a little about me, Isabella." Al-Masri gestured around the room. "I began my military career in rooms like this. They started us off with people who had tried to avoid their military service. Our instructions were to teach them a lesson and make sure they understood the price of letting their country down. Then they gave us more challenging tasks. Once it was a group of Algerian soldiers who had crossed the border; another time it was a computer programmer who was spying for Israel. It took me a month to get everything out of him. Then we executed him. I took great pleasure in doing it myself."

He spoke casually, as if the suggestion that he had killed a prisoner meant as much to him as commenting on the weather or deciding what to have for lunch. There was no weight to his words, no sign of remorse or hesitation. It was simply a fact, another task completed, as ordinary to him as any other part of his routine. It was supposed to frighten her, though, and she pretended that it did.

"You learn a lot about human nature in a room like this. You learn what is the real core of a person: what they believe, what they're willing to betray. People come into rooms like this thinking they are strong. But very quickly they learn that there is a price to pay for being strong."

He stood and took a stick—Isabella realised it was a riding crop—and reached out to place its tip on her forehead, pushing back to force her to look him square in the eyes.

"I get the sense that it may take something a little special to make you open up. Your friend says you work for the British. You are very young, though. *Do* you work for them?"

"I want to speak to my embassy," she said.

He ignored it. "How old are you?"

"My embassy."

"Nineteen or twenty—surely no older than that. The training you must have received will have toughened you up. Is that right?"

He pushed back hard with the riding crop, forcing her neck into an uncomfortable position.

"I see that you wish to save your words. Shall I tell you what I want to know? What I want is very simple: I want to know which part of British intelligence you work for and who you answer to. I want to know which other British personnel are stationed in Morocco. And I want to know—down to the *smallest* detail—what you were here to do and why you wanted to do it. You see, I don't believe for a second that you were really interested in helping this pathetic little group of activists with their spray cans and pipe bombs. Bashar has told me what you told them. Aicha told me, too. A group like that is too small for MI6 to care about. So, no. You have a bigger mission. The first step might have been me, but it wouldn't have stopped there. You would've gone on—wouldn't you?"

Isabella could hear the drip-drip of a distant pipe, eating away the seconds, and the sound of shouting in a nearby cell. A thought flitted across her mind: she'd resolved to kill Al-Masri. It was the only way to secure a future for Fatima, Latifa and the other children in the orphanage. Now here he was sitting several feet away from her. Bashar had a weapon, too; she might be able to use it to help her escape.

If she could persuade him to take off her handcuffs, why not kill him here and now?

"I'm surprised," she said.

"Why is that?"

"A man like you needs someone like me—a woman—to be handcuffed. And he needs to have his trained monkey with a gun in the room with him."

Bashar stiffened.

The general smiled.

"I like your spirit. And it doesn't surprise me. All the evidence points to you being an unusual and interesting young woman." He leaned forward so that he was only a few inches from Isabella's face. "Actually, that's not quite true. From what my men tell me, you are a very ordinary young woman for six days of the week. It is on Wednesdays that you turn into something quite different."

Isabella struggled to hide the flicker of concern. Wednesdays were the day she visited the orphanage. What had Al-Masri found out?

"The problem with your long and involved anti-surveillance routes is that it tells me you're doing something that is important to you. The rest of the week you are a normal young woman. You exercise on the roof of your building; you drink coffee; you walk around your neighbourhood. You pretend to be a model, which might fool some people, but a little digging has revealed that it is untrue. But there's nothing in any of that which interests me. I don't care. It is what you do on Wednesdays that interests me."

Time seemed to stand still. His eyes bored into hers. She tried to hide her discomfort at the direction the conversation had taken but wasn't able to do it.

A thin smile played across his lips.

"I would say that we are ninety percent of the way there. Take your most recent... excursion—let's call it that. We have identified most of your route. You thought you were clever, but we have cameras everywhere. It is just a matter of time before we complete our investigation and find out where it is you go. My guess? You go to meet your handler. We will find him and warn him off. I don't think we'll kill him—best to avoid an unpleasant diplomatic incident. But if he has a child, perhaps we'll have someone knock them off their bike. Or his wife may get mugged and badly beaten one night on her way home. We'll be imaginative." He smiled mirthlessly and tapped the riding crop against his palm.

Isabella had a sliver of time, but not much. If they'd pieced together her movements that far, there would be nothing to stop them tracing her route all the way to the front door of the orphanage.

It was just a question of time.

"What do you think about that?" He put the tip of the riding crop back against her forehead and levered her head up again. "Well?"

"You know what I think?" she said. "I think you're half a man. You have to cuff me because you're frightened. Take these cuffs off so we can have a proper conversation."

The general said something over his shoulder, and Bashar stepped forward. He took a key from his pocket and unlocked the cuff that secured her to the bracket while Al-Masri slowly stood, smoothing the crease of his trousers.

Isabella got to her feet and took a step toward him, straightening out her fingers so she could jab them into his throat.

He stepped back.

She felt a sharp prod from behind and then the searing shock as electrical current surged through her body. Her muscles seized, contracting painfully as her body locked in place. Her vision blurred, dark spots dancing in front of her eyes, and she could feel her legs give out beneath her; she was unable to stop the fall. She crumpled to the ground, hitting it with a dull thud, her limbs rigid and twitching involuntarily.

She saw Al-Masri's shoes right in front of her face. He bent down, grabbed her by the hair and then lifted and twisted her head so he was able to look down at her face.

"You silly little bitch," he said. "Coming here, to my country, and then trying to kill me? Did you really think you would be able to do it?"

"I got pretty close," she muttered.

He laughed. "Are you mad? You never stood a chance. And now I'm going to make you suffer for it."

Bashar jabbed her with the Taser again. The pain was overwhelming: like fire racing through her veins, stealing her breath. Her thoughts scrambled, disjointed fragments flitting through her mind as her body betrayed her. She wanted to move, to fight back, but it was impossible.

"Here is what is going to happen to you," Al-Masri said. "You will be taken back to your cell, and then, first thing tomorrow, you will be taken before a judge. We could hold you for two days and then ask for an extension, but we don't need to do that. We have everything we need to charge you.

The judge will order that you be detained, and then we'll send you both to Oukacha. We can hold you for two years without trial, but I doubt we'll need that long. And once you are in Oukacha..." He blew out a breath. "Well, Isabella, I think you'll look back on your stay here with fond memories."

He let go of her hair as Bashar tased her for a third time. Her jaw clenched shut, her fingers clawed uselessly at the air, and all she could do was suffer it. The seconds stretched into what felt like an eternity before the current finally stopped, leaving her limp and gasping for breath on the floor, every muscle in her body aching from the brutal jolt.

"Again," Al-Masri said.

The last thing Isabella remembered was the ticking of the discharging Taser and the cackle of Al-Masri's laughter.

67

Isabella woke slowly, her mind floating up through layers of thick fog. The sharp, burning ache in her muscles was the first thing she registered, followed by a pounding headache that throbbed in time with her heartbeat. Her limbs felt like dead weight, twitching a little as the aftereffects of the Taser pulsed through her body. Her mouth was dry, her tongue thick against her teeth, and the faint metallic taste of blood lingered from where she'd bitten down on it. She blinked, struggling to adjust to the dim light of the cell. They'd just thrown her inside, and the cold floor beneath her cheek felt harsh against her skin. She shifted her weight, groaning with the effort, trying to push herself upright. Her arms trembled, and every movement felt as if she were wading through molasses.

She didn't remember being taken out of the room and brought back here. Bashar must have used the Taser four or five times, and she had passed out from the pain.

She closed her eyes and concentrated on her body, trying to work out if that was all they had done. She thought so. She was sure there would be more unpleasant treatment later, but, for now, they had limited themselves to the Taser.

She slowly got to her hands and knees and crawled over to the bed, rolling onto it and flopping over onto her back. She looked up at the ceiling, where a cockroach was scuttling across the chipped and scabrous paint.

She needed to get out.

But she didn't know how.

Isabella woke to the sound of the bottom of the cell door scraping against the concrete floor. The light was barely enough to make out the two guards who stood in the doorway; their faces were unreadable, thrown into shadow by the glare of the fluorescent strips outside.

"Up," one of them said, motioning toward her. "Time to go."

"Where?"

"You're going before the judge."

Isabella sat up slowly, her muscles still stiff, swung her legs over the side of the bed and stood. The guards watched her closely, but it was with the same lack of concern that she had noticed throughout her time here. They didn't know what she was capable of, and that suited her very well. She was conserving her energy and patience for the right moment and doing nothing that would lead them to watch her more vigilantly. Now wasn't the time to resist.

"Enjoyed your stay?" the first guard said.

"It's been lovely. I'll be sure to leave a review."

The second guard thumped her on the back of the head. "She's got a smart mouth."

"Where she's going next?" the other guard said. "She'll think this was *luxury*."

The guard who'd struck her took a pair of handcuffs from his belt. Isabella held up her hands, and the guard fastened the cuffs around her wrists, tighter than necessary so that the sharp edges of the metal bit into her flesh.

"Where's my friend?" she asked.

"You don't have any friends."

They led her out of the cell and into the corridor. They set off, heading away from the room in which she had been interrogated, passing other cells. Some of them were empty, while in others she saw the silhouettes of prisoners lying quietly in the darkness.

Isabella thought of Aicha. She didn't know what had happened to her. It was possible that she had already been charged, but Isabella was fearful that her status as a Moroccan national would mean she was given a harder time. Isabella felt a fresh pang of guilt. It was inevitable, given Bashar's infiltration of the cell, that Aicha would eventually have found herself in a place like this; but there was no question that Isabella had accelerated that outcome, and that the charges she would face now would be more serious than what would otherwise have been the case. The cell had merely inconvenienced the state before; plotting to murder a general was an offence of an entirely different order. The death penalty hadn't been exercised in the country since the early nineties, and, while Aicha would likely escape the hangman's noose, Isabella had no doubt that she was looking at spending the rest of her life behind bars.

They carried on to the end of the corridor. The first guard spoke into the radio clipped to his shoulder and then stepped back to wait for the door to be unlocked. The mechanism buzzed, and the door swung back, revealing an outer yard.

The light from the early morning sun hit Isabella's face. Her eyes had grown used to the gloom of her cell, and the daylight, though filtered through the dusty air, was still sharp.

A black security van with the insignia of the General Directorate for National Security was waiting, the engine idling. Two additional guards stood near the rear doors, one holding a set of keys, the other tapping his baton impatiently against his leg.

The guard with the baton unlocked the door to the back of the van and gestured for her to step inside. Isabella ducked and entered, feeling the suffocating heat of the enclosed space immediately. The metal bench was hot against her skin, and there were no windows, only a small slit in the back doors that allowed a narrow strip of light. The guard followed her inside and shackled her cuffs to a metal bar fastened to the floor of the van. The doors slammed shut, and she heard the guards go around to the cab. Their doors opened and closed, and the van pulled away.

68

The ride back into the city was as uncomfortable as the one that had delivered her to the station. The van bounced and rattled, every pothole and bump jarring Isabella against the walls and the metal bench. She concentrated on maintaining her equilibrium. She closed her eyes and concentrated on the stuffy air moving in and out of her lungs, filling them and then slowly emptying them again.

She kept her focus and ran through the possibilities of what might come next. She had no clear picture of what the authorities had discovered or what they suspected but knew that it wouldn't make much difference. They'd caught her attacking the general and would have more than enough with Bashar's testimony to prove she'd been planning to kill him. As for the remaining gaps in their case, she knew they'd fill them with whatever they needed to make her guilt indisputable.

They had Aicha, too, and there was no telling what they'd made her say.

The noises outside changed as they entered the city, and

then, after a journey that might have taken half an hour, the van slowed and stopped. She heard the guards dismount from the cab, and then the back doors swung open. One of the men hopped up to unclip the shackle and then grabbed her by the arm, his fingers digging into her triceps as he led her down.

They were in an underground parking facility. This particular section was secured behind a wire mesh fence, with a gate to the left and a concrete ramp to the right. The guards moved Isabella quickly, one on each side with their hands on her arms as they led her down the ramp and into the belly of the courthouse.

It was cooler here. They reached a corridor and stopped in front of a small holding cell. Another guard unlocked the door, and Isabella was ushered inside. The room was empty except for a steel bench, there were no windows, and the only light was from a bulb on the ceiling that was protected inside a metal cage.

The door slammed shut, and she was left alone.

69

They left Isabella in the cell to stew. The minutes stretched out into what must have been an hour, but she kept her concentration on her breathing and challenged herself to keep her pulse at a steady fifty beats a minute. Her wrists ached from the handcuffs; she ignored the discomfort, focusing instead on what might come next. She knew there was no prospect of being released, so she resigned herself to the likelihood that she would either be taken back to the same police station where she had been held for the past few days or, as Al-Masri had promised, transferred to a prison while she waited for trial. It didn't make very much difference. She supposed, if she had to choose, she would rather be returned to an environment with which she had become familiar, with a better chance of being able to exploit the routines that she'd observed. The security at the police station had been reasonable, but she didn't think it was insurmountable. There would be a moment when the guards relaxed, and that would be the moment she'd make her attempt.

A prison, though?

That would be more difficult.

The door to the cell opened.

Isabella turned to see Aicha.

She was in a bad way: her face was pale, gaunt even, with dark circles under her eyes. Her lips were cracked, and her clothes were ripped in places. Her once lively eyes were hollow, and there was a limp in her walk as she was pushed into the cell.

Isabella stood. "Are you okay?"

Aicha collapsed onto the bench on the other side of the cell, leaning back against the wall and closing her eyes for a brief moment, as if just being still was a small relief.

"Aicha?"

She opened her eyes. "What?"

"Are you okay?"

"What do you think?"

"Did they..."

"Did they hurt me?" she finished. "Yes, they did."

"I'm sorry," Isabella said. "I should never have involved you."

"But you did, didn't you? And here we are." She closed her eyes, and when she opened them again, there was a bitter smile on her lips. "You know the funniest thing about all this? If you are who you say you are, this"—she waved an arm to encompass the cell—"will all be an inconvenience for you, but that's it. I imagine someone will make a phone call, and you'll be released. I'm surprised it hasn't already happened. It won't work like that for me, though, will it? No one's pulling strings to get me out. They'll throw the book at me. They'll give me the death sentence for what they'll say I was going to do."

"But they haven't executed anyone for—"

"For years," she cut over her. "I know. They still sentence

people to death, though. They'll let that hang over me while they leave me to rot. They'll say this is just a temporary pause, that the executions will start again soon and that I'll be one of the first they put against the wall. They'll torture me with it for the rest of my life."

"I told you," Isabella said, "I'll get you out."

"Fuck off," she said. It was the first time Isabella had heard her swear. "How the fuck are you going to do that? I'm Moroccan, not British. We're not the same. No one cares about what happens to me."

They fell into a strained silence. Isabella knew that they'd been placed in the cell together for a reason. It meant something; it was probably intended to rattle them before they were charged, maybe to get them to say something that could be used in the trial. She looked around, there was a camera up in the corner of the room, and she didn't doubt there were microphones, too.

"They interrogated me again last night," Aicha said, her voice steady but weak. "They want names. They want everyone tied to the group. I told them I don't know anyone else, but they don't believe me. They said they'll keep asking me until I give them what they want."

Isabella leaned forward and lowered her voice to a whisper. "I know you don't believe me, but I'll say it again anyway. I'll get you out."

She sighed and looked away. "Whatever, Isabella." She harrumphed. "Listen to me—'Isabella.' I doubt that's even your real name."

Isabella glanced around the dimly lit cell: the cold stone walls, the smell of sweat and damp, the discomfort of sitting on the cold metal bench. It was designed to wear them down, both physically and mentally. But she'd survived worse. She'd been in a Mexican prison, and then she'd been taken to the laboratory in Wiltshire and threatened with whatever they needed to do to wrest away the secret of her genetics.

It looked bleak now, but there would be options. There always were.

She just had to be ready.

70

Isabella sat on the narrow bench, her back pressed against the wall, staring at the floor. The flickering light overhead cast uneven shadows across the cell. Aicha was pacing, biting her lip, fidgeting with her hands.

The cell door was unlocked and opened, and a woman entered, stepping briskly inside. She was petite, no taller than Isabella's shoulder, with a sharp, focused expression. Her dark hair was pulled back into a tight bun, her eyes framed by rimless glasses that reflected the light. She wore a tailored black suit that looked out of place in the dingy surroundings.

"Isabella? Aicha?"

Isabella lifted her head. "That's right."

"I'm Nadia El-Haddad. I've been appointed as your defence lawyer for the hearing."

Isabella sized her up in a second. She didn't need to hear her out to know the outcome: she wasn't the kind of lawyer who would fight for them; she was the kind of lawyer who smoothed things over, made sure the process went as easily as possible for the prosecution. It was almost a relief. Isabella had no intention of fighting the charges; she knew it would be pointless. The deck was already stacked against them, and the path of least resistance was the right one, at least for now.

Aicha stopped pacing. "What's going to happen to us?"

Nadia glanced between the two of them. "The charges are serious, and the evidence the prosecution will present is... considerable. I don't see a realistic path to contest things at this stage. Your best option is to plead guilty and cooperate."

Aicha's face paled. "Plead guilty?"

"It's the only way to mitigate the consequences. Fighting will lead to a trial, and with the evidence they've gathered, you'd be looking at the maximum penalty. Years. Cooperation, on the other hand?" She shrugged. "That might result in a reduced sentence."

"How long?"

Nadia shrugged. "Ten years."

Aicha looked away and then down at the floor. "Not guilty. I want a trial."

"I don't think that's wise."

"I don't care."

Isabella nodded. "I agree. Not guilty for me, too."

"Fine." Nadia brushed her hands down her jacket as if trying to wipe away the atmosphere of the cell. "Show respect in the courtroom, answer only what you're asked, and don't make it more difficult than it needs to be. The judge will be more inclined to be reasonable if you cooperate from the start."

"We understand," Isabella said.

Nadia gave a curt nod. "The guards will be here shortly

to escort you both to the courtroom." She tucked her folder under her arm and made her way toward the door. "I'll see you inside."

71

F ootsteps echoed down the hallway. Isabella
stiffened, sitting straighter as the cell door swung
open. Two guards appeared.

"Time to go," one of them said.

Aicha rose slowly, wincing with the effort.

Isabella stood beside her, and together they were led out
of the cell and down the corridor.

The guards took them through another series of corridors, each turn seemingly identical to the last, and then up a
flight of stairs. They arrived at a set of heavy wooden doors,
one guard knocked, and after a moment, the doors opened.

The guards led them inside.

Isabella looked around: it was a courtroom, modest but
formal, the walls lined with dark wood panelling that gave
the space an oppressive feel. The judge was up high behind
a large wooden bench, wearing a simple black robe. His
expression was impassive, his eyes fixed on the documents
in front of him. A stern-faced man she took to be the prosecutor stood to the side, with several folders of documents
laid out before him. He was middle-aged, with a hawkish

nose and a sharp, calculating gaze that swept the courtroom and stopped on them. Isabella looked left to where Nadia was seated; she gave a cursory nod of acknowledgement, then looked away.

Isabella and Aicha were seated in the wooden dock. Isabella took in the rest of the room: it was half full. A group of reporters prepared their notepads, cameras were not permitted inside, so they would have to record the spectacle by hand. The rest of the public gallery looked to be filled with a mixture of curious onlookers and officials from the Moroccan government, including a few military officers who sat stiffly in the back, distinguished by their uniforms.

Nadia rose to her feet, her expression composed and calm, adjusted her glasses and glanced over at the prosecutor. They shared a look; Isabella caught it and knew for certain that what was about to happen had already been agreed.

One of the guards tapped Isabella on the shoulder. "Hands."

She raised her wrists, and the guard released the cuffs. The two men stood back, close enough to remind Isabella that they were still there.

Isabella looked up and saw that the judge was watching her. He looked at her with disdain, and she could see again that he had already been told what to do. He picked up a paper from his desk, his eyes scanning the page before speaking.

He cleared his throat. "This court will now hear the case against the defendants, Isabella Fischer and Aicha El-Sayed, charged with conspiracy to commit murder against General Abbas Al-Masri." He looked to the prosecutor. "Mr. Belkacem?"

The prosecutor, Belkacem, stepped up, opened a folder

and spread out several documents. "The defendants stand accused of conspiring to assassinate General Al-Masri, a respected figure within the Moroccan military. The evidence collected against them includes intercepted communications, witness testimonies, and materials recovered during their arrest. These elements collectively suggest a deliberate and coordinated effort to murder the general with the aim of destabilising the government."

The judge looked to Aicha and then Isabella, then back to the papers in front of him.

"What does the defence have to say?"

Nadia stood and reported that her clients denied the charges that had been laid against them.

Isabella took the opportunity to look around the room once more and wondered whether now—with her hands free—might be the time to try to get away. She decided against it. She knew that she would be in Marrakesh somewhere, but not exactly where; although she knew the city well, she'd be running blind.

Then she doubted herself.

Maybe she *should* try now.

It might be her best opportunity.

It might be her *only* opportunity.

She was confident that she would be able to overpower the guards and take a weapon, but then what? She wasn't going to shoot her way out, and, even if she was prepared to do that, she would have to leave Aicha behind.

She bit down in frustration on the inside of her cheek.

She had to do something.

She rested her hands on the lip of the dock, looked into the faces in the public gallery and stopped dead.

There was a man at the end of the second row. He was well built, wearing a suit that looked as if it was a size too small for him. His hair was cropped close to his scalp, and he was wearing a pair of spectacles with a heavy black frame. Those were new—she'd never seen him wearing them before—and he'd grown a thick beard, the brown shot through with streaks of silver and white.

She frowned.

It couldn't be.

Her mouth fell open in stupefaction.

It couldn't be. He was dead. She'd seen him go over the edge of the cliff and into the sea a hundred feet below...

But it *was*.

It was *Pope*.

72

P ope was watching her and, as their eyes locked, he raised an eyebrow and then gave an almost imperceptible tilt of his head. She knew she was gawping at him, and, for fear of giving him away, she looked down until she was confident she'd mastered the shock.

She looked back at him, his eyes were still on her, and as she looked, he mouthed a single word.

Ready.

Nadia finished, and the judge turned his attention to the prosecutor. "Mr. Belkacem," he said, "would I be right in thinking that the government would prefer that the defendants remain in custody?"

"Yes, Your Honour," he replied. "This is a matter of national security. Given the gravity of the accusations, we have no option but to insist that the defendants be detained while the investigation proceeds."

He carried on with his submission, but, to Isabella, his voice was little more than a drone. She reached forward and grabbed the metal balustrade at the front of the dock. Her heart was racing, and she was anxious that it was going to be obvious to anyone who looked at her that something beyond the proceedings had distracted her.

There was a dull thud from somewhere in the building, and then the shriek of the fire alarm. Belkacem stopped mid-sentence, frowned with irritation and then looked to the judge for direction.

"I'm sure this will just be a false alarm," the judge said. "We had one yesterday. It—"

Isabella watched as Pope reached an arm down to the floor. She couldn't see what he was doing but heard the clatter as something metallic bounced and then rolled down the steps and into the middle of the room. She heard a hiss and then saw a billowing cloud of thick smoke that began to spread, filling the room with a dense fog. Panic erupted as a second grenade released a torrent of white smoke that obscured everything in seconds.

Someone yelled out that there was a fire.

The journalists scrambled for the exits, knocking over chairs in their rush to escape, while the guards at the door shouted orders, trying to maintain some semblance of order, their voices muffled and disoriented in the chaos.

Isabella stood.

This was it.

Pope had given her an opportunity.

She had to take it.

The guards behind her were distracted, their focus split between the chaos in the courtroom and the instinct to protect themselves. Isabella got up and turned, picking out the nearest guard as he lumbered toward her, and driving her fingers into his throat. He staggered back, his hands reaching for his larynx as he gasped for air; he was distracted now, and Isabella drove her elbow into his jaw, sending him to the floor.

Her momentum brought her closer to the second guard. She caught his wrist, twisted it sharply and then yanked it up, forcing him to bend down. He grunted with pain as she forced his arm behind his back with a speed that left him powerless to stop her. She drove her foot into the back of his knee and dropped him and then, with one final wrench of his arm, drove him face-first into the wall of the dock.

Both men had pistols in holsters clipped to their belts; Isabella took both.

The smoke was thick, and visibility reduced to just a few metres. Isabella searched through the haze, catching glimpses of men and women stumbling blindly, coughing and gasping as the smoke filled their lungs. Nadia covered her mouth with her sleeve; Belkacem tripped and fell; the judge hurried through a door behind the bench into his private chambers.

Isabella spotted Pope as he vaulted the bar that separated the gallery from the rest of the room. One of the guards stood between him and the dock; Pope drove his elbow into the side of the man's head, following up with a right hook that knocked him to the floor.

Aicha clasped Isabella's wrist. "What's happening?"

Isabella turned to her; her eyes were wide with fright. "We need to go."

"I can't—"

"This is the only chance we'll get," Isabella insisted. "You either come now, with me, or stay here and let them send you to prison. Your choice—but you need to decide. I'm going. And we can't wait."

Aicha was wide-eyed with panic, and, for a moment,

Isabella thought she was going to have to leave her behind. She put her hands on the bar at the front of the dock and vaulted over it, turning back to see that Aicha had dragged herself over it to follow.

73

The smoke continued to pour out of the two cannisters, filling the courtroom, and the fire alarm continued to shriek. It was chaos. The public gallery was emptying out, but the narrow aisles between the seats were not wide enough for everyone to pass at the same time. One of the journalists stumbled down the steps and fell, causing a man in military uniform behind him to trip. There was a scream and then angry voices as others realised they were trapped.

Isabella looked for Pope but couldn't see him. The door through which they had entered would lead them straight back to the holding cells, and, given security was the main concern down there, she doubted they'd be able to leave the building that way. The main doors were blocked by the crowd, leaving just a fire door to the right—also blocked—and the door through which the judge had fled.

"Isabella!"

She turned; Aicha was standing still, frozen in shock, her breathing coming in shallow gasps.

Isabella looked for Pope again; he wasn't where he had

been sitting. The gallery was now almost completely lost in the smoke.

She grabbed Aicha's hand and dragged her into motion.

She felt a hand on her shoulder and, turning, raised her fist, ready to strike.

"This way," Pope said, pointing into the smoke to the right.

Isabella squeezed Aicha's hand. "Stay close."

Pope led the way, momentarily disappearing into the smoke. Isabella held onto Aicha's hand, pulling her along. The courtroom was out of control: guards shouted instructions while the men and women who had been in the gallery fumbled for an escape, knocking into one another as they coughed and spluttered.

Pope evidently knew the layout of the building. He reached a door Isabella hadn't been able to see from the dock and kicked it open. It swung wide, revealing a narrow service hallway lined with utility cupboards. Pope went inside, and Isabella and Aicha followed.

"Quickly," Pope urged. "We don't have much time before they realise what's going on. We need to be well away from here. I've got a car outside."

They followed him down the hallway. Pope led them around a corner to an emergency stairwell. He checked it briefly before motioning for them to follow.

"This way. Basement exit leads straight to the back alley. No cameras."

Isabella remembered how Pope had always filled her with confidence, he was calm and direct, and his planning covered every angle, every variable. An operation like this—complicated and with dozens of things that could go wrong—would have been something he would have spent as long as he could considering.

She wondered: how long had he known where she was, and why hadn't he revealed himself earlier?

They descended the stairs, sirens still wailing. The police would lock down the district once they realised two high-value detainees had gone missing. There wouldn't be much time.

They reached the basement. Pope cracked the door open to peek outside. The alley was deserted. "Quickly."

Isabella tugged Aicha, but she tugged back.

"We have to go," Isabella urged.

"I don't know who he is," she said, then, looking at her, "and I don't know who you are, either."

"Leave her," Pope said.

Isabella glared at him, then turned back to Aicha. "He's a friend. You can trust him."

"Listen to yourself," Aicha said. "Trust? Seriously?"

They heard footsteps from upstairs.

"Now," Pope hissed. "We need to go now."

Isabella let go of Aicha's wrist and shrugged: *It's up to you.*

Isabella turned away from Aicha as Pope opened the door and stepped out into the alley. Isabella followed, Aicha waited, and then, as the footsteps clattered down to the floor above, she came too.

"We have to cross two streets to get to the van," Pope said in a low voice. "Stay close." He pointed at Aicha. "You're Aicha, right?"

"Yes."

"Aicha—do *exactly* what Isabella tells you."

Aicha's face was a combination of emotions: anger, fear, confusion. She nodded her understanding, and they slipped out into the alley, hurrying to the main street.

The sun was beginning to set, casting long shadows

across the pavement. Traffic continued as usual, oblivious to the chaos in the courthouse. Pope led them through a series of narrow streets, avoiding the major intersections where police might have rallied.

Isabella saw a van parked in an inconspicuous spot between two buildings.

Pope unlocked the doors at the back. "Get in. We'll be out of the city in ten minutes."

Isabella hopped up, and Aicha followed. The van was empty.

She glanced at Aicha. "Okay?"

She nodded.

"Hold tight."

Pope climbed into the driver's seat and started the engine. The van rumbled to life; they pulled away from the curb, heading toward the city outskirts. Isabella kept a lookout through the tinted rear windows, looking for any sign that they'd been spotted or followed.

There was nothing.

Minutes passed in tense silence as Pope navigated through the narrow streets. The dense city blocks soon gave way to the more open roads that, in turn, led toward the highway.

"Where are we going?" Isabella said.

Pope glanced up in the rear-view. "I've got a safe house an hour from here. We'll lie low until I've figured out how to get out."

"I can't leave."

Pope's eyes narrowed. "You don't have a choice. Coming back to Marrakesh was stupid, but you got away with it."

"I'm sorry—"

"How many times did I tell you—you can't stay in one

place. You always have to stay on the move. They'll find you if you don't."

"Well," she said indignantly, "they didn't. And I don't recall you telling me anything for months. You let me think you were dead."

"Yes, I'll get to that. There was a very good reason for it." He tapped the wheel impatiently. "It doesn't change the situation now, though. You're well and truly blown. We get out of the country, and then we disappear. Permanently."

"And I told you," she said, "I can't. There's something I have to do."

"The kids," he muttered, shaking his head. "The orphanage."

Isabella looked over at Aicha; she was following the exchange with a confused expression on her face. She had no idea about Isabella's real motives, her cover story had always been tenuous, but now it was being exposed as a tissue of lies.

"Not now," Isabella said.

She'd managed to keep Fatima and the kids secret, and didn't want any possibility—through Aicha or anyone else —that what she was doing might have repercussions for them.

Pope realised she wanted discretion. "Fine. We'll go to the safe house, and then we can talk." He paused, then looked back into the mirror and locked eyes with Isabella. "Just me and you, though—we can't have passengers."

Isabella bit her lip. She knew they couldn't just leave Aicha. Her membership of a proscribed group—terrorists, in the eyes of the authorities—had been revealed, and now she was on the run. She would have to leave the country, too, and Isabella doubted that she would be able to manage something like that by herself.

"We can't leave her."

"Isabella..."

"We can't. She was helping me... to do something important. She's in this mess because of it."

Pope didn't reply, although she could see the growing tension in his shoulders as he stared out through the windscreen.

"Fine," he said. "But you might want to ask if she wants to come."

Isabella glanced at Aicha, who had fallen silent, staring out of the window.

"What do you want to do? You can come, or we can leave you somewhere."

"I'll come," she said. "I can't go home, can I? I need to work out what to do."

"Fine," Pope said again.

The road stretched out ahead of them, disappearing into the dusk as they left Marrakesh behind.

Isabella wondered if she would ever be coming back.

74

Pope drove carefully, making sure they kept a low profile, anxious to avoid attracting attention. The sun was beginning to set, casting a golden hue over the city. The chaos of the courthouse was behind them, but the tension in the van was palpable. Pope's hands gripped the wheel tightly, his eyes scanning the mirrors for any sign of pursuit.

"Where are we heading?" Isabella asked.

Pope didn't take his eyes off the road. "There's a small village about an hour outside the city. The safe house is there—we'll lie low until I can make the arrangements for getting out."

Aicha was still shaken. She sat quietly beside Isabella and seemed lost in thought, her hands clasped tightly in her lap.

"Checkpoints?" Isabella asked.

"It's possible. It's a question of how quickly they can get everything set up. With a bit of a tailwind, we'll probably be too quick for them."

"But if we do get stopped?"

"I'll work it out."

The streets grew quieter and the lights dimmer. Pope took them via smaller roads, choosing routes that avoided main highways, just in case roadblocks or checkpoints had been set up.

The van's tyres crunched over gravel as they finally exited Marrakesh, the city lights fading behind them. The landscape turned barren, with stretches of desert flanked by the occasional grove of olive trees. The sky darkened, stars slowly making their appearance as Pope pushed the van deeper into the countryside.

After nearly an hour, they approached a narrow, unmarked road that led into a small cluster of dwellings barely visible in the darkness.

Pope pulled the van to a stop and killed the engine. "We're here."

The safe house was a simple, one-storey building surrounded by high walls, with nothing particularly remarkable about it, a place where it would be easy to blend in and be overlooked.

They climbed out of the van, the cool night air a welcome relief after the confined space. Pope unlocked the gate and motioned for them to follow him inside. The house was basic but functional: sturdy wooden furniture, minimal décor, thick curtains over the windows.

"We'll stay here tonight," Pope said, locking the door behind them. "I'll have a think about what's next in the morning."

Isabella nodded; the weight of the day was finally catching up with her.

Pope went into the kitchen. "Hungry?"

"Very," Isabella said.

Pope found some bread, three tins of tuna, a can of

tomatoes, and a small block of cheese tucked away in the refrigerator. It was enough to throw something together, and after the day they'd had, even a simple meal would be welcome.

He pulled out a frying pan and lit the small stove. "I'll keep it simple," he said, glancing over his shoulder at Isabella and Aicha. "Just something to fill you up."

Isabella leaned against the doorframe and watched as he began to cook. Aicha sat at the small table, her hands wrapped around a glass of water, her eyes downcast.

Pope drained the tuna and threw it into the pan with a bit of oil, frying it gently as the aroma started to fill the kitchen. He cut the bread into thick slices and placed each under a small grill, browning them on both sides.

Isabella broke the silence. "I thought you were dead."

"I know," he said. "I'm sorry."

"You're *sorry*?"

"Very."

"You left me."

"I couldn't find you," he said. "It took me hours to get out of the water and then find a way back up the cliff, and by the time I did, you were gone."

"The police," she hissed, keen that Aicha didn't overhear. "I stayed as long as I could."

Pope glanced over at the table. "There's a lot to talk about. Shall we do it when she's not here?"

Isabella breathed in and out, suddenly burning with rage that Pope had let her think he was dead when he wasn't. "Tonight."

"You'll need to sleep."

"I won't be able to sleep until I know what's been going on."

"Fine. Eat first; then we can talk."

"Fine."

He glanced over at her. "I'm happy to see you."

She grunted.

"Are you happy to see me?"

"Moderately."

Pope's smile broadened as he added the canned tomatoes to the tuna, seasoning the mixture with salt and pepper, stirring it with a slow, steady rhythm.

Aicha leaned back in the chair and looked over at them. "Why are you helping us?"

Pope didn't look up from the pan as he answered, "Isabella and I have been friends for a while."

"Friends? You look old enough to be her dad."

"Nice to meet you, too."

"What are you, then? MI6?"

Pope looked over at Isabella for something that might give him a clue what he was supposed to say, she gave a tiny tilt of her head, and he nodded. "Something like that."

"That's what she told me," Aicha said. "You're working together?"

"I'm her handler," Pope said. "Best we leave it at that for now."

He slid the toasted bread onto plates, spooned the tuna-tomato mixture over the top, and grated some of the cheese over it. He turned off the stove and brought the plates to the table, setting one in front of each of them.

"Eat," he said, taking a seat himself.

They ate in silence for a while, the tension of a difficult day softened by the comfort of a warm meal. Isabella watched Pope carefully, trying to get a grip on the dozens of questions she needed him to answer.

75

Aicha said she was tired. Pope showed her through to the bedroom with two single beds and said she should make herself comfortable. Isabella tarried at the door, but it was obvious that Aicha wasn't in the mood to talk. They still had a lot to discuss, but it could wait until the morning.

She said goodnight, closed the door and went back into the living area, where Pope had produced a bottle of spirits. Isabella recognised it: Mahia, one of the most popular drinks in Morocco, distilled from figs and flavoured with aniseed. He unscrewed the top and poured himself a generous measure.

Isabella folded her arms. "What about me?"

Pope had raised the glass to his lips, but now he held it there. "Sorry?"

"You're not pouring one for me?"

"Since when have you been drinking?"

She stared at him as if that was the stupidest thing she'd ever heard. "I'm nineteen, Pope."

"I know," he said awkwardly. "But..."

"But I didn't drink before?"

"Well—you *didn't*."

"Before what? Before you left me and pretended to be dead?"

"Yes." He winced a little awkwardly. "Before that."

"Well, I drink like a fish now," she said. "Completely out of control. Something else you're responsible for."

Pope looked as if he was going to protest but must have caught the sarcastic uptick at the corner of her mouth. "Seriously, Bella. You really shouldn't—"

"Shouldn't be drinking?" she cut across him. "Shut up, Pope. You sound ridiculous."

He smiled, shook his head, and went back into the kitchen for a second glass. He unscrewed the bottle again, poured out another measure and handed the glass to her. He offered his glass, and she touched hers to it, put it to her lips and drank. She did drink, now and again, but not very much, and she had to work to hide her expression as the spirit stung the back of her throat.

"What you just said," he began. "About being nineteen…"

"You're going to say that you're sorry for missing my birthday."

"Sort of," he said.

"You're sort of sorry?"

"No—I mean I sort of missed it."

She frowned. "You've lost me."

"I was there," he said. "Not *there* there—not with you—but in the vicinity. Close enough to see you. You went for a run, and then you went and had a slice of cake in a café in the souk. La Patisserie de la…"

"La Patisserie de la Terrasse Spices," she finished for

him. It was her favourite patisserie in the city. "You were watching me?"

"I've been watching you the whole time, Bella. And yes, I realise that does make me sound like a stalker—"

"—it does—"

"—but it was for all the right reasons."

She stared at him across the table. "'The right reasons'? They must be important."

"They are."

"So important that you let me think you were fucking dead!"

She could feel her blood was up, and, judging by the way Pope held up his hands, he could see it was, too. "Will you let me explain?"

She leaned back and indicated with a flick of her hand that he should speak.

"First of all," he started, "I'm sorry. I mean it. You must've felt abandoned."

Isabella struggled to contain the emotions welling up, emotions that she'd kept the lid on for the last year. She was used to having people close to her disappear or die, but she'd never thought that Pope would be one of them. It had almost been easier for her to imagine that he *had* died. If she'd known all along that he was alive, that in some way and for some reason he'd chosen to leave her on her own, she might not have been able to cope.

"Disappearing like that wasn't planned," he said. "It was an opportunity, and I thought it was one I should take."

"I don't understand. What opportunity?"

"I need to start from the start," he said.

She finished her drink and held out her glass. Pope filled it and then his.

"Atari shot me," he said. "Buckshot, from close range,

from my shoulder to my wrist." He looked down at his right arm. "I couldn't do anything with it—the buckshot damaged the nerves, and I still don't have a full range of movement, even now. It gave him a chance against me. We struggled, I managed to get him over the edge, but he grabbed me and pulled me with him." He paused. "I thought that was that. It took three or four seconds to hit the water, and that was enough time for me to accept I was done. But then I was in the water, and I was still alive... I came up to the surface, but the cliff face was straight up, and there was nowhere for me to get out. I couldn't do much more than stay afloat so I let the current take me south until I saw an inlet where I thought I might be able to climb out. I was probably a mile away from you at that point, and by the time I climbed up to the top of the cliff and hiked north, you weren't there, and I needed to get my arm seen to."

"I waited as long as I could," she said.

"I know—I'm not blaming you."

"But we agreed," she said. "We said that if that happened, if we got split up, we'd meet at the rendezvous."

"I know—"

"And I must have gone back there every week for two months."

"I know," he said again. "You did."

She couldn't help staring. "You were there, too?"

He nodded. "And it was wonderful to see you, and incredibly difficult not to let you know, but..." He paused and took a sip of his drink. "But I'd decided to stay out of sight for as long as I could, and letting you know I was there would've meant we lost the opportunity."

"You keep talking about opportunities. *What* opportunity?"

"Two things, really. To let you stand on your own two

feet—that was important. I know I can be overprotective—
you always used to moan about that, didn't you—and I was
starting to get the feeling that, rather than helping you, I
was stifling you. This felt like a good chance to let you prove
to yourself that you don't need me. That you don't need
anyone."

"There are other ways to do that," she said. "I don't know
—maybe you could have told me you were going away for a
few weeks?"

"But then you would've known I was coming back. Isn't
it better that you didn't think you had a safety net?"

"That's weak," she said. "The other reason needs to be
much better than that if you don't want me to think you're a
total dick."

"You'll probably think that anyway," he said, with a wry
smile.

"Yeah," she said. "Probably. But why don't you let me
make my own mind up?"

"The other reason was because I wanted to make sure
you were safe." There was a pause as he sorted through his
thoughts, looking for the right place to start. "We both know
that there are a lot of people with a lot of money who would
love to spend time with you. The British already tried. But
there's the Americans with Daedalus, the Chinese... and
those are just the obvious ones. Private companies, too.
Manage Risk, for example. Jamie King's not a problem
anymore, but it's not like he hasn't been replaced by
someone just as bad, and he knows all about you. They all
want you. You're valuable. What they did to you and the
effect it's had—it's not just valuable, it's priceless."

"And?"

"And I decided, apart from letting you stand on your
own two feet, it'd be easier for me to stop those people from

getting to you if I could watch you without anyone knowing that I was there."

"Including me?"

"Especially you. I know your tradecraft is good, and I've seen how it's getting better, but knowing I was around would have meant you relied on me. It would be easy, under those circumstances, to relax. Not having me around kept you sharp—I saw it. And beyond that, if the people looking for you thought I was dead, there'd be no reason for them to think that they might be being watched themselves. And that'd make them easier for me to spot."

"And did you?" she said.

"Spot anyone?" He eyed her. "I did."

76

Isabella felt a little kick in her gut; first Al-Masri's team and now this. She felt like a fool.

"When?"

"Not for months, but then a team from Dubai got reasonably close a week ago."

"A team?"

"Two people—a man and a woman, playing as a married couple. You were followed in the medina when you came back from the airport—you'd taken your eye off the ball for just a moment, and they made you."

"I didn't see anyone."

"I know—because they were good. They would've followed you back to the riad, but I was able to intercept them long enough so they lost you."

"What does that mean?"

"I drove into their car, and then, when they were losing their shit with me, I put a tracker on it so I could follow them back to their hotel. I was interested in how they'd found you, and we had a good talk about it. They didn't know the ins and outs, but the impression I got was that they'd found out that Beatrix had a place here, and they decided it was worth sending a couple of agents to sniff around. They got lucky." He corrected himself. "Lucky up to a point, anyway."

"What happened to them?"

"They disappeared."

Isabella remembered reading in the paper: two tourists —a husband and wife—had been found dead in a hotel near the souk.

"You killed them?"

"They'd found you, Bella. They hadn't reported it, but they would've. I didn't have a choice. And they would've done the same to me. That's the game—they knew the risks." He finished his second glass. "The SIA will obviously send another team, so I decided it was time to come clean and see you again so I could persuade you it was time to move on. But you got involved with the general... and things got out of control after that."

"You've been busy," she said quietly.

He filled his glass for a third time. "I'm sorry if you think I should've been honest with you. It was difficult—there were times when I really doubted what I was doing, but I knew it was the right thing to do. I saw how hard you were working to create a life. I watched you play with the kids in the orphanage. I watched you exercise on the roof of the riad. The way you went up there to watch the sun rise in the morning. I was trying to hold the world at bay so that you could enjoy all of that."

"What?" she said. "Back up—you saw me on the roof?"

"The riad with the young lad who feeds the pigeons? You know that's a hotel?"

"Yes, I know. You were there?"

"I took a room on a long-term lease. Close enough to

keep an eye on you but not so close that I'd step on your toes."

"Fuck. I had no idea."

"That was the plan, Bella."

"What else?"

"I did enough to keep you safe, but not enough that it would've been intrusive."

"Did you go into my riad?"

"Now and again."

"What else?"

"I had a tracker on your bike."

"So you know about…"

"The arms cache? Yes—I've been there."

"And been inside?"

He nodded.

"You know about Broker?"

"I do, but it took me a while to work it out. Are you pretending to be me?"

She nodded.

"That's clever. The targets?"

"I only went after the bad ones—same as when you were doing it."

"I followed you to the airport the first time, but there was no way of knowing what flight you were there to get."

"The first time was Lagos," she said.

"Then Alexandria," Pope said. "Then Kinshasa."

"You said there was no way of knowing…" She paused, realising what he'd done. "A tracker?"

"In your suitcase," he said. "After the first time I thought I ought to be sure. And you always took the same one."

She could feel her temperature rising.

"What about Algiers?" he said.

She bristled defensively. "What about it?"

"You went twice. What happened?"

"The target..." She stopped, realising that he didn't know about Charlie and—weirdly—finding that she preferred to keep it that way. "The target wasn't what Broker said. He was supposed to be working for the Russians, but he's not."

"You would've realised that when you scouted him, though. Why did you go back?"

"Because I wanted to be sure."

She knew that if Pope had put a tracker in her suitcase, then he would also know that she had taken a trip to Sidi Bou Said to attend to Charlie's brother, but he seemed happy to leave things as they were, and she didn't want to mention it. She downed her drink, and before he could ask anything else, she held out the glass and waited for him to pour again.

He did. "You know we have to leave," he said as he put the cap back on the bottle.

"It's not fair," she muttered. "I *like* living here. It felt like things were almost normal."

"They're not, though, and they never will be. I know that's hard, but it's something you—both of us—are going to have to get used to. And you've poked the bear now. We need to find somewhere else."

"I can't yet," she said.

"Because of the general."

She nodded. "I can't leave until I know the orphanage is safe."

"He doesn't know that you came after him because of that?"

"I don't think so."

"Well, that's something. It'll give us a little time to plan."

"You'll help?"

"You wouldn't listen to me if I said it'd be better if we drove to the border now, would you?"

"And leave him to make their lives a misery? Are you mad?"

"So what choice do I have? Of course I'll help." He raised his glass, then looked at it and chuckled. "This feels weird."

Isabella grinned, raised her own glass and touched it to his.

"Do you forgive me?" he said.

She dragged out her answer in the hope that it might make him squirm. "I suppose so."

"I missed you," he said.

"I can forgive you, but don't think I'll forget."

"Wouldn't expect you to."

"Because you're still a dick."

"Guilty as charged."

He was reaching for the bottle to fill their glasses again when they both heard the sound of a door slamming.

Pope reached for his pistol.

"Shit," Isabella said, staying his hand. "Aicha."

77

P ope hesitated for a second, his hand still hovering over the pistol, before easing back. He gave Isabella a questioning look, his eyes narrowing.

Isabella hurried into the bedroom: it was empty. It wasn't a door that had slammed, but the sash window Aicha had used to leave the house. She went to it, pushed the sash up and slid outside into the scrubby patch of garden at the rear of the property. She hadn't got far when she heard the sound of an engine from the other side of the house and then the flash of high beams as they reached out down the road. Isabella ran, vaulted the fence and reached the road just as the van raced away. She started to run, feeling the power in her legs, and, as she picked up speed, she was close enough to reach out and touch the side of the vehicle.

Aicha must have seen her in the mirrors; she swung the wheel and brought the van across Isabella's path, forcing her to stop.

She paused to catch her breath, watching the van as it turned a corner and disappeared, heading back in the direction of the city.

Pope was waiting for her outside the house.

"She's gone," Isabella said, her voice tight with frustration.

"Why would she run?"

Isabella sighed, rubbing her temples. "She's scared. This whole thing has gone way beyond what she signed up for. I needed help, but I didn't tell her everything. The arrest, going to court, then this... She knows she's in big trouble."

Pope leaned against the doorframe, crossing his arms. "What do you think she'll do?"

Isabella paused for a moment, her thoughts briefly drifting back to Aicha's fear and determination. She didn't blame her for running. But the timing couldn't be worse. "I don't know," she admitted.

Pope nodded firmly. "We need to move. We can't be sure she won't go straight to them."

"She wouldn't—"

"Are you sure?" he cut across her. "She's scared—you said so yourself. Maybe she decides they'll go easier on her if she cooperates. We can't take the risk. She could lead them straight to us."

Isabella knew he was right. She didn't know Aicha, but knew she was angry—with reason—over the deception that had led them all to this juncture. She couldn't expect loyalty from her, and there was no way of knowing how she would react.

"I should've seen it coming," she muttered, more to herself than to Pope.

Pope straightened. "It doesn't matter. What's done is done. But we need to go." He eyed her again. "You're sure I can't persuade you to head for the border?"

"No," she said. "Not a chance."

"You want to go for the general?"

She nodded.

"It won't be easy. You won't be able to surprise him now."

"I know that," she said.

"Do you know where he'll be?"

"Now? Probably at home—it's like a fortress."

"Not there, then."

"But I know where he'll be at the weekend—Lagos."

"Why's that?"

"He's into polo," she said. "There's a competition—biggest in Africa. He's taking a team down."

"I'm not sure that's going to work, either," Pope said. "Nigeria must be three thousand miles away from here—I was going to suggest we get over the border into Tunisia by car, but it'd take four or five days to drive south. That means we'd have to fly, and I don't think it'd be a very good idea for you to be in an airport at the moment. They'll be looking for you there."

"We can fly," she said. "Just not commercial."

"Are you going to tell me how we'll be able to find someone willing to take us there at this short notice?"

"I have someone in mind," she said.

"You can tell me later," he said. "We can't be here. We need to be on the road."

Isabella pointed at the spot where the van had been parked. "With what? She took the van."

"Better steal another one, then."

78

P ope drove hard and fast along the desert highway that snaked in a northwesterly direction from Marrakesh into the desert. They had found a Suzuki four-by-four near to the safe house, and, with Isabella standing watch, Pope had quickly hotwired it. The Suzuki was old and uncomfortable, and it guzzled fuel; they ran low after the first two hours and pulled into a small roadside petrol station to refuel. A young boy barely into his teens appeared from nowhere, wiping his oily hands on a rag that he kept hanging from his back pocket. Half an unlit cigarette dangled from his lips. He filled the tank, his eyes never leaving Isabella.

As they pulled out, Isabella saw the boy saunter toward an office and talk to someone, pointing at the Suzuki as it disappeared into the distance.

"I wouldn't be surprised if he tells someone," she said.

"That might be paranoia," he said. "There's no reason to think they've got the word out yet, and certainly not to somewhere off the beaten track like that was."

"I don't know."

"He has a dull job," Pope said. "Ogling the women is probably what passes for entertainment."

There were a few lorries travelling both ways, as well as the occasional tourist bus. It wasn't hard to see what attracted people to this part of the country. The land on either side of the highway was flat and compacted, but in the distance, Isabella could see undulating dunes that stretched for hundreds and hundreds of miles.

"So," Pope said, "how are we getting out?"

"I know a pilot," she said. "His name's Charlie. Runs a small air freight business, mostly operating out of North Africa."

Pope glanced over at her. "And how do you know him?"

"I met him in Algiers. Broker sent me after him."

"Because he was working for the Russians?"

"Only he isn't. I went and checked him out—wanted to make sure he was what Broker said he was, and he isn't. He's a good guy. Nice. He does humanitarian work, too—flies medical supplies into places no one else will go. He's got a conscience. The intel Broker gave me didn't match who Charlie really was. Turns out that Broker—or whoever the client is—put another operator on him. They tried to sabotage his plane, and, when that didn't work, they tried to drive him off the road. I spoke to Charlie about it and worked out the only person with enough of a motive to get rid of him was his brother. There's money involved—an inheritance—and the brother doesn't think Charlie deserves it. Hence..." She spread her hands.

"And you're sure about him?"

"I am." He was staring at her. "What, Pope?"

"How old is he?"

"I don't know. In his twenties. I never asked."

"And you *like* him?"

"Jesus." She rolled her eyes and looked away, acutely conscious that the blood was rushing to her cheeks.

"I'm not prying. I'm just asking so I know what I'm dealing with."

"'What you're dealing with'? That sounds like something a dad might say. I don't need your approval, Pope."

"That's not what I meant," he said, flustered a little. "I meant operationally." He paused. "And there's the fact that I'd rather not look like a fool if there's something I don't know about you... you and him."

She looked out of the windscreen as she thought about what she should say. The truth of it was that she didn't know how she felt about Charlie. She knew she liked him, that she'd had fun with him when they had hung out, but, beyond that... she'd never had a boyfriend nor any kind of romantic entanglement. She realised, to her annoyance, that she lacked the emotional vocabulary to describe what she was feeling. And the fact that Pope was clearly uncomfortable—just as he'd always been—about the prospect of Isabella having a relationship presented complicated feelings: irritation that he had slipped right back into his paternal concern after letting her think that he was dead, and a warmth that he cared about her that much—like a father—when no one else in the world did.

Pope rescued her from the moment. "It doesn't matter," he said. "Do you trust him?"

"Yes."

Pope was quiet for a moment, his hands firm on the steering wheel as the Suzuki rattled over the rough highway. "That's all I need to know. You think he'll help?"

Isabella nodded. "I'm sure he will. He doesn't know it yet, but he owes me."

79

The Suzuki rumbled over the uneven dirt road, kicking up clouds of dust as Isabella and Pope neared the small airstrip. The airfield at Beni Mellal, nestled in the vast expanse of rocky desert terrain, shimmered amidst the barren landscape that surrounded it. A chain-link fence lined the perimeter, rusted at the edges and barely intact, with gaps wide enough for someone to slip through unnoticed. A single, weathered hangar stood at the far end, its metal siding pocked with dents and bleached by the sun, the paint peeling away in strips. Beyond it, they could make out the faint outlines of a narrow gravel runway stretching toward the horizon.

Pope drove them closer. Isabella spotted a lone Cessna parked outside the hangar, its white-and-blue fuselage streaked with dust from recent flights. A handful of makeshift shelters dotted the area, likely for mechanics and ground crew, but the place was eerily quiet. The only movement came from a lone figure pacing near the hangar doors, a cigarette glowing faintly in the growing dusk. The airfield felt forgotten.

"I like this," Pope said. "We aren't going to have any trouble getting away from here." He paused. "Provided your friend is true to his word."

"He will be."

Pope pointed to the parked Cessna. "That's not him?"

"No," she said.

Isabella checked the time. Charlie had been in Algiers when Isabella had called him, and he'd told her he'd set off as soon as he could. Isabella had tried to estimate how long it would take him to get here while Pope listened to Fleetwood Mac in the car, the map said there was around a thousand miles between the airfield and Algiers, and his Cessna cruised at around a hundred and seventy miles an hour. He should have been here already.

"What do we do?"

"Safer to wait here," Pope said. "We'll leave the car and go inside when he's here."

Isabella put the seat back so she could recline. Her feelings about Charlie were complicated, and she'd appreciated having time during the drive to sift through them in search of clarity. The issue for her was that the events of the last few days had brought into sharp focus the risks that she continued to bring to those close to her. She felt toxic; Pope had told her once that he'd felt the same way, as if he were emitting a kind of radiation that would always harm those he cared for most. Isabella knew what he meant. Even if she managed to keep her head down and not attract attention, she'd invariably stumble into something like the situation with Fatima and the orphanage and feel compelled to act. She'd accepted long ago that a normal life, if such a thing existed, was out of her reach; recent events had underlined that. It was one thing for her to embrace that reality for herself, but it was another thing altogether to force it on someone like Charlie. She realised that she had been unconsciously sketching out what a relationship between them could look like, but now she could see it for what it was: a naïve pipedream.

SHE STILL COULDN'T HELP but feel a jolt of excitement when, thirty minutes later, she spotted a dot in the sky that grew into the Cessna that Charlie flew. She put one hand on Pope's shoulder to point it out to him. They both got out to stand with their eyes shielded from the sun as the plane banked and turned toward them.

Charlie angled the Cessna toward the small airstrip, a thin ribbon of tarmac surrounded by barren land that stretched out beneath him. He descended slowly, bringing the plane in low and circling once to ensure the strip was clear before aligning for his final approach. He levelled off for landing, and the Cessna's wheels skimmed the tarmac, sending up clouds of dust in their wake. The plane bounced once before settling, the screech of the tyres mixing with the burble of the engine.

Pope opened the door of the Suzuki. "Did you tell him we'll leave straight away?"

"Yes," she said. "But won't he need to refuel?"

"Probably. Come on."

Pope started the engine and drove them both through the facility's unguarded gate and to the scattered buildings. The Cessna had come to a stop at the end of the airstrip, and Charlie was turning it so he could taxi back to the fuel bowsers. They arrived at the same time, the propeller slowed to a halt, and Charlie popped the door open and hopped down to the asphalt. Pope parked the car, and

Isabella got out, jogging over so she could intercept Charlie before Pope could get there. She wasn't embarrassed; she just wanted a moment of privacy with him to say hello.

Charlie was wearing a pair of well-worn cargo pants, a black T-shirt, and a sturdy leather jacket with patches on the elbows and scuffs across the shoulders. He was wearing aviator sunglasses, and, as she approached, he pushed them up above his forehead. His smile was wide, and, reaching him, she threw her arms around his neck with a force that caught him off guard.

"Thank you," she said.

"Are you all right?"

"I'm fine. Just... really pleased to see you."

Charlie looked over her shoulder to where Pope hovered awkwardly in the background.

"And that's...?"

"My dad," she said.

"Your... dad?"

"It's a long story. I've got a lot of explaining to do—I know that."

"I've got to refuel," he said. "There's a café inside, and I'm starving. You can tell me all about it."

C harlie went to make the arrangements for the plane to be refuelled. Pope and Isabella went in search of the facility's café. The building, a low, one-storey structure with weathered whitewashed walls and a flat roof, sat just beyond the main hangar with faded signs written in French and Arabic announcing it as "Café de l'Aérodrome." They went in and found a table where they could watch as the bowser was driven out to the Cessna. The café had a handful of mismatched wooden tables and plastic chairs set out on a concrete floor that showed scuffs and stains from years of traffic, a layer of desert dust clinging to the corners. Old aviation posters were stuck to the walls, yellowed from exposure to the sun, and a ceiling fan lazily spun above, providing only the faintest relief from the heat. The air smelled of stale coffee, mingling with the scent of mint tea and tobacco smoke from the lone patron sitting near the window, smoking a cigarette and gazing idly at the tarmac outside. The only sign of modernity was the small television in the corner, tuned to a local news channel, the volume low enough to blend into the background.

Pope sat down at one of the tables while Isabella went to the counter and ordered croissants and *msemen*, though neither looked fresh, and three bottles of Orangina. She delivered them to the table just as Charlie arrived at the entrance.

"Be nice," she muttered to Pope.

Charlie sat down, and Isabella pushed a plate with one of the *msemen* across the table.

"Thank you," he said, taking a bite.

Pope handed him one of the Oranginas. "All okay?"

Charlie nodded. "It'll take half an hour, and then we can be on our way."

"Thank you," Pope said. "It's good of you to help like this."

Charlie cracked the lid of the bottle and took a swig. "It's not a problem. But I am curious. This is all very mysterious."

"I should probably apologise," Isabella said. "It was urgent... and I haven't told you everything. About me, I mean."

"Okay," he said slowly. "That's ominous."

She didn't want to lie, but now she had reconciled herself to the fact that a normal relationship with Charlie—with anyone—was out of the question, she needed to let him down gently, and lying was the only way to do it.

"I've been in a relationship with a man in Marrakesh for the last six months. He's involved in the mafia. He has a lot of money and a lot of influence."

She hadn't mentioned the story she had concocted to Pope, but he embellished it with disturbing ease. "The Mafia Maghribiyya," he said. "They grow hashish in the mountains. Usually, they're Berbers who migrated to Holland and Belgium and then go back."

Isabella took over again. "I've been trying to get away

from him for weeks, but he wouldn't let me. It got worse when I got back home after the last time I saw you. He said I was seeing someone and using my modelling as an excuse. He told me I couldn't do it anymore and that I had to move to his place in the mountains. I mean, obviously, I wasn't going to do that, but I told him I would, and then I called my dad so he could help get me out."

Charlie looked at Pope with a curious eye. "Can I ask what you do?"

"I work in private security," he said. "I was in the military before that."

"I thought you might say something like that. You have the look."

"Tried to scrub it off," he said with a shrug. "Easier said than done."

"So you helped Isabella?"

"That's right. I picked her up and drove her out of the city. But I spoke to a friend of mine who works in intelligence, and he said that the mafia will have someone at all of the main airports. I didn't feel confident that we'd be able to get out without being stopped or followed. It was Isabella's idea to ask you for help. A very good idea, I thought. And I'm grateful to you for saying yes."

Charlie must have been disappointed—that Isabella wasn't quite what she'd said, that she'd lied to him, that she'd been in a relationship—but if he was, he hid it well. "I'm happy to be able to help. I've only known her for a little while, but I think she's great. We've had fun."

"Lots of fun," Isabella said.

"Can I ask something?"

"Of course," Pope said.

"Why Lagos?"

"I served in Nigeria when they were dealing with Boko

Haram. I have some good friends there—people I trust. I was due to go to see them anyway, but this made it seem like an even better idea. They'll put us up for a couple of weeks until we're sure that we got out without Abeqquy knowing where we've gone."

"Abeqquy?"

"The man I was seeing." Isabella took over.

The two of them—Isabella and Pope—were so smooth it was as if they'd never been apart. Isabella didn't know how she felt about that, about the ease with which they lied, about the fact that she found it so simple and natural to take advantage of Charlie's guilelessness.

They paused for a moment to look out of the window as the hose from the mobile bowser was disconnected from Charlie's plane and the vehicle was driven away.

"Looks like they're done," Pope said.

Charlie didn't appear to hear him. "I have some news, too," he said.

Isabella raised an eyebrow. "Oh?"

"All that stuff with my brother." He quickly explained what had happened with Jack for Pope's benefit. "He called me up a few days ago to apologise. He said he wouldn't oppose the will and that whatever my grandmother decided was fine by him."

Isabella kept her face as neutral as she could. "That's quite a change of heart."

"Tell me about it," he said. "I would've said that was impossible."

"Did he admit to what we said he'd done?"

"What's that?" Pope said.

"I think he tried to have Charlie killed," Isabella said. "There were a couple of things, all very suspicious given what they were arguing about."

"How awful," Pope said, his face impassive.

"He didn't say anything," Charlie said. "But I wouldn't have expected him to. He's hardly likely to implicate himself in something like that, is he?"

"No," Isabella said, her mind flicking back to her visit to Jack's bedroom. "I suppose not."

Charlie got up. "Well," he said, "all I know is that I had a problem with Jack for months, and it was only when I met you that things seemed to get better. I know it's just a coincidence, but I can't help thinking you're my lucky charm." He pointed out of the window toward his plane. "And I'm happy I'm able to help. The plane's ready—we can make a start if you're ready."

81

The heat shimmered off the tarmac, and the wind carried fine grains of sand across the runway. Charlie explained that they couldn't just take off without adhering to the minimal, but necessary, administrative protocols. Even in a place as remote as this, the rules had to be followed, or at least enough of them to avoid drawing attention.

Charlie had already filed a basic flight plan before leaving Algiers, which included their destination—Lagos, in Nigeria—and the estimated duration of their journey. He told Pope and Isabella that the Cessna didn't have the range for the full flight, and that they would stop at Dakar to refuel. The plan had been submitted to the regional aviation authority through a coded radio call, and, to avoid suspicion, he'd made sure to state the purpose of the trip as a cargo transport run. Although the local airstrip officials were few and far between, there was always the risk that someone could be watching, so they couldn't afford to bypass that step completely. Pope had fake passports for them both: Isabella was travelling as Isabella Fischer, while

Pope was flying under the name Thomas Fischer; Isabella had taken her assumed surname *after* Pope's disappearance, and it was a reminder that he'd kept a close eye on her and that she hadn't noticed. Charlie added both identities to the airfield's logbook, a formality that might never even be reviewed unless an inquiry came through.

There was the possibility of cargo checks, and, to maintain their cover, Charlie had stowed a couple of sealed boxes in the rear of the Cessna and labelled them as 'Technical Equipment' on the cargo manifest. They ought to serve as plausible evidence should anyone ask too many questions.

With the paperwork, identification, and cargo in order, Charlie and Isabella walked over to the small airfield office, where a single official sat behind a battered desk, idly flipping through old flight schedules. Pope made his way to the plane to wait, giving them another few moments of privacy. In the office, Charlie handed over the documents, received a perfunctory stamp in return, and, with a nod, they were cleared for take-off.

"Your dad's nice," he said as they made their way back along the airstrip.

"He can be a bit..."

Charlie smiled. "Defensive?"

"That's one way to describe him. Or grumpy. Possibly rude."

"Don't worry—I get it."

She looked over at him and frowned. "Get what?"

He winked. "I'd be defensive, too."

She paused. "About what I said," she started eventually. "Or what I *didn't* say. About... my situation."

"Forget it," he said. "We'd only just met. Why would you tell a stranger about what was happening? I'm just glad I'm able to help get you away from him."

The three of them boarded the Cessna as the sun began to dip low over the horizon, casting long shadows across the desert floor. Charlie ran his final checks of the aircraft while Pope and Isabella settled in. All three were quiet, preoccupied with the weight of the journey ahead of them.

Charlie's voice sounded in Isabella's headset. "Ready?"

"Ready," she said.

Pope nodded. "Ready."

The engine roared to life, and the propeller turned. Charlie sent them racing away down the airstrip and into the air, turning to face south. Isabella looked back as the airstrip disappeared into the distance and knew she was probably leaving Morocco for the last time.

PART VIII

82

The Cessna's engine hummed steadily as it cut through the humid, darkened skies. Isabella glanced out of the window. The inky blackness stretched out below, interrupted occasionally by patches of shimmering light marking the scattered towns and villages below. They'd been in the air for hours, departing Morocco in the early evening, making a brief refuelling stop in Dakar, and now, after midnight, they were approaching Lagos.

Charlie's voice crackled through the headset, pulling Isabella out of her thoughts. "We're about twenty minutes out. You two ready?"

"Ready," Pope said, leaning forward, his eyes narrowing as he peered out of the cockpit window. "Any issues on approach?"

"It's quiet. Air traffic control's giving us the green light. Should be a smooth landing."

Isabella nodded. She and Pope exchanged a brief look, everything had gone according to plan so far, but the real work would begin once they were on the ground. She shifted in her seat, rolling her shoulders to ease the tension that had settled there during the flight. Charlie had chosen a small private airstrip on the outskirts of Lagos, far from the prying eyes that would be attendant upon a major airport. It wasn't exactly legitimate, but Charlie's plan ought to have ensured their arrival wouldn't draw attention.

Charlie made a smooth descent, the plane's nose tilting downward as the altimeter dropped. The airfield came into sight, a dark strip of tarmac nestled between rows of trees, illuminated by a handful of lights. It was barely more than a clearing in the jungle, with just enough infrastructure to accommodate a few small planes.

"Runway's clear," Charlie said, his voice steady and calm. "Hold on."

Isabella tightened her grip on the armrests as the plane descended further, the hum of the engine growing louder. The wheels touched down with a gentle bump, the plane rolling forward before Charlie slowed to a crawl, steering them toward a dimly lit hangar at the far end of the strip. It was quiet, no sign of movement except for a lone figure standing by the hangar, smoking a cigarette.

The plane rolled to a stop, and the man walked over, tossing his cigarette to the ground and crushing it under his boot. Charlie powered down the engine, the hum fading into silence. He unclipped his harness, glanced back at Isabella and Pope, and grinned. "Welcome to Lagos."

POPE WAS the first to step out. Isabella followed, the heavy, humid air of the Nigerian night washing over her as she climbed down the short steps. She took in their surroundings: the airstrip was quiet, just as they'd hoped. The man, dressed in a faded shirt and cargo pants, nodded at them, his expression bored but watchful.

Charlie walked over and put his hand out. "Charlie," he said.

"Albert."

The man looked from Isabella to Pope and back to Charlie again. "Your friends?"

"That's right," he replied. He turned to Pope and Isabella. "This is Albert—he'll take care of things here."

Albert nodded, then gestured toward a battered pickup truck parked near the hangar. "We've got a few minutes before anyone else shows up. Best get your gear and go."

Pope turned toward the pickup and nodded to Isabella to encourage her to follow, and then, with unusual tact, realised that she wanted a moment with Charlie. "I'll be over there," he said, pointing.

"I'll be here for a day or two," Charlie said to him. "If you need anything, you've got my number."

"Appreciate it," Pope said, clapping him on the shoulder. "Thank you."

Isabella waited for Pope to set off before turning to Charlie.

"Are you going to be okay?" he asked her.

"I'll be fine," she said. "Thank you."

He waved that away. "I'm just happy I could help."

She reached out and took his hand. "You didn't have to. You're very kind."

He smiled a little bashfully, and, before she realised what she was doing, Isabella took a step toward him and kissed him on the lips.

"That was nice," he said with a smile.

"Will I be able to see you again?" she asked.

"Are you going to kiss me again?"

"I might."

"No reason why not, is there? I mean, you're away from Morocco now."

Isabella hated the fact that they had had to lie to him but agreed with Pope; there really hadn't been anything else for it. She didn't know whether it would be possible for them to see each other again but hoped that it might be. Pope probably wouldn't be keen on the idea, but she was an adult now and could make her own choices.

"Let me work out what we're going to do," she said. "I'll call you when we've sorted it all out."

"I'll look forward to it."

"What are you going to do now?"

He shrugged. "Diving's not great here, but I always wanted to try Ghana. Busua Beach is supposed to be amazing. I might give that a try." He paused, smiled and shrugged. "Could charter a boat and enough gear for two?"

She smiled back at him. "Maybe next time."

ALBERT CLIMBED into the driver's seat and turned the ignition. The truck sputtered to life, its engine barely masking the chorus of crickets and the distant, muffled sounds of Lagos. They drove off, heading down a narrow, bumpy dirt road that led away from the airstrip; Isabella leaned back against the seat, her mind already shifting to what lay ahead.

She glanced across at Pope, who was staring straight ahead, his jaw set and his eyes focused. She knew he was running through the plan they'd discussed, preparing for what was to come. She was glad he was here; there was no one she trusted more than him.

83

The truck rumbled down the uneven streets of Lagos, weaving through a mix of faded colonial buildings and newer, glass-fronted structures crowded along the busy roads. Pope and Isabella sat quietly in the backseat. The city was alive with a chaotic energy, vendors shouted from street corners, motorbikes zipped in and out of traffic, and the scent of grilled meat wafted through the open windows.

Albert drove with practiced ease. "There's a hotel just up ahead," he said, his voice cutting through the background noise. "Not too fancy, but it's clean, and they don't ask too many questions."

Pope nodded, satisfied. "Thanks."

They pulled up to a modest building that looked a little worn around the edges but was well-maintained. The neon sign above the entrance flickered, casting a soft glow onto the sidewalk. A bellhop stood by the door, half-heartedly waving away a man selling cheap watches. Isabella and Pope climbed out of the truck, and Pope handed Albert a few bills.

"Thanks for the ride."

Albert nodded, then turned the truck back toward the street and drove off. Pope and Isabella walked toward the entrance; the bellhop greeted them with a tired smile, opening the door without a word.

The air was cooler inside, a welcome relief from the humidity on the street. The lobby was small but clean, with a handful of leather chairs arranged around a low coffee table. A television mounted on the wall played a muted local news channel.

They approached the reception desk, where a woman with neat braids and a crisp uniform stood behind the counter, her expression professional but disinterested. "Good evening," she said, glancing up from a logbook. "Do you have a reservation?"

"No," Pope said. "We'll need two rooms."

She nodded. "I have two rooms on the third floor."

"That'll work," Pope said, handing over one of the burner cards he carried, which was unlikely to be traced back to anything significant.

The receptionist checked them in, sliding their key cards across the counter. "Enjoy your stay," she said, her eyes flicking briefly to Isabella. "Breakfast is from six to ten, and there's a bar on the ground floor."

"Appreciate it," Pope said, taking his key card and turning toward the lift.

The ride up was silent, the lift humming softly as they ascended to the third floor. Isabella leaned against the wall and ran through the plan. They would rest for a bit, then head out to the safe house to collect the weapons and gear they needed. They would scout the polo club tomorrow and work out how to get close enough to attend to Al-Masri.

Their rooms were small but serviceable, with a double

bed, a tiny desk, and a window that overlooked the busy street below. Isabella stood at the door to Pope's room while he checked the locks on the door and windows. Satisfied, he turned to Isabella. "Not bad," he said.

She nodded. "We've stayed in worse."

"We need to get moving soon," he said. "I don't want to be out there with the kit when the streets start getting busy. The sooner we have everything back here, the better."

"Agreed."

Isabella went to her own room and freshened up, then met Pope downstairs after thirty minutes. The hotel was quiet, only a few guests wandering through the lobby as they made their way outside. The night air was still warm, but the humidity had lessened, making it easier to breathe. Pope led the way down the street, keeping a steady pace as they walked toward a nearby street where Albert had told them it would be easier to catch a ride to the outskirts.

There was a line of taxis waiting; Pope went to the car at the front of the line and told the driver where they wanted to go. Isabella glanced around, on edge. Lagos teemed with life, just like Morocco; but unlike Marrakesh, she had never been here before, and the unfamiliarity gave her reason to be nervous.

84

Pope navigated the narrow streets, his eyes flicking from the cracked, uneven pavement to the bustling throng of people pushing past them. He led Isabella down a series of winding alleys, each narrower than the last, until they arrived at a plain concrete building with iron-barred windows and faded paint.

"This is it," Pope muttered.

"You've been here before?"

"Years ago," he said. "I'd just transferred into the Group. We had a job here—the quartermaster had just set it up."

Isabella knew about the safe houses from what Pope had told her before. He'd described them as emergency fallbacks: some were for agents who needed to get off the street, while others were caches of equipment and ammunition.

"Not much to look at," she said.

"That's the idea."

He led her around the back, where a stack of rusted metal barrels created a makeshift barricade. He moved them aside and located a door partially concealed by a tattered tarpaulin. Pope pulled the tarp aside; the door was made of thick metal and had a faded, weather-beaten keypad mounted next to it.

Isabella leaned in to watch as Pope punched in a code.

The keypad clicked, and the door opened into darkness.

Pope led the way inside and flicked a switch; a dim fluorescent light buzzed to life, casting a pale glow over the room. It was a modest space, not much larger than a walk-in larder. Metal shelves lined the walls, each of them holding sturdy, dust-covered cases. In one corner, a cot lay folded against the wall; next to that was a grimy sink and an empty crate that served as a makeshift table.

"Still here," he muttered with a hint of relief. "I always used to worry that I'd turn up at one and find someone else had been there first."

He opened one of the cases and pulled out a compact FN SCAR assault rifle. Its matte-black surface gleamed under the light. He examined it, tested the action, then placed it on the crate before opening another case to reveal a set of Beretta M9 pistols, each meticulously cleaned and stored with accompanying magazines.

Isabella ran her fingers over a combat knife, its serrated edge still as sharp as the day it had been stashed here.

Pope moved to another shelf where he found a box of radios and a basic first aid kit. "These supplies were supposed to last until we could get out of the country."

Isabella pulled out a satchel bag, filling it with ammunition, a couple of grenades, and a collapsible baton.

As they worked in silence, Pope reached for a small wooden box tucked away on the bottom shelf. Inside was a collection of identification documents and a decent number of Nigerian naira.

He handed Isabella a passport stamped with the name 'Rachel Beckett.'

"No photo," she said, holding the page out for him to see.

"How would they know to have one for you? We'll get photos for both of us and stick them in. They won't be perfect, and they won't do if we try to use them to get over the border, but they'll do if they're just flashed at someone. We'd need to find an expert to make them a little more presentable."

She pocketed the passport. "Know anyone?"

"I might know someone who knows someone."

Pope lifted a heavy, padded case from beneath a stack of crates. Flipping the latches, he opened the lid and took out a surprisingly long rifle.

"What's that?" Isabella asked. "I don't recognise it."

He held it up. "A Zastava M91. Serbian, but plenty of them find their way down here. They're reliable, and you can throw them around without causing too many problems."

Pope carefully lifted the disassembled rifle from its case. The dark steel barrel gleamed under the dim light as he laid it on the crate. He worked methodically, attaching the 7.62mm barrel to the receiver, securing the bolt, and adjusting the high-precision scope. Isabella watched, noting the ease with which he handled the components, every movement practiced and efficient.

"I'll have to zero it later," he said. "But it looks good."

"Give it to me," Isabella said.

She felt the heft of the rifle as she examined it. The steel barrel was long and sleek, designed to minimise recoil and keep her shots steady, even at long distance. She ran her fingers along the contours, noting the smooth action of the bolt, the clean lines of the adjustable stock, and the simple bipod attached to the front. She nodded her approval and then began disassembling it, her hands moving instinctively as she removed the bolt, magazine, and sight. Piece by piece, she laid the rifle out in sequence, ensuring everything was in its place and would be just as quick to reassemble when the time came.

"I think that's how we'll end up doing it," Pope said. "We'll find your general and put a couple of rounds in him from range."

"When he's in the middle of a match," Isabella said.

"Depends on the lay of the land, but yes—that seems like it'll be the best idea."

Isabella looked at the bulky case and knew it would draw the wrong kind of attention. "We're not carrying it like that," she muttered.

Pope found a canvas garment bag folded on a shelf. He took it down, shaking out the dust, and turned to Isabella. "This'll do."

They removed the padded inserts from the case, placing the rifle components into the garment bag's various pockets and lining them with folded pieces of fabric to keep the parts cushioned and hidden. The barrel, scope, and stock fit snugly along the bag's length, each segment tucked behind a layer of lining. Pope zipped it up, slung it over his shoulder, and adjusted it to look like an inconspicuous bag of clothes.

Isabella laid out the equipment they'd chosen and took a sturdy duffel, the kind that could pass for an everyday travel bag, and arranged the items inside: extra magazines, ammunition, and a basic cleaning set. She added a compact medical kit, a utility knife, together with water and a small stash of energy bars.

They checked that they hadn't forgotten anything and, happy that they hadn't, went back out into the alley. Pope closed and secured the door, put the tarpaulin back in place and rearranged the barrels. Isabella took the rucksack and slung it over her shoulder, feeling the edges of the magazines dig into her side. Pope picked up the garment bag, and the two of them made their way back to the busier streets and found a taxi to take them back to their hotel.

85

They spent the day in the hotel for the most part, venturing out for breakfast and lunch while they planned what they were going to do that evening. Pope suggested that they go and look at the polo club in advance of the tournament tomorrow. Isabella agreed. The more they could familiarise themselves with the terrain, the better their chances of success. They had done everything they could do online, including a careful assessment of the grounds with the satellite coverage provided by Google, but there really was nothing to beat visiting a place on foot. It would be much easier to find a suitable shooting position to carry out the assassination, and there was no substitute for feeling the atmosphere of a place in person.

There had been hours spent waiting, and Pope had taken the chance to tell Isabella more about what he had been doing in the time they had spent apart. He had been in Marrakesh for most of it, staying in a hostel to start with until he was able to find a room close enough to observe her riad. She had asked him how closely he had been watching her, and he'd told her: most of the time he'd restricted himself to watching from the other riad, but there had been times when he had been inside her property in order to satisfy himself that she was safe.

She believed he had been honest with his answers, and rather than the annoyance she had initially felt—almost certainly fuelled by her embarrassment that she hadn't noticed him being in the city with her—now she felt a renewed affection for him that he cared enough to do what he had done. She was still cross with him for letting her think that he was dead, but she was starting to see his logic. She didn't agree with it and told him that—several times—but she could understand it.

He went on to tell her about his family. His wife, Rachel, had insisted that they separate after the danger that had been brought down upon her and their two daughters in the aftermath of Pope and Isabella's escape from Syria, and Pope had respected her wishes. The family had been hiding in Vietnam, but she and the girls had returned to the United Kingdom to move in with Rachel's parents. Pope was obviously uncomfortable with the decision but accepted that it was her choice to make and wouldn't interfere. Isabella had asked whether he had been to visit them, and he shook his head, then looked away. Rachel had made it very plain that their marriage was over and had told him she didn't want to see him or face the peril that seeing him would entail. Isabella could see that her decision had wounded him, but he had accepted it.

Pope's voice had softened as he talked about his daughters, and Isabella recognised the man underneath the layers of control and discipline. She had wanted to reach out to him, to offer some comfort for what he had lost, but she held back. Their relationship had always been rooted in pragmatism; there was little space for vulnerability.

"I couldn't risk her life again," Pope had said quietly. "Or the girls'. You saw what happened after Syria... They'll always be targets as long as I'm around."

"And me?" Isabella had asked. "I'm a target too."

He had looked at her. "You're different," he had said. "You know how to protect yourself. But I won't let anything happen to you, either."

That final statement lingered between them, heavy and unresolved. They both knew that the risks they took—together and apart—were constant, and that their lives would never be simple or safe. But in this moment, with Pope confiding in her, it felt like a fragile kind of trust had been re-established between them.

86

I sabella sat in the passenger seat of the rental car, gazing out the window as they approached the entrance to the Royal Oak Polo Club. The sun was setting, casting long shadows across the road, and the air outside was heavy with the humidity that clung to everything, even this far out from the city. As they drew closer, she could see the faint outlines of the club's main gates, two towering pillars of whitewashed stone that framed a wrought-iron arch. The gates were intricately designed, with a brass emblem in the shape of a horse at the centre, polished to a bright sheen.

Pope slowed the car as they passed through the gates.

The guard approached and indicated that Pope should wind down the window.

"Tickets?"

Pope took out the printout with the two tickets they had purchased for all three days of the competition. The guard looked at the tickets, then at Pope and Isabella, then grunted. "In you go."

Pope moved away again.

Isabella eyed the long, tree-lined driveway that stretched out ahead of them, leading toward the main clubhouse. Flanked on either side by manicured lawns and rows of palm trees, it was obvious that the owners of the club valued first impressions. Even in the dimming light, the grass was a deep, vivid green, maintained with a precision that suggested money, lots of money.

The clubhouse came into view: a sprawling colonial-style structure with wide verandas and tall French windows, painted a stark white that stood out against the lush green-ery. The building was surrounded by meticulously land-scaped gardens, with bursts of colour from bougainvillea and hibiscus flowers. Soft, ambient lighting illuminated the paths, giving the whole area a serene and inviting feel.

"It looks like a resort," Isabella said.

"Lot of money in Nigeria these days," Pope said. "Wasn't like this the last time I was here."

Isabella observed everything, cataloguing the details. As they drove past the entrance, she noticed a line of luxury cars parked neatly along the driveway, sleek, expensive models with darkened windows, their drivers standing nearby, discreetly talking among themselves.

The field itself lay beyond the clubhouse, stretching out into the distance. Isabella could see the carefully marked lines of the polo pitch, the tall goalposts standing sentinel at either end. Floodlights stood at the four corners, no doubt powerful enough to allow play well into the evening. The grass was cut short and even, pristine. A few horses trotted along the sidelines, their riders warming them up for their match later tonight.

"Here we are, then," Pope said, breaking the silence.

"What do you think?"

He glanced around. "Security is average."

"Might be more tomorrow."

"Maybe."

Isabella looked across the property, noting the small details. A trio of guards stood at the entrance to the club-house, casually watching the few guests who were arriving, but they didn't seem particularly vigilant. They were dressed more like attendants, in dark suits with earpieces, blending into the background. There were also a few security cameras mounted discreetly under the eaves, their red lights blinking intermittently.

"The security's subtle," she said. "Not too aggressive. They want people to feel comfortable, not watched."

"Agreed. We ought to be able to move around without drawing too much attention—as long as we're careful."

They parked near the far end of the lot, away from the main entrance, and got out. Isabella took everything in: the various exits and entrances, the layout of the pathways, the way the grounds were divided into sections.

A faint murmur of voices and laughter drifted toward them as they made their way closer to the clubhouse. A group of guests stood on the veranda, drinks in hand, their voices rising and falling in animated conversation. They were dressed in expensive evening wear: tailored suits and elegant dresses, old money and influence.

Isabella and Pope continued their slow circuit.

"We'll need somewhere high," Pope said as they moved past the clubhouse, his eyes shifting from the field to the buildings around them. "A clear line of sight to the field, but out of view from the main walkways."

Isabella glanced up at the roof of the clubhouse. It offered a decent view of the pitch but was too exposed.

They walked a little further, making their way around to the back of the clubhouse where a row of low buildings stretched out: stables and maintenance sheds. Isabella's gaze lingered on one of the sheds.

"That might work," she said, tilting her head slightly toward it. "What do you think?"

Pope followed her gaze. "Maybe."

They casually walked over to the maintenance sheds. As they got closer to the nearest one, Isabella saw that one end was partially obscured by trees. It was in a quiet corner of the property, away from the bustle of the main clubhouse and the spectators arriving for the tournament.

"I like it," Pope said quietly. "We can get in and out without passing through the main areas. Should have a good view of the field from there, too."

They kept walking. Isabella kept looking back to the shed. "It's set back just enough that no one would think to look there if they heard a shot. By the time they figure out where it came from, we could be gone."

Pope nodded.

They took another detour, walking around the far end of the field. Isabella could see that the shed offered a wide view of the entire pitch.

"It'll work," she said. "Good cover, good angles, and we can get in and out quickly."

Pope didn't respond immediately. He was scanning the area, noting the guards positioned around the field, the way the pathways twisted between the buildings, and how people were moving in and out of the different areas. Finally, he nodded. "I think so, too."

She and Pope kept their pace casual. Isabella glanced back toward the stables, where grooms were tending to the horses. The stables were large, well-kept, with enough space to house dozens of animals. She could see the shadows of horses moving inside, their silhouettes flickering against the illumination from the lights fixed along the walls.

She glanced back toward the field. The floodlights had come on, bright and harsh against the darkening sky, and she could see the players assembling near the centre, their horses restless, snorting in the cooling air.

She was still watching when she saw someone she recognised.

He was on the other side of the field, but her attention was snagged by the way he walked: with a limp, favouring one side of his body over the other. He was bent over to the left as a result of the beating that Isabella had given him in the alleyway outside the orphanage.

"There," she said, with a discreet point. "The man with the limp."

"I see him," Pope said. "Who is it?"

"One of the general's men."

Pope eyed him and nodded. "Sure?"

"Sure."

They were both still looking when Al-Masri himself appeared from around a corner. He was leading a beautiful chestnut horse, and as Isabella watched—agog—he handed the lead rope to a groom and turned to speak to the guard.

Pope noticed that she was distracted. "Is that him?"

"Yes."

"What are you thinking?" he said. "Change of plan?"

"It'd be useful to know where he's staying. It'd give us the option."

Pope mulled it, then nodded again. "He'd recognise you?"

"For sure."

"But not me." He sucked his teeth. "All right. We'll follow

him. Go back to the car and get ready. I'll keep an eye on him, and we can follow."

ope sat in the driver's seat, hands relaxed on the wheel, eyes locked onto the rear-view mirror. Isabella was beside him, her gaze fixed forward, scanning the street ahead of them. Al-Masri and the guard had just exited the polo club and made their way to a black SUV parked near the entrance.

Pope pointed to the guard and winced. "What did you do to his face?"

"I was gentler than he deserved."

"Remind me not to annoy you."

"Annoy me *again*," she corrected.

Pope started the engine. "You're not going to let that go, are you?"

"Ask me in a few weeks."

The SUV pulled out of the car park and rolled through the iron gates, joining the traffic on the main road. Pope let a truck pass before he eased their car into motion, maintaining a discreet distance. It was early evening now, and the light from streetlamps cast long shadows, filtering through the leaves of the acacia trees that lined the road. The polo club gradually receded behind them as they merged onto a busy boulevard.

The SUV navigated a roundabout, heading west toward the heart of Lagos. Pope followed, weaving through the throng of cars, motorcycles, and pedestrians who crossed the streets at will. They passed street vendors peddling everything from roasted plantains to knockoff sunglasses, their makeshift stalls set up on the sidewalks. A group of young boys played football on a patch of open ground, their shouts rising above the rumble of traffic.

The SUV slowed slightly as it approached a traffic light, and Pope instinctively eased off the accelerator, making sure to keep at least two cars between them.

The light turned green, and the SUV surged forward, cutting through a narrow street that ran parallel to a bustling market. Isabella's eyes flicked to the market stalls and the colourful fabrics that billowed in the breeze, the stacks of dried fish and pyramids of ripe mangoes.

The SUV took a sudden left, heading down a quieter, tree-lined avenue. Pope waited a few seconds before following. The buildings here were taller, their façades gleaming with modern glass and steel. They passed a high-end shopping mall, its neon sign flickering as the evening settled in, and then a sleek office complex. The traffic had thinned out, and the road ahead was clear.

They continued to follow as the SUV turned onto a street lined with embassies and diplomatic residences. The architecture shifted again, this time to a blend of colonial and contemporary styles. Tall gates and lush, manicured gardens surrounded the buildings. They followed the SUV down a long, tree-lined boulevard until it eventually slowed, pulling into the driveway of an imposing building. Isabella read the name on the sign out front: The Lagos Continental.

"There we go," she said.

The building stood tall against the city's glittering skyline. It dominated the surrounding area, with clean lines of glass and steel stretching upward, reflecting the lights from its neighbours. The ground floor was elegantly designed, with a broad driveway leading up to a grand entrance under a gleaming, curved overhang. Valets moved briskly, directing cars, while uniformed doormen welcomed guests.

Pope brought their car to a stop just down the street, out of view of the entrance. They watched as the SUV was driven off by the valet to a side parking area, leaving the guard to disappear into the lobby.

"Would be good to know which room he's in," Pope said.

Pope turned the engine off, and they both stepped out. The air was warm and thick, a slight breeze carrying the hum of the city. They made their way across the street and approached the hotel entrance. A doorman in a crisp uniform greeted them with a nod.

Isabella flashed a polite smile, taking the door to the side of the entrance, peering through the glass first to see if she could catch sight of the general or his guard. Pope was just behind her.

"There," she murmured.

Al-Masri had made his way to the reception desk, and they watched as he spoke briefly to the clerk, handing over an ID card. After a moment, the clerk nodded and handed him a small envelope. The general glanced around the lobby before heading toward a bank of elevators.

"He's going upstairs," Pope said. "Stay here. I'll message you."

Pope left her side, jogging across the lobby to wait for the next lift with the general and his guard.

Isabella wasn't prepared to wait.

She was willing to bet the general would be staying in one of the penthouses. She saw a door marked Private and, gambling that it would offer an alternative way up the building, opened it with the kickplate and went inside. She was on a service landing. The walls were painted a dull beige, stained from years of neglect, and the faint scent of industrial cleaner lingered in the air. The floor was covered with scuffed linoleum tiles, and she noticed signs of wear along the edges where equipment had been pushed through countless times. A dull hum emanated from somewhere further down the hallway, likely the building's ventilation system.

There was an lift marked with a warning sign that it was for staff use only, and, next to that, a metal staircase spiralled up to the higher floors. Overhead, harsh fluorescent lights flickered occasionally, casting unsettling shadows against the walls.

Isabella paused to listen, but there was no sound of footsteps or voices. She ran up the stairs without stopping, and, even with her physical gifts, she was still out of breath when she got to the top. She opened the door and looked outside into the elevator lobby. The hallway stretched out in both directions, lined with soft, cream-coloured carpet that muffled the sound of her steps. It looked like it probably skirted the building in a rectangular route, with rooms on either side. Dim wall sconces cast a warm, golden glow; she took a moment to look up and down the corridor, scanning the numbers on the doors. Each room was marked by a small brass plaque, the numbers polished to a shine: even on the right, odd on the left.

She felt her phone buzz in her pocket and took it out to see that Pope had texted her.

>> Where are you?

She called him back. "Can you speak?"

"You're out of breath," he said. "Please don't say you—"

"Top floor," she cut over him.

"What? I told you to—"

"I'm not just going to sit and wait. Where are you?"

"Still on the ground floor. They wouldn't let me get in the lift."

Isabella heard the ding of an lift as it reached the floor. She ducked back into the stairwell, closing the door to leave just a crack that she could look through.

She heard the general's voice as he came out, and saw him walk past, his phone pressed to his ear. The guard followed two or three paces behind him.

"He's here," she said.

"Bella, you—"

"This is our best chance," she said.

"*Bella.*"

"Get the car ready. I'll call you."

She ended the call, put the phone in her pocket and opened the door again.

The general and the guard were halfway down the corridor, following it in an anti-clockwise direction.

They went around to the left.

Isabella moved quietly, her eyes darting to each room as she passed, making a mental note of anything that seemed out of place. She tried to look like she belonged there, just another guest on her way to her room. The last thing she needed was to draw attention to herself.

She passed a housekeeping cart left unattended near the end of the hallway—the faint scent of cleaning products lingering—and continued down the corridor.

She turned left, like they had.

She kept close to the wall, her eyes narrowing as she tried to spot any signs of heightened security. Nothing. No guards, no cameras beyond the standard ones mounted on the ceiling. Al-Masri was cautious, but it looked like he trusted that his location was secure enough.

She turned the corner and spotted a double door on the right, different from the rest: more ornate, with a brass knocker and a 'Do Not Disturb' sign hanging from the handle. That had to be it. It was in the corner of the building, suggesting a suite.

The faint ding of the elevator's arrival echoed softly behind her, and then she heard the sound of voices. Someone else was coming.

Al-Masri took out a key card, held it against the reader next to the double doors and, as Isabella heard the buzz of the lock, opened the doors and went inside. The guard held the door for a moment, speaking with the general with his back to Isabella.

The voices were still coming her way.

Isabella was trapped between the newcomers and the guard.

The voices—both male—drew closer. Two men, speaking in Arabic. Isabella glanced at the reflection in the glass panes of the window at the end of the corridor and saw the two men as they approached. Big, dressed in suits, laughing at a joke one had shared with the other.

More of the general's guards?

She muttered a curse.

She watched in the glass as one of the newcomers stopped, opened a door and went inside.

The other man continued on.

The guard at the door to the suite had taken out his

phone and was staring at the screen, his attention still angled away from Isabella.

Isabella looked left and right and saw a door with a room service tray left outside it. She knelt down, took a dirty knife from the tray and inserted the flat edge between the door and the frame, positioning it right at the latch. Holding her breath, she angled the knife and wedged it deeper with a gentle twist. She applied pressure, pressing the latch back just enough. The lock gave a soft click as the latch released, and she pushed the door open.

She slipped inside, closing the door quietly behind her.

She called Pope.

"Isabella?"

"He's up here. At least one man outside the door, with at least two more up here."

"Abort," Pope said. "Stick with the plan. We'll do it tomorrow."

She was frustrated, but knew he was right.

"Isabella?"

"I'm coming out."

She reached for the handle at the precise moment it was opened from the outside.

She didn't have time to hide but stepped back and raised the knife in her fist.

The door pushed all the way back, and she saw him: Bashar.

88

His gaze locked onto hers, and a flicker of recognition flashed across his face.

For a moment, time seemed to stretch, the room narrowing until it felt like there was nothing but the two of them.

Shit.

Bashar froze.

Isabella didn't.

She reached for him and, with both hands, hauled him inside before he could raise the alarm. She pivoted and flung him into the room and then followed, the knife raised.

He reached a hand into his jacket to where, Isabella guessed, he had a weapon in a shoulder holster.

She bounded forward, taking one step and then another until she was able to reach out and grab Bashar's wrist. His jacket fell open, and she could see the butt of a pistol, still holstered, his fingers around it. She shoved him back, and he hit the edge of the bed, toppling back.

Bashar tried to free his hand, his face changing from one of surprise to alarm when he felt the power in Isabella's grip and realised that she was stronger than him. He changed tactics, drawing back his left fist and firing out a jab. It wasn't effective, he was on his back and punching up with his weaker hand, and Isabella was able to bring up her own hand and divert his clumsy strike.

He tried again to loosen her grip, abandoning his attempt to withdraw the pistol and then, instead, raking her face. She felt blood on her cheek but held on. She could feel the tension in his arm, his muscles bunching as he tried to wrestle free. He reared his head back and butted her, and she let go, seeing stars, and stood; he leapt up, dipping his shoulder and charging at her, the impact driving her against the wall.

Bashar's weight bore down on her, but she braced her feet and pushed back, keeping him off balance, then looped around and grabbed him again.

Bashar growled in frustration; Isabella had to end this quickly before the sound of the disturbance brought out the other guards. He twisted his body, trying to throw her off, but she moved with him, maintaining her grip. Bashar stumbled, gasping, and she used the moment to rabbit punch him in the side of the head: once, twice, three times.

She tightened her grip.

Bashar backed up, and Isabella went with him, slamming into the opposite wall. Her head snapped back and bounced off the wall, but she held on tighter. There was a side table with a vase of flowers on it, the impact jolted the table, and the vase tumbled off it, smashing against the tiled floor.

It was loud; surely the guards would have heard it.

She tightened her hold even more, leaning in to press her advantage.

His eyes were wild, his breathing ragged. She could see

his surprise—how could a girl like her be as *strong* as this? —as he tried to process the mess he was in, looking for a way out, but Isabella didn't give him a chance.

Bashar brought his free hand up and tried to claw at her face again, but she twisted her head away, blocking the swipe with her shoulder. She felt his fingers brush against her hair, but she didn't let it distract her. She encircled his throat with her arm, putting his larynx against the inside of her elbow and then tightening her grip. She grabbed her right wrist with her left hand and cinched in the choke as tightly as she could. Bashar struggled for breath, his body jerking as he realised the danger he was in and tried to pull free.

Her phone buzzed. She ignored it.

Bashar was getting weaker; Isabella was close to over-powering him.

"You had this coming," she muttered, her lips brushing against the side of his ear.

She could feel his strength fading, and then he fell forward onto his knees; Isabella shifted her weight, pressing her forearm harder against his neck, cutting off more of his airflow. Bashar's mouth opened, his lips forming silent words, but no sound came out. He clawed at her arm, his nails scraping against her skin, but his movements were losing their coordination, becoming more frantic and desperate.

The phone was still buzzing.

Bashar's eyes rolled, his legs giving way beneath him. Isabella held him up for a moment, waiting until the last bit of resistance drained away, and then she eased him down to the floor, keeping her grip tight. She felt the tension leave his muscles, his head lolling to one side; she kept the choke in place for another thirty seconds until his breathing stopped, and then she released her hold, letting his body slump against the wall.

Isabella got up, went to the door and looked through the spyhole.

Nothing.

Could she really have been lucky enough that the guards hadn't heard them?

She answered the phone.

"Isabella? What's happening?"

She stepped back, her heart pounding, watching him for a moment to make sure he was dead.

"I'm coming up."

"*Wait*," she said as she gulped for breath. "Wait."

"What happened?"

"It was one of the guards—Bashar. He came into the room where I was hiding." She took another breath and willed her heart to slow. "I'm fine."

"Him?"

"He's been better."

Isabella crouched next to Bashar's lifeless body, the muted glow from the bedside lamp casting long shadows across the room. His neck was twisted at an unnatural angle; there was no question that he was dead.

Isabella heard the sound of a door opening and closing and then muffled conversation.

"So—where have you found?"

It was Al-Masri; Isabella recognised his voice.

"Somewhere nearer the polo club."

"Because this place is *awful*," Al-Masri complained. "I can't believe they thought a room like that would be suitable for me."

"I am sorry, General."

Isabella's heart fell. Al-Masri was *leaving*.

She clenched her fists in frustration.

"The next place had better be good," Al-Masri said. "You've already wasted too much of my time."

There was a knock on the door.

Fuck.

She put her eye to the peephole and saw three men outside: the guard she had beaten before, the guard who had been with Bashar, and the general.

She was outnumbered.

But then she remembered: Bashar had a pistol.

She went back to the body, turned him over and reached down to the holster. Her fingers closed around the grip of Bashar's gun, and she withdrew it, cool and heavy in her hand. She took a steadying breath, her mind racing through the possibilities. Three men outside, and they had the advantage of strength in numbers; on the other hand, she had the element of surprise.

Now might be the best chance she would ever get to be done with Al-Masri.

The knock came again, this time harder.

One of the men outside muttered something impatiently in Arabic.

She went to the spyhole and looked through it again.

"Where is he?" Al-Masri said.

"He said he was going out," the bruised guard said over his shoulder.

Al-Masri stood with his arms folded. "Where?"

"He has a woman here."

"A whore, you mean. Does he know where we are going?"

"I told him."

"Then we will see him there. I'm not waiting."

She tightened her grip on the butt of the pistol and visualised: open the door; aim and shoot Al-Masri; track left and shoot the guard with the bruised face; track right for the other man.

The men backed away.

Isabella took a breath and centred herself.

A couple—a man and a woman—passed into and then out of view.

Al-Masri and the others were no longer there.

She held the gun behind her back and, with her left hand, reached for the door handle. She pulled it down, opened the door and put her head outside into the corridor. The couple were ambling away to the left, but the three men were nowhere to be seen. She paused in the doorway, knowing that she could pursue them but that that was not ideal: there would be witnesses now if she shot them.

She swore under her breath and went back into the room again.

"He's coming down," she reported.

"On his own?"

"With two guards. He's leaving."

"The hotel?"

"He's checking out and going somewhere else."

"Do you know where?"

"He didn't say."

Pope cursed. "It's starting to feel like we're losing control of the situation. This was worth a punt, but I think we need to abort and stick to the plan for tomorrow."

"You could follow."

"What about the body? They'll find it, Al-Masri will be told, and then he'll run."

She knew he was right. "Fine," she said reluctantly.

"We need to move it," Pope said. "We need to get him out of the hotel."

"How?"

"I'm thinking."

Isabella thought, too. "There's a housekeeping cart down the corridor."

"Big enough?"

"I think so."

"Go and get it."

"After that?"

"I'll figure it out."

89

I sabella took a last look around the room, making sure there were no obvious signs of a struggle. The vase had shattered, and the shards would need to be collected, but, apart from that, everything looked as it should. She smoothed down her clothes and crossed the room to the door. She put her eye to the peephole again, looking for any movement outside. The hallway was quiet; she carefully cracked the door open and looked left and right.

It was empty.

She put the door on the latch so it couldn't close on itself, slipped out and made her way down the hall to where she had seen the cart. It was still there: a standard housekeeping model, common in any larger hotel, made of durable black plastic, with two large yellow vinyl bags attached to either side for collecting linen and a smaller, black one for rubbish. The front had two doors that could be latched shut and, when open, allowed for the linen to be unloaded without dragging it out of the top. The cart sat on four sturdy wheels, making it easy to manoeuvre even when fully loaded. There were tools and cleaning supplies inside it: a dustpan and brush, a broom, plastic bin bags, and bottles of shampoo, conditioner and shower gel to replenish the bathrooms.

She scanned the area for any sign of staff, but the hallway remained deserted. It was a stroke of luck, and she wasn't about to waste it.

Pope's voice crackled through her AirPods. "Talk to me."

"I've got the cart. Heading back now."

She wheeled it toward Bashar's room, moving quickly but trying to keep her movements casual, as if she belonged there. The wheels squeaked faintly against the carpet, and she winced at the sound, glancing nervously around. She reached the room, pushed the cart up against the door, and slipped back inside, closing the door behind her.

She bent down, gripping Bashar under the shoulders, and with a grunt, hoisted him up enough to get him next to the cart. She opened the doors and tried to push him inside. His body was limp, and she couldn't manage it. She stepped back to survey her options, then wheeled the cart into the widest part of the room and tipped it over onto its side. She grabbed Bashar again and dragged him up until he was on top of the cart, his backside falling through the open doors. She pushed and pulled his body until, with the aid of gravity, he was inside. She moved to the bed, grabbed the bedspread and stuffed it inside so that it partially obscured the body. She went into the bathroom, collected two large towels from next to the shower, and used them to fill the remaining gaps until she was happy that his body would only be visible if someone removed the linen.

She grabbed the edges of the cart, bent her knees, and then heaved it until it was upright.

"Ready," she said.

"Take the service lift. Do you know where it is?"

"Yes," she said.

"Go down to the basement level. There's a back exit to the alley. I'll be there."

She used the dustpan and brush to clear up the shattered vase and dumped the shards, and the disturbed flowers, into the cart's rubbish bag. She pushed the cart back out into the hallway and wheeled it down to the service elevator, her pulse pounding in her ears. She pushed the button, waiting nervously as the lift arrived. The doors slid open, and she quickly manoeuvred the cart inside. She hit the button for the basement, holding her breath as the doors closed. The elevator ride was painfully slow, and she counted the floors as they ticked down.

The lift chimed, and the doors slid open to reveal the dimly lit basement. Isabella pushed the cart out, glancing around to orient herself; she saw storage rooms, utility cupboards, and housekeeping carts like the one she had taken. The smell of detergent and bleach hung heavy in the air. She spotted a large, green double door at the far end of the corridor, the emergency exit sign glowing faintly above it.

"I'm in the basement," she said. "Where are you?"

"Heading to the alley now. I'll meet you at the exit."

Isabella pushed the cart down the hall. She reached the emergency exit and hesitated, listening for any sounds on the other side. She could hear the faint hum of traffic and a distant conversation, but nothing close enough to be a threat. She pushed the door open and wheeled the cart out into the alley.

Their car was reversing into the alley. It stopped, and Pope got out.

"We'll need to put him in the boot," he said, going around to the front of the cart.

Isabella took position on one side of the cart as she and Pope prepared to lift Bashar's body out and carry it the rest of the way to the car. With a steadying breath, she gripped his shoulders while Pope took hold of his legs, and together they manoeuvred him carefully, lifting him out of the cart and onto the ground. Bashar's lifeless body felt even heavier now than she remembered, his weight cumbersome and awkward as they adjusted their grips.

Pope shot her a nod. "Ready?"

She nodded back, and they hoisted Bashar up and made their way toward the car with deliberate but unhurried steps, mindful of the occasional sound of traffic on the main street beyond the alley. Pope hit the button to open the boot, managing to balance Bashar's legs as he did so. Isabella adjusted her grip and helped slide the body inside. The suspension squeaked under the dead weight, and she winced at the sound, glancing instinctively over her shoulder to make sure they hadn't attracted any unwanted attention. She checked her surroundings, noting the faint glow of streetlights reflecting off nearby walls, but the alley was still and quiet, empty save for the two of them.

Once Bashar was in, Isabella took the bedspread and draped it over his body, tucking it neatly around him to cover any exposed parts. Pope closed the lid quietly, giving her a quick thumbs-up before heading around to the driver's side.

She slipped into the passenger seat as the engine rumbled to life, low and steady, and Pope guided the car out of the alley. He kept his speed deliberately casual, blending seamlessly into the light evening traffic as they drove away from the hotel.

"I'm annoyed," she said.

"Why?"

She gestured up to the hotel. "Because he was in there, and we blew it."

"We just got unlucky." He shook his head with certainty. "We tried, the opportunity wasn't there, so we rely on Plan A. We'll do it tomorrow at the tournament."

90

They drove out of the city until they found a quiet stretch of road between Iteku and Agelete. Pope turned onto a track that cut into the forest, slowly edging along the uneven surface until they were out of sight of the main road. They both got out and went around to the back, Pope opened the boot, and they lifted Bashar's body out, swinging it once and then twice and then a third time, releasing it so that it fell into a thick clutch of hibiscus.

Isabella wiped her hands against her shirt. There was a grim satisfaction in dealing with him this way; the beating he'd given her wouldn't have been his first, nor would it have been his last. She'd seen a sadism in his eyes that had been given free rein in Al-Masri's service, and the general would have continued to indulge it. No more. Bashar had paid the price for crossing her; his patron would be next.

Pope leaned against the side of the car. "Back to the hotel," he said. "We need to be rested for tomorrow."

A bushshrike called out somewhere in the canopy overhead.

"What's the plan?" Isabella asked.

"I'll get inside and get on the roof nice and early."

"What about me?"

"You can't be inside, can you? You said it yourself—if he sees you, it's off."

"I could take the shot."

"No," Pope said. "You can run interference if I need it, and you can pick me up once it's done."

She glared at the ground.

"I know you want to do it," he said, "but he's dead either way, isn't he?"

"Whatever," she said sullenly.

He opened the door and lowered himself into the driver's seat. "Come on. I want a beer, and then I want to get to bed."

91

Isabella found it difficult to get to sleep. The room was dark and quiet, but her mind was anything but still. It churned with fears and uncertainties, her thoughts unspooling at a speed that made it impossible to find rest. She lay on her back and stared up at the ceiling, trying to make sense of everything that had happened in the last few days.

Pope's reappearance had thrown her for a loop. She'd accepted that he was gone, made peace with it in her own way, and had plotted what she would do without him. His death had left a scar, but it had also forced her to think independently, to plan a future on her own terms. But now he was back, and everything she'd worked toward was up in the air again. They were going to have to negotiate a relationship that, while of huge importance to her—and to him, she knew—was only going to get more complicated. She wasn't the same person she'd been before. She was older, more experienced, more determined to take control of her own life. And Pope, ever the careful strategist, with his plans for her safety and his overwhelmingly protective instincts, wasn't going to easily let go of the reins. She knew the tension would build between them again, and she wasn't sure how long it would be before it snapped. His protective instincts might clash with her desire for independence, but she wasn't a child anymore. She needed to be allowed the space to figure out who she was outside of his shadow.

She turned onto her side, the sheets twisting around her legs as her thoughts turned to Charlie. There was something about him—his quiet strength, his loyalty—that drew her in, and she'd found herself developing feelings that went beyond friendship. But it was dangerous, especially for him. Charlie wasn't a part of her world, and if she let herself get too close, she'd be dragging him into something he wasn't prepared for. His run-in with his brother had been bad enough, but it was nothing compared to what might happen if people came after her and found him instead. How could she live with herself if she put him in harm's way?

And then there were Al-Masri, Aicha, Fatima, and the children. So many people whose lives intersected with hers, all of them pulling her in different directions. Her mother had always told her she couldn't allow her actions to be dictated by her emotions. Beatrix had drilled it into her head time and time again: emotions cloud judgement, make you reckless, make you vulnerable. She had warned her that if she let herself get too attached, it would only be a matter of time before she found herself in a position where she had to make a choice: save the people she cared about or save herself.

But despite knowing that her mother was right, she couldn't help feeling the weight of the decisions she had made. The children at the orphanage needed her, Fatima needed her, and who knows what had happened to Aicha.

Isabella had stepped into the fray willingly, knowing full well the risks, and now there was no turning back.

Pope had always told her that she wasn't in a position where she could allow her actions to be ruled by her feelings, and that, if she did, there would come a time when people she cared about were put in harm's way. He had explained that she would feel obliged to step in and help and that, if she did that, she would find herself in a position where she had no choice but to step out from wherever she was hiding so that the men and women who were looking for her were given an opportunity to close in that otherwise might not have been there. He had been right about that, just like he was right about most things, and now she worried that her hard-won independence was under threat.

She sighed, frustrated by the tangled mess of her thoughts, knowing that sleep would be difficult. The world was closing in on her, the stakes getting higher, and she wasn't sure how much longer she could keep all the plates spinning before something—or someone—broke.

92

Isabella and Pope sat across from each other, the hotel restaurant bustling around them as guests enjoyed their breakfasts. The smell of fresh bread and the hum of nearby conversations did nothing to ease the knot that had settled in Isabella's stomach. She stirred her coffee absently, her mind racing with thoughts about what they were about to do. She knew Pope well enough to know that he'd never normally agree to an operation with this little preparation, and the knowledge that he was only doing it because of her stubbornness made her feel a pang of guilt. He'd always been cautious and methodical, and this rushed, high-risk plan was the opposite of everything he stood for. Yet here they were, ready to push ahead with it anyway, because he knew that if he didn't, she would do it alone. She glanced up at him. It wasn't that he didn't trust her, it was that he couldn't bear the thought of her getting hurt. That only made her guilt worse. He was putting himself on the line for her, taking a risk he would never normally consider.

"Last run-through," he said.

She finished her coffee and put the cup back in the saucer. "Okay."

"We drive to the club. I get inside over the fence at the back and set up position on the shed overlooking the field. What about you?"

"Wait in the car park," she said, her tone clipped as though this wasn't the hundredth time they've gone over the plan.

"Ready to move," he added. "I'll take the shot, leave the rifle and exfiltrate the same way. You pick me up, and we leave town."

"I know all that," she protested. She hated feeling like he was treating her like a novice, even if she knew it was just his way of making sure they were both on the same page.

"I want to make sure it's clear," Pope replied.

"You want to make sure I do as I'm told," Isabella said, rolling her eyes.

"That too," he said.

ISABELLA SLID into the driver's seat of their car. She glanced at Pope, who was already checking his gear in the passenger seat. His expression was rigid.

She started the engine and pulled out of the hotel car park, merging into the flow of traffic that clogged the street. The noise of the city buzzed in her ears, but she tuned it out. Her eyes flicked to Pope again; his silence was heavy, full of thoughts that neither of them had the time nor the inclination to voice.

They crossed one of the busy bridges, the neon signs of the city reflecting off the water below, and Isabella felt the weight of the moment press down on her.

"You know the spot?" Pope asked, breaking the silence.

"Yeah," she said, gripping the wheel a little tighter as they neared their destination. "The side road just past the trees that runs along the fence. I'll drop you off there."

Pope nodded.

The streets gradually grew quieter as they moved away from the centre of the city. The towering buildings gave way to smaller shops and houses, and eventually, the polo club came into view.

Isabella slowed the car as they approached the turnoff. The road narrowed, lined with overgrown bushes and trees that provided some cover. She pulled off the main road.

"This is it," she said, pulling the car to a stop.

Pope opened the door and got out. He collected the bag with the broken-down parts of the rifle and slung it over his shoulder. "Comms check when I'm over the fence. Stay sharp. I'll see you when it's done."

Isabella nodded and watched as he disappeared into the shadows between the trees.

She put the car into gear and pulled back onto the main road. Her heart beat a little faster as she drove toward the car park, trying to ignore the nagging voice in the back of her mind that was whispering all the things that could go wrong. She couldn't afford to think like that, not now.

Isabella heard the static buzz of the radio, then the familiar click and then Pope's voice. "Angel, this is Archangel. Comms check. Over."

Isabella adjusted her earpiece and pressed the transmit button. "Archangel, I hear you. Five by five. Over."

"Good. No interference on my end. I'm over the fence and heading for the shed. It's quiet—looks good. Stay sharp. Over."

Isabella glanced in the rear-view mirror. "Roger that. Waiting for your move. Out."

The club's main entrance loomed ahead. Isabella slowed the car as she approached the entrance, blending in with the other vehicles arriving for the tournament. She gave a quick nod to the security guards at the gate, who waved her through without a second glance.

She pulled into a spot near the back of the car park, far enough from the entrance that she could wait without drawing attention but close enough that she could move quickly when Pope gave the signal. She shut off the engine and leaned back in her seat, her eyes scanning the rows of cars and the polo field beyond.

93

Isabella shifted in the driver's seat, glancing at the dashboard clock. Two hours had passed since Pope had gone over the fence and disappeared into the polo club. Al-Masri had arrived just a few minutes after she had parked the car, his black SUV sliding into a space a hundred and fifty metres away. Isabella had watched him disembark with itchy fingers, tempted almost to the point of distraction by the thought of intercepting him, pulling her pistol and doing him there and then. She hadn't. Pope had radioed her to check in just as her hand had drifted to the door handle, and she had stopped, reminding herself that they had a plan, and it would be best to stick to it. She watched Al-Masri instead: he was laughing and joking with another man—a teammate, perhaps—while his security followed behind him.

She drummed her fingers on the steering wheel, eyes flicking to the entrance of the club every few minutes, her mind replaying the plan on loop. The car park was quiet save for the occasional arriving car; no one seemed to pay any attention to her rented car.

She lifted the radio to her mouth, ready to check in with Pope, when his voice crackled through the earpiece, breaking the silence.

"Angel, this is Archangel." Pope's voice was low and tense. "We've got a problem. Over."

Isabella straightened in her seat. "I'm here. What's going on? Over."

There was a pause, just long enough to make her uneasy; then Pope spoke again. "The general had a conversation with one of his men. Looks like they've got wind of something. He's pulling out. Over."

Isabella swore under her breath, glancing toward the club entrance again, her mind already racing through the implications. "Do you think they've made you? Over."

"Unlikely," Pope replied. "But he's spooked. He's heading for the exit with his guards, moving quickly. Looks like someone warned him—might be the guy from last night; maybe they've worked out what happened. How thorough were you when you cleaned the room? Over."

"Pretty thorough."

"Are you sure?"

She paused. "I was rushed. There was a vase that broke —maybe I didn't get all of it. Over."

"Doesn't matter," Pope murmured. "You need to get eyes on him. He's with his men, heading toward the SUV on the east side of the lot. If he leaves, it'll be on you to keep him under surveillance until I can get to him. Over."

"Copy that. I'll intercept."

"You'll follow," he corrected. "I'll find transport, and you can guide me in. Tell me you understand, Bella. Over."

The general turned the corner and entered the lot. He moved with purpose, his head swivelling from side to side; whatever had spooked him, it was clear he didn't feel safe here any longer. He was with two of his guards, the men flanking him as they made their way toward a black SUV parked near the edge of the lot.

"Bella—*tell me you understand.*"

"I understand. Over."

Al-Masri climbed into the SUV, the door slamming shut as his guards took up positions in a second vehicle just behind. The convoy began to roll forward, slowly at first, then picking up speed as it headed for the exit.

She put the radio down on the seat beside her, her heart pounding. The plan was unravelling, and they were running out of time. The general was scared; it meant he would be more difficult to reach.

They were close. Too close to let him slip away now.

94

Isabella idled the engine of their car and waited for Al-Masri to move off. The small convoy turned onto the drive and then raced down it toward the main road; she let them go and then pulled out, sliding into the line of traffic a few cars back. Her hands were sweaty, and she could feel the thunder of her pulse.

"Isabella," Pope said in her ear, "report. Over."

"I'm on him," she said. "He's heading toward the highway—looks like he's aiming straight for the airport. Over."

"Copy that. Keep your distance, but don't let him out of sight. Over."

"No shit," she said, partly amused and partly irritated that he felt he still had to remind her of the basics.

"I'm over the fence," he said. "I'll find transport and rendezvous with you. Out."

The SUV cut through traffic, its tinted windows concealing the occupants. The trail vehicle—a BMW—was directly behind, and Isabella counted three men inside it.

Traffic thickened as they left the quieter suburban

streets, merging onto a busier avenue. Isabella clenched her jaw, scanning the surroundings for any advantage: a red light, a bottleneck, *something* she could exploit. But Al-Masri's driver was moving with intent, slicing through lanes with no regard for the angry blasts of the horns from the drivers left in their wake.

"Isabella." Pope's voice crackled in her ear.

"I'm here. No change. Over."

"I've just checked on the map. I can see you. Over."

"You're tracking me? Over."

"I might have linked to your GPS last night—just in case. Out."

She couldn't help herself responding, "Jesus, Pope"

"Just as well I did," he said.

She ground her teeth; he was still as paternalistic as ever.

"You're going to hit traffic," he said. "Looks like there's construction—five miles north of your position. The roads are red. They'll have to slow down. Over."

She nodded. Her eyes were fixed on the dark silhouette of Al-Masri's SUV as it sped down the road. "Roger. That might be the opening."

"Do not engage. Acknowledge. Over."

"Yes, Dad."

"Isabella—I'm serious."

"So am I," she said. "Where are you? Over."

"Fifteen minutes behind you."

"So you won't get to me in time, will you?"

The convoy surged forward, taking advantage of a break in traffic.

"Probably not."

"So we'll lose him. I know what you're going to say, and

you know I'm going to ignore you. It has to be me. He gets away if I just stick behind him like this."

Isabella pressed down on the accelerator, careful to maintain her distance yet keeping them within sight.

"All right," Pope said at last. "Fine. The roadworks will be your best bet. But do it carefully. I'll be there as fast as I can. Out."

Five miles until the traffic would thicken, she repeated to herself, visualising the road ahead. The minutes and miles ticked by; her hands were steady on the wheel as she matched the pace of the traffic around her.

There.

Flashing signs announced the construction zone, forcing all lanes to merge into a single, narrow path flanked by concrete barriers. Traffic slowed as vehicles funnelled into the crawl. Isabella could see the SUV's brake lights flaring as it was forced to reduce speed, taking up its place in line as the lanes converged.

The SUV was boxed in on either side by cars.

Now or never.

She had one shot, and she'd have to act fast.

She swung the steering wheel to the left and accelerated, overtaking the backup vehicle before it could react. She manoeuvred her car up alongside the SUV, pressing in close. The guard in the passenger seat looked over at her in surprise as she yanked the wheel and sideswiped the SUV's rear quarter.

The impact was enough to jolt the car sideways, its driver wrestling to regain control. The backup vehicle honked furiously but was blocked from advancing by Isabella's car.

She turned the wheel and hit the SUV again, harder this time, sending it veering toward the barrier on the right. The driver tried to correct, but the narrow lane left him with no room. The car scraped along the barrier, sparks flying as metal ground against concrete.

Isabella hit the brakes and leapt out, drawing her weapon.

The rear door of the trail car flew open, and one of Al-Masri's guards disembarked, gun in hand. Isabella dropped him with a quick shot to the shoulder, sending him crumpling to the ground.

The driver of the BMW opened his door and got out; Isabella shot him through the window.

She turned back to face the SUV, watching as the general opened the door on the other side and ran.

She heard Pope's voice again: "Isabella?"

"He's running. I'm going after him."

Isabella pivoted, her eyes locking onto Al-Masri as he bolted across the narrow lane, weaving through the stalled traffic. The sound of horns and shouting drivers faded into the background as she focused solely on him, her pulse quickening as she moved into pursuit.

Al-Masri darted through the construction, kicking up dust as he slipped between the barriers. She sprinted after him. The uneven terrain made the pursuit difficult, with broken asphalt and scattered gravel threatening to trip her, but she didn't falter; this was her one chance, and she wasn't about to let him escape.

Al-Masri glanced over his shoulder, his eyes wild with fear. He shoved a construction worker aside, sending the man sprawling, and ducked under a low scaffold. Isabella lengthened her stride at the same time as quickening her pace; she was lightning fast, and he was older and slower and never stood a chance of staying ahead of her for long.

They reached a narrower section of the site, where half-finished concrete walls rose on either side. Isabella used the opportunity to close in, cutting the distance with a burst of speed. He was just metres away now, his heavy breathing loud enough for her to hear.

He ducked around another barrier, his pace slowing as exhaustion began to take its toll. Isabella rounded the corner after him, gun raised, her finger steady on the trigger. She saw his hesitation—a single, faltering step—before he tried to scramble up a small embankment at the side of the road, hoping to put some distance between them.

Isabella closed in. Al-Masri staggered against a stack of concrete blocks, chest heaving from the chase, his gaze darting around for any means of escape. His eyes widened as he noticed her, but there was no fear—only a hardened resolve and a glint of arrogance. He straightened up, squaring his shoulders and preparing to fight.

Isabella looked down at the gun and put it aside.

Al-Masri sneered at her, his face heavy with contempt. He swung first, a heavy punch aimed at her head, but Isabella ducked, slipping to the side. She caught his wrist with one hand and twisted it sharply. The general's face contorted in shock and pain as her grip tightened, far stronger than he'd expected.

He tried to break free, twisting and jerking his arm, but Isabella didn't let go. She stepped in closer, pulling him off balance and sending him crashing to his knees. Al-Masri looked up at her, his gaze flickering with disbelief.

"What... are you?" he gasped, struggling against her hold.

He surged up, swinging his other arm in a desperate attempt to break her grip. Isabella absorbed the blow without flinching, feeling it graze her shoulder. She released his wrist, only to pivot and drive a knee into his abdomen. The blow knocked the wind out of him, and he doubled over, coughing and gasping for air.

She grabbed him by the collar, hauling him upright with ease.

His eyes widened, a spark of fear now evident as he realised he was badly out of his depth. He threw another punch, but it was wild and uncoordinated, a move born out of desperation rather than skill. Isabella sidestepped it, grabbed his arm, and twisted it behind his back with a sickening pop.

Al-Masri screamed.

"Why are you doing this?" he spat, panting heavily.

He tried to turn his head to look at her, but Isabella only leaned in. "You had this coming the moment you threatened the kids at the orphanage."

She drove the point of her elbow into the back of his neck, sending him sprawling to the ground. He lay still, his breathing shallow and ragged, every ounce of fight gone. She waited, watching him struggle to lift his head, to find any last scrap of defiance or strength, but there was nothing left.

She picked up the gun from where she'd put it down.

Al-Masri's gaze met hers one final time, and she saw his confusion; she had a raw power, something that made no sense to him. His mouth moved as if to speak, but no sound came.

She held his gaze for a second longer and then shot him.

"Isabella?" Pope's voice crackled through her earpiece.

She stood over him, her breathing steady, barely touched by the exertion. "It's done. I got him."

"Get away from the road. Keep going north. There's a shopping mall half a mile away. I've got another car. I'll pick you up there. Out."

EPILOGUE

Isabella felt the tension easing from her shoulders as they pulled into the car park of the small, unassuming hotel just across the border in Togo. They had driven through the night, leaving the chaos of Lagos behind and slipping out of Nigeria under a haze of adrenaline and exhaustion.

"Thank God for that," Pope said, leaning back in the seat. "I thought we'd never get here."

The drive had taken six hours but had felt twice as long. Pope had picked up Isabella not far from the spot where she'd shot Al-Masri, and, as they'd raced west, every mile of the road between them and the city felt like another layer of safety.

Pope had navigated their way through back roads to avoid the possibility of checkpoints, always keeping an eye out for anyone who might have been trailing them. They'd steered well clear of the official crossing and approached the border under the cover of darkness, following a narrow unpaved track Pope had mapped out earlier. The track was barely visible, cutting through dense thickets of underbrush and trees, where only the occasional worn tyre tracks spoke of the smugglers who had used it before them. Pope had explained: he had travelled along the route when he had exfiltrated from Nigeria at the conclusion of the business that had brought him here before, and had been banking on it still being passable. They had both exhaled with relief when they saw that it was. The terrain had been rough, and Isabella had gripped the dashboard as the car jolted and rattled over rocks and uneven ground. They kept the head-lights off, relying instead on a handheld flashlight Pope occasionally flicked on to illuminate obstacles ahead. There was one point where they had to slow to a crawl to avoid a group of local farmers returning from their fields; they cast curious glances but paid them no mind.

Finally, after nearly an hour of slow progress, Pope steered them across the invisible line into Togo, marked only by a change in the road's texture and a distant glow from the nearest village.

The hotel was modest, a faded structure with peeling paint and a cracked sign above the entrance, but it was exactly what they needed: anonymous, quiet, and far from anyone who might be searching for them. Isabella looked around, her senses still heightened, half expecting some-thing out of place. But the sounds here were calm: distant laughter, the murmur of voices, the rustle of palm leaves in the breeze.

They checked in, paying in cash and avoiding eye contact, and made their way up to their adjoining rooms on the second floor. Isabella sank onto the bed and allowed the weight of the past few days to crash over her.

She was asleep within minutes.

Isabella awoke five hours later. She showered, put on her dusty clothes from yesterday and saw the rust-coloured splatter of dried blood on her shirt. She went to the bathroom and scrubbed the stain in the sink, the water turning faint red. Isabella hadn't been cut; the blood must have belonged to Al-Masri. The shirt was wet, but the morning was already hot, and she knew it wouldn't take long to dry.

She had noticed a small business centre when they checked in, and went down to see if it was empty. The space was tucked away in a corner, equipped with a few computers, a printer, and a modest setup meant for guests needing to check email or print boarding passes. It was early, and the centre was empty. She took a seat at one of the terminals, reached into her pocket and took out the USB drive containing her secure operating system. She inserted it into the port and restarted the machine, waiting for it to boot into her custom environment, separate from the hotel's network.

Isabella navigated to her bank's website, pulled up her account balance and took a moment to consider the figure. She'd saved enough of the money Beatrix had left her to sustain her modest lifestyle, but she had bolstered the balance with the fees from Broker, and, anyway, she could manage with less.

She initiated a transfer, carefully checking the details of Fatima's account. She hesitated for a moment, her finger hovering over the confirmation button, then pressed down firmly. She wired half of her balance, knowing it was going somewhere it would make a real difference.

She opened her email and saw that she had a message

from Charlie. He told her he hoped she was okay, that he had been thinking about her, and, when she was able, he would like to see her again. She started to compose a reply, but realised, as her fingers were suspended above the keyboard, that she had no idea what to say. She found her thoughts going back to Chloe and Jean-Claude, both murdered by the Chinese asset sent to bring her in, and knew that she would be putting Charlie in grave danger every time she saw him. And worse, she couldn't even tell him why; there was no way of explaining why she was so valuable, and what the people looking for her would do to find her, not without admitting that she was different from him in ways that would be impossible for him to understand.

She closed the window with her undrafted reply and then deleted his email.

It was better this way.

She was maudlin as she logged out, erased all traces of her activity from the system, and removed her USB drive, tucking it back into her pocket.

ISABELLA WAS GOING BACK UP to her room when Pope came down the stairs.

"Morning," he said.

"Morning."

"Sleep well?"

"Not bad," she said, deciding there was no point in burdening him with the nightmares that had jolted her awake three separate times.

"Want to get some breakfast?"

She nodded.

They walked together to the hotel's small dining area, where a buffet was set up, offering local and international choices. The aroma of fresh coffee drifted through the air, mingling with the scent of warm pastries and spices from the local dishes. Isabella picked up a plate and surveyed the spread. There were baskets of fresh croissants, pain au chocolat, and crusty bread rolls next to a selection of local jams and honey. Further down the line, they found a colourful display of fresh fruit: pineapple, mango, and papaya sliced and ready to eat. There was also a warm section, offering spicy scrambled eggs, grilled tomatoes, and fried plantains, alongside more typical options like bacon and sausages.

Isabella filled her plate with a croissant, some mango slices, and a spoonful of the scrambled eggs; Pope piled his higher, adding fried plantains and a serving of the spiced eggs with a thick slice of bread.

They found a quiet corner and sat across from each other, the early sunlight filtering through the windows and casting a soft glow over the table. They ate in comfortable silence. Isabella appreciated the simplicity of the moment and found peace in how quickly the two of them had fallen back into their unusual relationship: like father and daughter, but with baroque additions making it something else entirely.

"We'll need to move on today," Pope said. "We're too close to the border. I don't think it's urgent, but we'll stand out here."

"Where were you thinking?"

"I don't know Togo very well," he said. "I was in and out of here in a day the last time. I was thinking the Ivory Coast or Liberia. I've been to both, and I know them reasonably well."

"Not Marrakesh?"

"No," he said. "Not anymore. You've already been located there, and now you'll have the government looking for you, too."

She nodded, looking down glumly at her plate.

"Do you have anything there you need?"

She shook her head. The only thing she cared about was the pendant that her mother had given her, and that was still around her neck. She was sad to leave the riad and the city, but she knew Pope was right; she couldn't go back now. She was sad that she would never be able to visit the orphanage, too, but at least the money she had sent would be put to good use.

"I was thinking," she said. "We'll need money."

"Some," he said. "But Liberia's not an expensive place to live."

"I wasn't thinking about us. I sent some money to the orphanage this morning. It was a lot—but it won't be enough for what they need."

"And you'd like to send more?"

She nodded.

"You're thinking about Broker?"

"No," she said. "I don't think we can trust him. I think he lied to me."

"I can see why you'd think that," he said.

"Do you know anyone else?"

"No," Pope said. "That's a very particular line of work. There aren't that many people offering the kind of jobs we'd find acceptable."

"Why couldn't we look for work ourselves?"

He frowned. "How'd you mean?"

"I mean there are people everywhere you look who are out of their depth. People who are being abused or taken advantage of. My last job with Broker was to eliminate two people in Croatia—"

"The Vaughns," he said.

"You know about that?"

He gave a tilt of his head.

"Of *course* you do," she said, snorting with fake indignation.

"Do I think there are people who we could help?" He eyed her over the rim of his coffee cup. "Yes. I do. But they might not be able to pay for the help."

"They wouldn't," she said, "but I'm thinking we could take our payment from whoever it is deserves our attention."

"Steal from the rich and give to the poor?"

She shrugged. "Why not?"

"Might be a little too noble for me," he said.

She grinned. "Bollocks."

Pope took a moment to consider her proposal. "It's risky. Going after people who have resources worth taking means they could put a price on our heads."

"I know," Isabella replied, her gaze steady. "But if they're corrupt, if they're taking advantage of people who can't fight back, then they deserve to lose what they've got. We can do some good and keep ourselves funded at the same time."

"And fund the orphanage."

"And that."

He looked out the window, watching the sparse activity on the quiet street outside. "It's... unconventional. Not exactly what I had in mind when I thought of keeping you safe."

"Since when have we ever done things conventionally?"

He chuckled, shaking his head. "Touché." He set his

coffee cup down, eyes serious as he met her gaze. "All right. But we'll need to be careful—*very* careful—and we'll have to pick our targets wisely. No sense in drawing unnecessary attention. And I'll want to have the final say."

"Deal," she said.

She extended her hand, and Pope took it.

"So," she said, "where do we start?"

Isabella Rose and Michael Pope will return.

Building a relationship with my readers is the very best thing about writing. Join my Reader Club for information on new books and deals plus a free copy of Milton's battle with the Mafia and an assassin called Tarantula.

You can get your content **for free**, by signing up at my website.

Just visit www.markjdawson.com.

ALSO BY MARK DAWSON

IN THE JOHN MILTON SERIES

The Cleaner

Sharon Warriner is a single mother in the East End of London, fearful that she's lost her young son to a life in the gangs. After John Milton saves her life, he promises to help. But the gang, and the charismatic rapper who leads it, is not about to cooperate with him.

<u>Buy The Cleaner</u>

Saint Death

John Milton has been off the grid for six months. He surfaces in Ciudad Juárez, Mexico, and immediately finds himself drawn into a vicious battle with the narco-gangs that control the borderlands.

<u>Buy Saint Death</u>

The Driver

When a girl he drives to a party goes missing, John Milton is worried. Especially when two dead bodies are discovered and the police start treating him as their prime suspect.

<u>Buy The Driver</u>

Ghosts

John Milton is blackmailed into finding his predecessor as Number One. But she's a ghost, too, and just as dangerous as him. He finds himself in deep trouble, playing the Russians against the British in a desperate attempt to save the life of his oldest friend.

<u>Buy Ghosts</u>

The Sword of God

On the run from his own demons, John Milton treks through the Michigan wilderness into the town of Truth. He's not looking for trouble, but trouble's looking for him. He finds himself up against a small-town cop who has no idea with whom he is dealing, and no idea how dangerous he is.

<u>Buy The Sword of God</u>

Salvation Row

Milton finds himself in New Orleans, returning a favour that saved his life during Katrina. When a lethal adversary from his past takes an interest in his business, there's going to be hell to pay.

Buy Salvation Row

Headhunters

Milton barely escaped from Avi Bachman with his life. But when the Mossad's most dangerous renegade agent breaks out of a maximum security prison, their second fight will be to the finish.

Buy Headhunters

The Ninth Step

Milton's attempted good deed becomes a quest to unveil corruption at the highest levels of government and murder at the dark heart of the criminal underworld. Milton is pulled back into the game, and that's going to have serious consequences for everyone who crosses his path.

Buy The Ninth Step

The Jungle

John Milton is no stranger to the world's seedy underbelly. But when the former British Secret Service agent comes up against a ruthless human trafficking ring, he'll have to fight harder than ever to conquer the evil in his path.

Buy The Jungle

Blackout

A message from Milton's past leads him to Manila and a

confrontation with an adversary he thought he would never meet again. Milton finds himself accused of murder and imprisoned inside a brutal Filipino jail can he escape, uncover the truth and gain vengeance for his friend?

Buy Blackout

The Alamo

A young boy witnesses a murder in a New York subway restroom. Milton finds him, and protects him from corrupt cops and the ruthless boss of a local gang.

Buy The Alamo

Redeemer

Milton is in Brazil, helping out an old friend with a close protection business. When a young girl is kidnapped, he finds himself battling a local crime lord to get her back.

Buy Redeemer

Sleepers

A sleepy English town. A murdered Russian spy. Milton and Michael Pope find themselves chasing the assassins to Moscow.

Buy Sleepers

Twelve Days

Milton checks back in with Elijah Warriner, but finds himself caught up in a fight to save him from a jealous and dangerous former friend.

Buy Twelve Days

Bright Lights

All Milton wants to do is take his classic GTO on a coast-to-coast road trip. But he can't ignore the woman on the side of the road in need of help. The decision to get involved leads to a tussle with a murderous cartel that he thought he had put behind him.

Buy Bright Lights

The Man Who Never Was

John Milton is used to operating in the shadows, weaving his way through dangerous places behind a fake identity. Now, to avenge the death of a close friend, he must wear his mask of deception once more.

Buy The Man Who Never Was

Killa City

John Milton has a nose for trouble. He can smell it a mile away. And when he witnesses a suspicious altercation between a young man and two thugs in a car auction parking lot, he can't resist getting involved.

Buy Killa City

Ronin

Milton travels to Bali in search of a new identity. He meets a young woman who has been forced to work for the Yakuza in Japan, and finds himself drawn into danger in an attempt to keep her safe.

Buy Ronin

Never Let Me Down Again

A human rights activist has vanished without a trace and his dying mother is desperate to know the truth. When the mysterious disappearance leads Milton all the way to the Western Isles of Scotland, he sees an opportunity to find an old friend and finally make amends for a mistake that cost him dearly. Milton is determined to track both men down, wherever his search may lead.

Buy Never Let Me Down Again

Bulletproof

Captured and imprisoned by the organisation he once worked for, Milton must do one last job in exchange for his freedom. Bullheaded billionaire fixer Tristan Huxley is brokering a weapons deal between Russia and India. He needs protection and he wants Milton by his side. Huxley has trusted Milton with his life before but these days his world is more decadent and his enemies more dangerous, in ways that nobody could ever have suspected.

Buy Bulletproof

Uppercut

John Milton is on the run again. Chasing clues to help him understand the new risks he faces, he finds himself in Dublin. Before he knows it, he is involved with a woman who has fallen foul of a dangerous local family.

Buy Uppercut

Bloodlands

John Milton is on a mission that will bring him face-to-face with enemies old and new. When his friend, Alex Hicks, finds himself pursued by mysterious adversaries, the two men are thrust back into the web of international espionage.

Buy Bloodlands

IN THE BEATRIX ROSE SERIES

In Cold Blood

Beatrix Rose was the most dangerous assassin in an off-the-books government kill squad until her former boss betrayed her. A decade later, she emerges from the Hong Kong underworld with payback on her mind. They gunned down her husband and kidnapped her daughter, and now the debt needs to be repaid. It's a blood feud she didn't start but she is going to finish.

<u>Buy In Cold Blood</u>

Blood Moon Rising

There were six names on Beatrix's Death List and now there are four. She's going to account for the others, one by one, even if it kills her. She has returned from Somalia with another target in her sights. Bryan Duffy is in Iraq, surrounded by mercenaries, with no easy way to get to him and no easy way to get out. And Beatrix has other issues that need to be addressed. Will Duffy prove to be one kill too far?

Buy Blood Moon Rising

Blood and Roses

Beatrix Rose has worked her way through her Kill List. Four are dead, just two are left. But now her foes know she has them in her sights and the hunter has become the hunted.

Buy Blood and Roses

The Dragon and the Ghost

Beatrix Rose flees to Hong Kong after the murder of her husband and the kidnapping of her child. She needs money. The local triads have it. What could possibly go wrong?

Buy The Dragon and the Ghost

Tempest

Two people adrift in a foreign land, Beatrix Rose and Danny Nakamura need all the help they can get. A storm is coming. Can they help each other survive it and find their children before time runs out for both of them?

Buy Tempest

Phoenix

She does Britain's dirty work, but this time she needs help. Beatrix Rose, meet John Milton...

<u>Buy Phoenix</u>

IN THE ISABELLA ROSE SERIES

The Angel

Isabella Rose is recruited by British intelligence after a terrorist attack on Westminster.

<u>Buy The Angel</u>

The Asset

Isabella Rose, the Angel, is used to surprises, but being abducted is an unwelcome novelty. She's relying on Michael Pope, the head of the top-secret Group Fifteen, to get her back.

<u>Buy The Asset</u>

The Agent

Isabella Rose is on the run, hunted by the very people she had been hired to work for. Trained killer Isabella and former handler Michael Pope are forced into hiding in India and, when a mysterious informer passes them clues on the whereabouts of Pope's family, the prey see an opportunity to become the predators.

<u>Buy The Agent</u>

The Assassin

Ciudad Juárez, Mexico, is the most dangerous city in the world. And when a mission to break the local cartel's grip goes wrong, Isabella Rose, the Angel, finds herself on the wrong side of prison bars. Fearing the worst, Isabella plays her only remaining card...

<u>Buy The Assassin</u>

The Avenger

Living under new identities in rural France, Isabella Rose and Michael Pope are trying to lay low. Tired of hiding, all Isabella wants is the chance to live an ordinary life. But Isabella is an extraordinary young woman and the people pursuing her will never, ever, give up. Her unique abilities have attracted the attention of the Academy of Military Science in Beijing. And it's not only Isabella who needs to stay in the shadows. Pope has his fair share of enemies and a family that he's desperate to protect.

<u>Buy The Avenger</u>

Pretty Face

Isabella is building a new life in Marrakesh, supporting herself with contract work and finally looking to put down roots. But when one of her contracts isn't quite what it seems, things quickly descend into chaos.

<u>Buy Pretty Face</u>

IN THE CHARLIE COOPER SERIES

Sandstorm

Group Fifteen operative and ex-MI6 officer Charlie Cooper is working undercover as a political negotiator. Attending a conference surrounded by diplomats, businessmen and lobbyists, nobody would suspect what he really does for a living. Also in their midst is Aisha, a Saudi activist whose protests against human rights abuses have made her an enemy of her country's regime.

Buy Sandstorm

The Chameleon

Masquerading as an analyst, Cooper manipulates his way into the company and soon finds himself en route to Istanbul. The stage is set for a high-octane showdown on Sidorov's private island. With geopolitical tensions on a knife's edge, Cooper must navigate a labyrinth of deception and danger to complete his mission.

Buy The Chameleon

Blood Brothers

Cooper travels to Israel to find his estranged half-brother, Freddy, who has mysteriously disappeared. Freddy's ties to NetGuardian, a cybersecurity firm implicated in dubious activities, propel Cooper into a dangerous web of corporate espionage, state-of-the-art surveillance technology, and the ruthless world of intelligence.

Buy Blood Brothers

Dead of Winter

Charlie Cooper is sent to Prague to investigate - and eliminate - the leader of a group of far right hooligans guilty of the murder of an Interpol agent. Cooper is on his final warning and is expected to get in and out with minimal fuss, leaving just the body of his target in his wake.

Buy Dead of Winter

Code Blue

Cooper is thrust into a high-stakes mission when a fellow operative, codenamed NORTH STAR, vanishes in Macao. The trail leads to a shadowy team of Russian mercenaries with a chilling agenda: to expose Group Fifteen, the clandestine organisation that operates beyond the reach of conventional intelligence agencies.

Buy Code Blue

North Star

After barely escaping an assassination attempt in Iceland, NORTH STAR, a former Group Fifteen operative turned Russian asset, vanishes. Driven by guilt and a thirst for revenge, Control tasks Charlie Cooper with tracking him down.

Buy North Star

IN THE ATTICUS PRIEST SERIES

The House in the Woods

Disgraced detective Atticus Priest investigates the murder of a family on Christmas Eve. He's been employed to demolish the police case against his client, but things get complicated when the officer responsible for the case is his former girlfriend.

<u>Buy The House in the Woods</u>

A Place to Bury Strangers

A dog walker finds a human bone on lonely Salisbury Plain. DCI Mackenzie Jones investigates the grisly discovery but cannot explain how it ended up there. She contacts Atticus Priest and the two of them trace the bone to a graveyard in the nearby village of Imber. But the village was abandoned after it was purchased by the Ministry of Defence to train the army, so why have bodies been buried in the graveyard since the church was closed?

<u>Buy A Place to Bury Strangers</u>

The Red Room

When a man's fatal fall from Salisbury Cathedral spirals into a scandalous case involving the victims of a sex ring, Atticus Priest and Mackenzie Jones uncover more bodies and incriminating videos. Racing against the clock, they confront personal demons and tangled emotions as they try to catch the murderer before he can strike again.

Buy The Red Room

All the Devils Are Here

Atticus Priest is employed by an estranged husband to dig up dirt on his wife. But when she goes missing after swimming in the River Avon, Atticus uncovers a conspiracy between five lifelong friends that goes back years.

Buy All The Devils Are Here

ABOUT MARK DAWSON

Mark Dawson is the author of the John Milton, Beatrix and Isabella Rose and Atticus Priest series.

For more information:
www.markjdawson.com
mark@markjdawson.com